"An enchanting must-read."

   —*Publishers Weekly*, starred review, on *Satisfaction Guaranteed*

"A truly funny rom-com that's full of heat and heart."

   —*Kirkus Reviews*, starred review, on *Satisfaction Guaranteed*

"*Satisfaction Guaranteed* is a standout romance with humor, heart, and two characters who step out of their comfort zones together."

                         —*BookPage*, starred review

"Incredibly satisfying."

                —*Washington Post* on *Satisfaction Guaranteed*

"This book is sapphic, it slaps, and it's singlehandedly giving sex toy rep in romance. More of that please!"

                —Elite Daily on *Satisfaction Guaranteed*

"Highly recommended."

              —*Library Journal*, starred review, on *Worth the Wait*

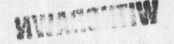

Behind the Scenes

Behind the Scenes

KARELIA STETZ-WATERS

FOREVER

New York Boston

Forever
Hachette Book Group
1290 Avenue of the Americas, New York, NY 10104
read-forever.com
twitter.com/readforeverpub

First Edition: January 2023

Forever is an imprint of Grand Central Publishing. The Forever name and logo are trademarks of Hachette Book Group, Inc.

The publisher is not responsible for websites (or their content) that are not owned by the publisher.

The Hachette Speakers Bureau provides a wide range of authors for speaking events. To find out more, go to www.hachettespeakersbureau.com or email HachetteSpeakers@hbgusa.com.

Forever books may be purchased in bulk for business, educational, or promotional use. For information, please contact your local bookseller or the Hachette Book Group Special Markets Department at special.markets@hbgusa.com.

Library of Congress Cataloging-in-Publication Data

Names: Stetz-Waters, Karelia, author.
Title: Behind the scenes / Karelia Stetz-Waters.
Description: First Edition. | New York : Forever, 2023.
Identifiers: LCCN 2022026253 | ISBN 9781538709252 (trade paperback) | ISBN 9781538709269 (ebook)
Subjects: LCGFT: Novels. | Romance fiction.
Classification: LCC PS3619.T47875 B44 2023 | DDC 813/.6--dc23
LC record available at https://lccn.loc.gov/2022026253

ISBNs: 9781538709252 (trade paperback), 9781538709269 (ebook)

Printed in the United States of America

LSC-C

Printing 1, 2022

To Fay. You are my happily-ever-after.

acknowledgments

First, thank you to all my readers. Thank you for reading. Thank you for taking a chance on sapphic romance when you hadn't read one before. Thank you for writing to me to let me know how you connect with my books and for sharing your life stories with me. Thank you for inviting me to your book groups and recommending titles I should read.

Thank you also to all the podcasters, bookstores, TikTokers, and Bookstagrammers who shared *Satisfaction Guaranteed* with their fans. I can't tell you how touched I am by your praise and how much I appreciate what you do for readers and writers like me. And a special shout-out to the Haus of Bad Bitches at the Bad Bitch Book Club, the Steamy Lit book club, Reader Seeks Romance, the Fresh Fiction Podcast, Powell's Books, Jan's Paperbacks, Grassroots Books, and The Ripped Bodice.

Thank you to all the friends who support and celebrate with me. Thank you, Liz, Liz, and Scott, for social-distancing in my winter garage. I thought playing the fireplace channel on the TV would warm us up but it was your hearts that did. Thank you, Shannon, for parking-like-police with me— that's parking driver's-window-to-driver's-window—when it was too rainy to sit outside and too COVID-y to be inside. Thank you, Maria, for Zoom-crafting through the pandemic.

Thank you, Terrance, for your wise counsel and for having no objection to lunch at Ma's Dairy Farm Tavern. Thank you to my friends and colleagues in the English department for staying true and strong when we were apart.

Thank you, Cas Taylor @_olygirlfilms, for talking to me about the life of an indie filmmaker. Thank you, Ross Smith, for talking to me about sound production.

Thank you to my editor, Madeleine Colavita. And thank you to everyone at Forever. Thank you also to my agent, Jane Dystel, who has been with me throughout my publishing career, and to everyone at Dystel, Goderich & Bourret.

Thank you to my students, especially my creative writing students in the Golden Crown Literary Society Writing Academy, for reminding me what a privilege it is to be a writer and how important it is to support one another.

Thank you to the queer community. I love your strength, your perseverance, your openheartedness, the way you approach challenge with joy. Thank you, Keith and Jerred, for making Pride happen in rural Oregon and for 3D printing me a clitoris-shaped cookie cutter.

Thank you to Willa the Pug for working from home with me. I think my students really appreciated your insights into technical report writing. I'm sorry you got so attached that whenever we leave the house now you have to sleep in the Grief Closet by the front door.

And the biggest thank-yous of all…

Thank you to my parents for instilling in me the love of reading, for supporting my dreams, for modeling a loving marriage, and for so, so much more.

And thank you to my wife, Fay. Thank you for fighting for social justice every day. Working from home with you these past two years, I see just how much you do, how powerful you are, and how many lives you touch. And you still cook me a gourmet dinner every night. I'm not sure that me doing the dishes and picking snakes out of the yard is an equal trade-off, but I will always pick snakes out of the yard for you. I am luckier in love than anyone could expect. Thank you, sweetie. You're my happily-ever-after.

Behind the Scenes

chapter 1

〓

Rose Josten sat at a table under a patio umbrella gazing out at a sea of pugs. She wouldn't have been able to pick hers out of the crowd except for the Gucci dog coats her sister Gigi had given them in honor of Rose's birthday. Thirty-eight. Rose was not in middle-aged pug lady territory yet, but middle-aged pug lady territory was visible in the distance. Her dogs were visible in the distance because they were wearing coats with bows that made them look like fat butterflies.

Rose's three sisters—Gigi, Ty, and Cassie—sat around the table, sipping lemonade from commemorative Portland Pug Crawl pint glasses.

"Designer labels are part of the capitalist conspiracy." Ty, the youngest, hopped up onto her chair, folding her skinny body—she hadn't inherited the Josten curves—onto the seat like an elf on a mushroom. The comment wasn't directed at Rose. "Resist the machine." Ty pulled at her T-shirt, which read, conveniently, RESIST THE MACHINE.

Gigi waved her perfectly manicured nails and dropped her voice to a stage whisper. "Rose is turning thirty-eight and all she has are those two little mutants. I had to go big."

"I can hear you," Rose said.

"Gigi, don't tease your sister." Cassie had four kids, and it was hard for her to turn off her maternal instincts. "And thirty-eight is a great age."

Thirty-eight was exactly 2.8 years less than half the average life span of American women. Rose had checked.

"They are not mutants," Rose added. "They are the product of three thousand years of inbreeding. You're looking at the birth of GMO. And I have everything I want."

Her dogs. Her health. An Athena profile that got hits when she bothered to set her status to SEEKING. A townhome that looked like a page from the Pottery Barn catalog because everything had come from the same page in the Pottery Barn catalog. And a job that allowed her to buy seven-hundred-dollar end tables without thinking about it. And she'd bought the Artisan Hand Painted Earthenware Vases and the Faux Silver Dollar Eucalyptus Branches, too. She probably had over three hundred dollars in Faux Silver Dollar Eucalyptus branches. (That was definitely part of the capitalist conspiracy.) And she had her sisters. Their never-ending four-way texts. Their long talks. Their laughter. Birthdays and holidays and evenings in Cassie's she-cave. Complain about her life and she'd earn herself a Wikipedia page titled "First World Problems."

"But are you sure you don't want to do more for your birthday?" Gigi asked. "I know how you feel about flying, but LA is just an hour away. I have Ativan."

Like that would keep the plane from crashing.

Also the flight to LA was two hours and ten minutes. Rose knew. She'd just sent her assistant there to discuss supply-chain logistics with the Crestwell Transportation Company.

"Crush Bar is having a Pants Off Dance Off," Ty suggested.

"It's a dance party where people don't wear clothes. You might meet someone."

"Naked wearing only my shoes," Rose said. "Please tell me people wear their shoes."

"So that's a yes?" Ty asked.

"Optimist. That is an *I celebrate YOU doing that*. And there's nothing better than hanging out with my sisters and a million pugs."

The tide of pugs moved toward their table, swarming around Gigi's chair. Gigi eyed them the way she eyed bad haircuts that she'd like to get into her salon for fixing up.

"This is all I want," Rose said.

This moment. Rose took a deep breath, part of her mindfulness practice, and released it slowly. The spring sunshine. Ty and Gigi play-bickering and Cassie mothering them all. The herd of adorable dogs. The promise of dinner at her favorite Thai place. The three days she'd taken off work...to do what?

"I've got everything I need."

She felt a familiar pang of longing. This was her life. And it was wonderful, and it should be enough.

"I think Cupcake's eating out of the trash," Rose said.

She wasn't just deflecting her feelings. Her dogs, Cupcake and Muffin, had flapped their designer wings over to the banquet of delicacies spilling from an over-full dumpster. Rose hurried over.

There were ketchup packets and beer-soaked napkins strewn about. Cupcake and Muffin had never had anything so wonderful. It was Michelin-starred. They saw Rose coming. They loved her, but they had to make a choice: their mother and goddess or a paper tray that had once held a hamburger. With surprising speed, Cupcake picked up the tray and dodged left. Muffin, realizing the desperation of the situation, swallowed half a hot dog whole, then wedged himself between the dumpster and the warehouse building behind it. Rose knelt and reached for him.

"You bottom feeder. You living trash compactor." She grabbed Muffin's bow, but he slipped away. "I am very disappointed in your life choices."

Muffin had the audacity to wag his tail cheerfully, just an inch out of Rose's reach. The air behind the dumpster smelled like the underworld.

"I will not accept that it was your brother's bad influence." The calm, reasonable tone that convinced clients there was only one good course of action and it was the one she had suggested did not work on Muffin. "There is a shred of free will left in that walnut-size brain, and you could have used it."

Behind her, she heard metal clang. She stood up quickly. A woman had emerged from a steel door in the warehouse wall.

"Can I help you find something?" the woman asked.

She was pretty, with curly dark hair shaved on the sides and pulled back in a ponytail. She was about Rose's age, but she wore ripped skinny jeans and a Siouxsie and the Banshees T-shirt faded enough to be a 1990s original, a look that should have been reserved for twenty-somethings in a band but looked good on her nonetheless. Ty would have fallen in love with her immediately. Rose could admit this wasn't the kind of woman you wanted to meet while fishing around behind the trash, but she'd long since gotten over being nervous around attractive women...if she'd ever been nervous around attractive women. It was possible she'd missed that developmental stage. Maybe Ty had gotten all the nerves-around-women genes.

"Just getting this demon out of the trash."

The woman blinked against the sunlight. She looked like she'd been up for days. The door closed behind her, the words

STEWART PRODUCTIONS stenciled in gray paint on the metal. Excited to meet another human, Muffin bounded out from behind the dumpster. Rose scooped him up.

"Why are there so…" The woman lost her words. She rubbed her eyes, looking perplexed. "There're hundreds of them."

"It's a fundraiser for the Humane Society," Rose said.

The woman reached out and petted Muffin, who had never met anyone so wonderful.

"So you're making bad life choices? But there was so much good stuff back there." The woman ruffled the wrinkles on his forehead. "How could your mother take that away from you? How could she stand in the way of joy?" The woman shot Rose a friendly, albeit fatigued, smile. She tweaked the bow on Muffin's coat. "Gucci."

"How did you guess?"

"The *G*." The woman showed her the pattern on the underside of the bow. "Is it this year's season?" The quirk of her smile said that she was teasing.

"Probably. It was a birthday present." Rose rolled her eyes. "For me from my sister. Does that make it better?"

"Better than what?"

Being 2.8 years away from middle age and the kind of person who owns designer dog coats?

"Better than taking them to Nordstrom and then having the coats tailored?"

"Oh, you should always tailor pugs," the woman said to Muffin, ruffling his neck fat. He goggled at her adoringly. "They have such big, manly shoulders, and such little spindly waists. I had a hairless cat." The woman looked up. "We had sweaters custom-knitted for him, but, to be fair, that was my ex. I would have been fine with off-the-rack."

She grinned, and the smile made faint laugh lines around

her eyes and creases beside her mouth. She was definitely attractive. Tall. Lanky. Braless (not that Rose noticed) in a way that said *I forgot to put on a bra* not *I want to show you my nipples.* She had the sexiness of a cool hipster without the annoyingness of a cool hipster because she wasn't twenty-two and didn't take herself too seriously.

Rose liked how quickly *we* turned into *ex.*

Which was none of her business.

She reached for a reason to prolong the conversation. *Could you give me the name of your cat-sweater knitter? Do you come here often? I'll buy you a beer? Can you hold this dog while I look for his evil twin?* For a moment, with the sun shining and the city glowing with new spring, it felt like anything could happen. Maybe she'd walk back to her sisters and by the time she reached them, she'd be the kind of woman who went to LA and danced naked in sneakers.

The woman gave Muffin a parting pat.

"Remember"—she directed the comment to Muffin—"you're not overdressed; everyone else is underdressed." To Rose she added, "Have fun."

Then she was walking away with a slight limp and two enormous laptops Rose hadn't noticed before tucked under her arm. And Rose was Rose Josten, senior associate at Integral Business Solutions, faithful sister, fearful flier, thirty-eight, holding a dog in a Gucci coat covered in dumpster grease.

chapter 2

Ash Stewart leaned forward on the couch, the only piece of furniture in her spacious, atrium-style living room. Buying furniture was so taxing. A television and Xbox sat on the floor in front of her. She blinked as she met an untimely demise. The rocks protecting her stronghold exploded as Amphib the Destroyer and his minions swarmed. Her health status dropped to zero.

"Go again?" Ash's friend Emma sat cross-legged on the sofa, looking like a prep school boy in her rugby jersey.

"How do you do it?" Ash tossed the controller on the sofa. "You don't even play Death Con Six."

The game's theme song played. The screen asked if they wanted to restart from the last chapter.

"You're old." Emma grinned. "I've been playing since I was in the womb. You got an Xbox when you were, like, an *adult*."

Ash was forty. She should defend forty. Forty was prime of life. But she'd stayed up until four a.m. drinking Mountain Dew, which should have made her feel like one of Emma's young gamer friends, but it didn't.

"I was playing Super Mario Bros. before you were a dirty thought," Ash said.

"You want to play Pong?"

Who knew the word *Pong* could be imbued with so much loving condescension?

"Damn you, Gen Z." Ash picked up her beer.

"Millennial by one year," Emma said. "You want to play again?"

"As much as it's nice to be crushed by a man with a frog's head..." Ash nodded to the screen. "No."

On-screen, Emma's character flexed his muscles, waiting for the game to resume.

"I need to get back to work." Ash sighed. She had to bring the rough cut of the Portland Outfitters commercial to the owner to see if it struck the right balance of hip and rustic. Then she had to study Senate candidate Grayson Beller. Shooting his campaign ads would be good money, but she wasn't going to work for him if he had some cut-school-funding, kill-the-trees voting record. She had to finish storyboarding the Wag and Browse Bookstore and Dog Kennel ad. If there was any way to make that not sound like the strangest combination ever, she'd find it.

And then there was the other project. The most important one. The impossible one. Her movie: *Inevitable Comfort.* Her last chance at getting back into directing when no producer would touch her except maybe, just maybe, iconic, iconoclastic, devil-may-care billionaire Irene Brentworth. The longest of long shots. Ash should stop thinking about it.

"And I've got to get us ready to shoot that historic preservation bit in St. John's," she said, continuing the to-do list out loud. "There's the lighting...maybe a new filter for the Canon 4K...make sure we've got everything charged. I should go back to the studio. Did I plug in the Canon 4K?"

"There's something interesting about that," Emma said.

"What's that?"

"That's *my* job."

Yes. Technically. Emma was her cameraperson. And yes, Emma was awesome. If something needed to be charged or repaired or updated or light-tested or sold on the black market or conjured out of thin air by sheer force of will, Emma would have already done it, which was why Emma felt fine playing Amphib the Destroyer all afternoon. All afternoon was how long Ash had promised Emma she'd relax. But all afternoon? That was a long time to go without the distraction of work.

"Amphib the Destroyer wants to dominate you again," Emma said.

"I can't take the pain."

"Okay." Emma drew out the word like Ash was in trouble. "I have a different game." Emma logged Ash out of the Xbox and pulled up her own credentials on autofill. "You'll like it. It's really slow...like the nineties."

A moment later, a pastel farm scene appeared on the screen. Balloon-like animals bounced in place.

"I think you're more of the bunny." Emma clicked the bunny and nodded for Ash to pick up the controller.

"A kids' game?"

"Nope."

The bunny wrinkled its nose. "I'm hungry. Let's get some carrots," it said.

"Really?" Ash raised an eyebrow.

"Go on."

Ash moved the joystick. The bunny bounced slowly out of the frame.

"Slow down and enjoy the day," it said.

Sunlight streamed through the two-story windows. The

hardwood floor gleamed. (The almost total lack of furniture showcased the hardwood.) The smell of pines blew in from the forested hill below Ash's deck and her spectacular view of Mount Hood. There was a lot of peacefulness floating in on the breeze, a lot of time for thoughts.

Ash moved the joystick again. The bunny floated away.

"Woah, too fast," it said. "Let's breathe together. In." The bunny inflated as it drifted back down. "Out. In. Out."

"The game teaches you to slow down and breathe," Emma said.

"I don't need to slow down and breathe."

"Literally anyone who says they don't have to slow down, has to slow down. Namaste."

Coming from Emma, *namaste* sounded like something you called to your teammates before you tackled someone. Emma threw an arm around Ash's shoulder.

"Work-life balance. You're such a millennial...by one year." She shook Emma off with a smile so Emma knew she was just playing. "Work-life balance is where success dies."

"It's biofeedback," Emma protested. She waved the game controller. "It's because science."

"Is Death Con Six biofeedback?"

"I'll give you some biofeedback." Emma gave Ash a friendly shove. "Play."

The buzz of Ash's phone saved her from the floating bunny.

Ash flipped the phone over. Her heart stopped. BRENTWORTH OFFICE flashed on the screen. They were calling to say no to *Inevitable Comfort*. They'd heard the logline. They'd read the treatment. But no, they hadn't read the script. No, they hadn't advanced the idea to Irene Brentworth. A romantic comedy with a queer disabled ex-firefighter was too niche. Maybe if it was a man or an able-bodied woman, think Lara Croft Tomb

Raider except a firefighter in the Pacific Northwest with bigger breasts and one arm that was a machine gun.

"Ash Stewart Productions," Ash answered.

"This is Mark from Irene Brentworth's office."

Ash mouthed *Brentworth*. Emma's eyes went wide.

"I . . . yes . . . I mean hello . . ."

Time slowed down. Ash tried to catch her breath. In a second, she was going to know. Was it advertisements for life or did she have a chance at filmmaking again? A second chance at her career. A chance for all her crew to soar. Yes, she hoped they'd stay with Stewart Productions, but after a Brentworth production they could do anything. And maybe they'd all stay together. They'd look back on today as the start of an empire. But Brentworth wasn't going to back *Inevitable Comfort*. Ash had to face the news. This was the moment when she had to give up the last shred of hope.

"Brentworth would like to see the whole pitch deck," the man said, a little wearily. "That'll include green-locked script, budget, any actors you've attached, résumés for any crew you want to bring with you, storyboards, marketing plan, comps. And a ten-minute proof of concept."

"Yes. Of course. I . . . let me find a pen."

Emma rolled her eyes and opened the voice recorder on her phone.

"Tell it to me," she whispered.

"Okay, um, yes," Ash said. "Can you say that all again?"

She knew what went in a pitch deck. It was just that every cell in her brain was busy celebrating and panicking at the same time. She was going to pitch to Irene Brentworth. She couldn't handle it. She'd crack. She'd fail spectacularly. She'd win. She'd be one of the best directors in the world . . . again. Her ex-wife would come back. *We were good together, Ash. Let's make movies again.* She'd never have to film another screaming used car salesman commercial again.

She repeated the items the man listed.

"Brentworth would like to see you at three thirty p.m., June tenth."

"Of course."

"In LA. I'll email you the details."

The man hung up. Ash stared at her phone.

"I...we...that..." she said.

June tenth ricocheted through her mind like a bullet. She couldn't do a proof-of-concept film that fast. She didn't have actors. She hadn't scouted locations. She barely had enough crew to make commercials. And the business side of filmmaking. That had always been her ex's job. Victoria was the producer. Ash was a director. How did you even figure out a budget for a film?

"Irene fucking Brentworth wants to hear your pitch!" Even Emma, who managed to look cheerfully nonplussed about everything, stared at Ash, mouth agape. "You did it."

It had taken years to write the script. A year to work up the courage to tell Emma she hadn't given up her dream of being a director...to which Emma had offered an anticlimactic *No shit*. Ash had labored for months over the treatment and longer over the logline. How could it be that hard to write two sentences? And Brentworth was going to hear their pitch, and if Brentworth wanted the movie she'd fund it. People would fall in love with the leads and their story of redemptive love.

Was it possible?

"I have to text everyone I've ever met," Emma said. "We have to have a party."

"We don't have time for a party. We have to get to work!"

Ash leapt off the couch. "I'm going to the studio. No more floating rabbit."

"You have to play with the floating rabbit," Emma said more seriously than those words should ever be spoken.

"I don't have time."

Emma was quiet for a moment, then very slowly, in a tone Ash had never heard her use before, she said, "We're not going to finish the pitch deck in time, and we're not going to get the money."

"Trust me," Ash said. "I'm going to throw myself into this one hundred percent. Every. Waking. Minute. I will make this happen."

Emma stood up, too. She put her arms around Ash in a real embrace. Ash stiffened. Emma didn't do real hugs. She gave noogies and headlocks. Those Ash could tolerate; the soft weight of Emma's arms made her stomach tighten.

I'm fine.

"You," Emma said quietly, then released Ash, "are the reason we won't win the pitch."

Her words hit Ash in the gut. Everyone else in Hollywood knew Ash as the woman who tanked a twelve-million-dollar movie because she couldn't get her shit together. But Emma never reminded her. Emma never said anything mean. She teased. She poked at Ash like a little sister trying to get her big sister's attention. But behind that was the no-nonsense love of a good friend. She never went too far. But this was too far.

"I can. I'm fine," Ash snapped.

"You're an amazing artist and an amazing employer," Emma said. "And when we're shooting something, even if it's just that guy who yells at you to buy new tires, you bring everything you've got. But you're dropping the ball. You're saying you'll do things, and you forget. You're doing half our jobs for us, or trying to."

"Is it because I messed up the reservations in Burns?"

"That hotel was a biohazard, but no. It's not Burns. It's this." Emma gestured to the Xbox.

"It's dead to me," Ash said. "No more Death Con Six until we've won the pitch."

"You don't get it. We *want* you to play Death Con Six. Pilot, me, Jason, the whole crew, we want you to stay home for one day and let us do our jobs. You're dropping the ball because you're trying to do everything yourself. You have to relax. Go to a party at the Aviary. Get on Athena. Go on a date. Watch some of those weird ASMR videos you like."

"Don't yuk my yum."

"I *want* you to watch videos of some woman handling cantaloupes." Emma put her hands on Ash's shoulders and gave her a little shake. "It's weird, but I love you, and you love cantaloupe woman. And you said she helps you relax."

"I don't *love* her."

"I'm calling in the friend card. Something's got to change."

Of all the people she had known in her life before the accident, Ash wouldn't have guessed it'd be the scrappy young production assistant who'd stick around. But Emma had. Like a stray puppy that followed you around until you fell in love with it.

"We have to get you some help," Emma said.

"I don't need help!" Ash said louder than she meant to. She flashed back to the last morning with her ex. *I can't spend my life taking care of you, Ash.* Ash cleared her throat. "I'm fine. And the friend card isn't about business. It's when you need someone to pretend to be your girlfriend at your sister's wedding."

"The friend card is about anything." Emma folded her

arms. "That's the whole point of the friend card. Whatever it is, whenever it is…I call the friend card and you do whatever I ask."

"So what are you asking? Drop our customers? Don't do the pitch?"

Emma was not going to pull some your-mental-health-is-more-important-than-this-film bullshit, was she?

"I'm not sure what I'm asking," Emma said. "But when I do, you have to say yes, and it's going to have something to do with you taking a break and not having a heart attack."

chapter 3

≋

Ash waited until she was sure Emma was out of the neighborhood and not lingering in the scenic viewpoint pull-off waiting to catch Ash going back to work, then drove back to the studio. She worked for a few hours, poring over the script, looking for the scenes she wanted to use for the proof of concept. But Emma didn't have any reason to worry. Ash only stayed for a couple of hours. A few hours. Okay, seven hours. Ash left the studio at two a.m. Maybe it was three. Or four. She didn't look. There was so much to do. She would have stayed longer, but inevitably Emma would have come in early and caught her and given her another lecture on work-life balance, which would be wasted on Ash because Ash didn't *want* work-life balance.

She wanted to win this pitch. She wanted to make movies again.

Around five, she stepped out of the studio, laptops in hand. She paused on the concrete step, checking to make sure she had her keys before letting the steel door close behind her. She glanced at the dumpster. She couldn't help but smile, even if she was oscillating between panic and feverish, self-destructive ambition. She couldn't forget the woman pulling her dog from behind the trash can, and it had been years since Ash had noticed a woman. And if the woman had just been pretty or just had a nice ass, Ash wouldn't have noticed in the first place, let alone thought about her now when she should be working harder than she ever had in her life. Or at least spinning her wheels very, very fast.

It was the dignity with which the woman had fished out her dog. Leaving aside the dumpster and the sticky pug, she'd looked perfectly polished in a linen blazer. Her light-brown hair fell to her shoulders in soft waves, looking natural and also like she'd never had a hair out of place. It was the hair of a politician, the kind who funded arts in schools and could throw down on the Senate floor. She was tall and curvy. She took up space with a languid grace that said *I could kick your ass in the boardroom, but I don't feel like it right now.* All that could have been pretentious. She was wearing white linen to an event that seemed to involve drinking beer and watching pugs scavenge fair food. But there was something in her wry, amiable smile that said, *Yes. I know. I'm the woman wearing linen to the Pug Crawl.* It had made the lecture she'd directed at her dog even funnier than it would have been otherwise. *I am very disappointed in your life choices.* Ash had almost felt like the woman was trying to make her laugh. And it was that blend of authority—the woman was clearly the boss of whatever she did in life—and good humor that kept her passing through Ash's mind. Not that that meant anything, even though Emma would probably say Ash thinking about a woman was an *emotional breakthrough.*

Ash took a deep breath, maybe the first that day. The spring air was sweet, even in the warehouse district where she'd rented the cheapest studio space she could find. She breathed in the smell of distant flowers. Her heart ached as she made her way down the empty street toward the lot where she'd parked her car. It was a beautiful night, even here in the industrial zone. It would have been nice to have someone to turn to and say, *Can you smell the spring?* She pushed the thought away.

Back at home, she opened the fridge, took out a protein shake, and carried it to the deck. Portland glittered below a line of trees. Here the smell of blossoms mingled with wet earth. The stars twinkled. It'd be getting light soon. She had to get some sleep. She finished the shake and dropped the carton in the sink, then headed for bed. She stripped and put on a long T-shirt. Then she reached under her bed for her virtual reality headset.

The ASMartist Ash liked—the cantaloupe woman, as Emma called her—didn't film in VR, but Ash still liked the feeling that there was nothing in the world except her and the woman known to the ASMR community only by her handle: Cherry Covered Apron. No one knew her real name. Comments on her website hung in limbo waiting to be *approved by the administrator.*

Ash selected Cherry Covered Apron's longest video, settled the headset over her eyes and ears, and lay back in bed. The video began with the woman's sweet voice welcoming her.

"I'm so happy you're here, sweetheart."

She lingered on the *s*'s. The sound slid over Ash's skin. It tingled in her ears and then down her arms, up her spine, and along the tight muscles of her shoulders, relaxing them slowly.

"You've had such a stressful day."

No one had ever seen Cherry Covered Apron. The videos showed her from the hips up and chest down, mostly focused on her hands and whatever object she was touching. In this video it was walnuts. She stirred the hard shells against one another. The rhythmic clacking became a wordless mantra. Click. Click. Click. It was like a lullaby. Some of her videos were more erotic. There was no pretending Cherry Covered Apron's fingers squishing around the cantaloupe seeds didn't look sexual. But this video was chaste, like a backrub from an old friend...if Ash had been the kind of person who let friends give her backrubs.

"You're safe with me," Cherry Covered Apron whispered.

She must have had an amazing microphone. Ash could hear the dampness of Cherry Covered Apron's lips as she spoke. Cherry Covered Apron could have kissed the microphone and there wouldn't have been any feedback or distortion. It was gorgeous sound, and Cherry Covered Apron had a lovely voice. A lot of the other ASMartists were just feathery, like someone trying to sound sexy when they didn't feel it. But Cherry Covered Apron's voice was rich and kind and meaningful.

"Sweetheart," she drawled. "Close your eyes." The walnuts clicked together. "You feel totally at peace."

Ash felt her heartbeat slow to a normal rate.

"You work so hard. Listen to the sound of my voice and let go. I'm scooping you up in my arms, sweetheart. You're so special."

If only. Ash closed her eyes behind the VR headset, letting Cherry Covered Apron's voice caress her. She wasn't embarrassed about liking ASMR even though she protested when Emma mentioned it. Yes, it was weird to fall asleep to the sound of a stranger telling her she was special while rattling walnuts in a bowl, but it was innocent and private. It wasn't like she went to WinCo and fondled walnuts in the bulk aisle. She just fell asleep pretending that a woman with a beautiful voice cared that she was tired.

chapter 4

Rose's assistant, Chloe, was already at work at eight, looking comfortable in her prim tweed suit. Rose set a coffee on Chloe's desk.

"You're the best." Chloe looked up with a smile. "You know you can never leave Integral, not until I retire."

That was a daunting thought. Chloe was only twenty-five.

"Anything interesting?" Rose asked, nodding to Chloe's computer and the emails Chloe scanned for her every morning.

"I've got one to beat the marijuana sushi delivery business."

Anyone could request Integral Business Solutions' services. That didn't mean everyone got them. It certainly didn't mean everyone could afford them. The office kept a running list of the funniest submissions to come through the client inquiry portal. Ridiculous dreams that would never come to fruition.

"Go on." Rose leaned against the doorframe, sipping her black Americano.

"It's an advertising production company. Stewart Productions. Normal enough, but it's not Stewart who contacted you, and it's not about making advertisements." Chloe read from her screen. *"My boss, Ash Stewart, doesn't know I'm writing to you. I promise I'll tell her before you start consulting for us."*

"That usually helps," Rose said.

"I work for Stewart Productions. It's an advertisement production company: local shops, political campaign stuff, IG reels for influencers. Boring stuff. What we all want to do is make movies, especially Ash. It's her dream. BUT WE NEED AN INTERVENTION. That last part is in all caps, by the way."

"Ooh. An all-caps intervention." Rose shook her head. "Are we going to blindfold her and take her to the wilderness?"

"Maybe." Chloe read on. *"Ash is a director, and she's written an amazing script. It's all about love, forgiveness, suffering, our connection to nature, and it's really funny, too."* Chloe glanced over the rim of her glasses. "I love funny movies about human suffering. She goes on, *She sent her logline to Irene Brentworth's office. You probably haven't heard of her but if you were in the film industry you would have. She has a ton of money, and if she backs your project, you've made it. But she almost never calls you back, and if she does you have to be ON.*

"Ash sent her the logline and Brentworth's office actually CALLED. All caps. *They want to see a full pitch deck and a proof of concept in a MONTH.* Also all caps. *That basically means you need to know everything you could possibly know about the project, figure out how you'll sell it, and film a sample of it. The problem is Ash is an amazing director, but she doesn't know how to do all that producer stuff. But she'll try, and she'll try to do it by herself because she's got a hang-up about her ex-wife and asking for help. She's going to have a heart attack and die. Then I'm going to have to make the film in her honor, and it'll be crap. I'll always wonder if I could have saved her, which is a lot of emotional baggage. So I'd like to meet with you as soon as possible. We'll be able to pay you when we get the contract with*

Brentworth. I can't wait to meet you. Your résumé looks amazing. Sincerely, Emma Gilman."

"Complicated," Rose said.

"*P.S.*" Chloe finished the letter. "*Trigger warning: The movie is very sex-positive and consent-based. There's a scene with ferns.*"

"Right." Rose drew the word out. "Ferns. I'm out."

An advertising company pitching a comedy about sex, suffering, and ferns to a fickle investor. A boss who didn't know her associate was trying to hire a consultant. (What did Emma Gilman do at Stewart Productions anyway?) Emma who was already planning the emotional baggage she'd have if her boss died.

Who was Rose to judge? If nothing else, Ash and Emma had interesting lives.

"Shall I send them the usual?" Chloe asked.

Thank you for your interest in Integral Business Solutions' services. Unfortunately, we are not able to take on all prospective clients et cetera et cetera.

Emma's letter was so earnest.

"I'll write to her," Rose said. "Maybe I can recommend someone else or a book on healthy workplace relationships."

Rose put it off. Real work called. It was four o'clock before she knew it. A knock on the wall beside her open door broke her focus.

"Working hard as always." It was the founding partner, Howard Melnor. "Happy hour," he added cheerfully.

Once-a-week drinks in the elegantly decorated front office was Integral Business Solutions' version of family dinner. Once a week, on company time, with free top-shelf alcohol, everyone gathered and talked about the same things they talked about by the watercooler but with snifters of Uncle

Nearest Whiskey in hand. Rose usually spent the time gazing out the window, twenty-four stories down to the bustling street.

Everyone at Integral Business Solutions was nice. They had 2.2 kids. They liked the Blazers. Their dogs were named Rufus. Howard Melnor played golf, didn't cheat on his wife, was a little cultish about his alma mater, Texas A&M, and treated all the associates with respect and professionalism although no one had been able to train him out of calling the women gals. It was a nice place to work, a perfectly fine place.

"Listen up, everyone," Howard said, drawing the group's attention.

Rose turned from the window.

"I think a little announcement is in order," Howard said. "Rose?"

Rose looked around. It wasn't her birthday. She wasn't getting married.

"Rose is too cool to brag," Howard went on. "Beltliner International Dehydrated Foods saw Rose's proposal for their corporate restructuring plan, and they love it. Rose, here's to you landing the biggest client this year."

Oh, that.

"Or should I say the biggest client ever," Howard added.

Cheers and congratulations went up.

"And she's not even a partner," one of the other partners said.

Someone else said, "I wonder how long that'll last."

"That is something we will have to discuss," Howard said with melodramatic seriousness.

As if there was a question.

Of course she was making partner.

She would study Beltliner, run all aspects of their operations through her twelve-point metric, and help the company *opti-mize their profits with values-aligned strategies for growth potential.* Then she'd make partner, work half as hard, and make twice the money...for the rest of her life. The thought settled in her stomach like a ball of ice.

"Are you going to Philadelphia?" another colleague asked.

On-site visits were central to the Integral Business Solutions' Collaborative Solutions Method.

"There's no need for Rose to go to Philadelphia," Howard said.

Everyone knew Rose would rather die than get on an airplane. The two things were basically the same. Die or get launched into the air in a tube filled with pressurized oxygen and gasoline and die when it crashed to the ground. Why waste the money on a ticket?

"Everyone goes on-site," someone said, but they weren't being mean. They were just setting Howard up for the comeback.

"When you're as good as Rose, you can Zoom in from your basement and they'll still want you."

chapter 5

Rose let herself into Cassie's house without knocking. Cassie's oldest daughter, Delilah, looked up from her laptop and whatever macabre game she was playing with her best friends, all of whom lived in Finland. (No one could explain that.) The girl pointed at her eyes and then at Rose in an I-see-you gesture that barely escaped from beneath heavy black bangs. Rose blew her a kiss, which Delilah pretended to ward off with fingers in a cross, then returned. Cassie's husband, Kenneth, walked by with the twins under each arm. Cassie sat at the kitchen table with her arms wrapped around her middle boy. He was clutching his favorite American Girl doll, who now sported a kind of sideways mullet.

"The twins cut her hair," Cassie explained and kissed the top of his head. "It'll be okay, sweetie. Aunt Gigi will fix it." Cassie waved to Rose. "Gigi and Ty are already here."

It was Thursday night in the she-cave. Rose trailed her fingers along the smooth banister that led to the cozy attic room. She'd made the down payment on this house. She didn't personally want to live in a six-bedroom bungalow with half an acre of lawn that needed mowing, fertilizing, dethatching, weeding, and resodding. There were nuclear power plants lower-maintenance than that lawn. But she loved the house for Cassie. She loved watching the kids race across the grass.

Rose paused for a moment before opening the door. She could hear Ty and Gigi bickering cheerfully. Inside her sisters sat on opposite ends of the couch, their legs stretched out next to each other.

"They all got their jewel boxes cleaned up," Gigi was saying.

"Vulva!" Ty wailed.

"You mean the lavender candy bag?" Gigi grinned. "Or are we talking about the love oyster?"

Ty threw her head back in despair.

"My new waxer is amazing. The bride said it didn't hurt at all. Azalea Salon is going to be Portland's number one premier waxing salon."

Rose flopped down in her favorite easy chair. "Are you talking about Brazilians again?" she asked. "I can't see how it didn't hurt *at all.*"

"Pain makes you feel alive!" Gigi said.

"Being chased by cougars makes you feel alive," Rose said.

"Waxing perpetuates the myth that all women should look like porn stars," Ty complained.

Gigi pointed an accusing finger at both of them. "Don't tread on my dream."

Cassie appeared in the doorway.

"Girl doll okay?" Rose asked.

"Maybe Gigi can make the style work for her." Cassie shook her head. "Poor kid. Middle kids have it hard."

Gigi waved the comment away. "How about mentoring you all into adulthood. Now, that was hard."

There was a heartbeat of silence. Gigi was the oldest, but it hadn't been like that. It was Rose, the second oldest, twenty at the time, who'd held it all together when their parents died. Cassie glanced at Rose. Ty leaped up and squeezed herself into Rose's chair and gave her a kiss on the cheek the way she had when Rose was walking her to elementary school on Rose's way to class at PSU.

"Fine. We'd all be monumentally fucked if it weren't for Rose," Gigi said.

They all laughed. Cassie got a box of wine out of the mini fridge. She filled four vaguely skull-shaped goblets. Her daughter, Delilah, had made them in ceramics class, and she hadn't perfected her black-magic chalice making. Cassie took her place in the big armchair. She'd nursed all her children in it before she and her husband moved it upstairs to be the throne of the she-cave.

"To Rose," Cassie said. She took a swig of wine then treated them to an animated telling of the saga of the American Girl doll and her plans for restorative justice among children. Ty described a story one of her students had written at the McLaughlin Academy where Ty taught as a graduate teaching fellow getting her MFA or at least pretending to write the novel that would earn her an MFA when...if...she finished it. Gigi elaborated on the Brazilians until Cassie covered her eyes and said, "Do not take me all the way into the flippits and flappets," and Ty buried her face in a pillow, moaning, "It's called the vulva."

Cassie poured more wine into their skulls. There was a comfortable lull in the conversation. They all smiled at the sounds of Cassie's children playing downstairs.

"What about you, Rose?" Cassie asked. "Any word on the partnership?"

The sisters told one another everything. But with the box wine warming her, the twilight fading in the skylights, happiness radiating out of every floorboard of Cassie's house, Gigi and Ty bickering about *vulva* versus *lady bits*...Rose didn't want to spoil the evening talking about work. But there was no getting around it.

"Howard told the office I'm getting it." She offered her sisters a smile that felt convincing.

"That's wonderful." Cassie leapt up and gave Rose a hug, enveloping Rose in her #1 MOM sweatshirt. "I'm so proud of you. I knew you'd make it."

"If they didn't give it to Rose..." Gigi made a cutting motion. "I know people."

"You don't," Cassie said.

It was best they all believe that.

"I thought I'd get it," Rose said, looking down at her lap, "but there are a lot of qualified people at the firm, so it's nice to hear they're excited about me."

"They'd be totally wrong not to give it to you," Cassie added. "But sometimes life isn't fair. I'm so glad it's fair this time."

"We should do something with your hair," Gigi said. "Or maybe permanent eyeliner. I want to celebrate this. You are a true glass-ceiling-busting boss lady."

Rose hadn't tried to bust the glass ceiling. She'd tried to make money to put Ty through college, to help Cassie buy the house, to subsidize Azalea Salon before it turned a profit. She looked at her sisters. Their faces glowed. They were happy for her. Not figure-of-speech *happy for her*, really truly *happy* because this was Rose's dream and Rose had made it!

Because Rose had spent every day since she switched her major from music to business convincing them that she wanted this so there'd be nothing to take the shine off Cassie's banisters, nothing to make Ty feel guilty about the student debt she didn't owe, nothing to make Gigi offer Rose a lifetime of free Brazilians in exchange for everything Rose had done.

chapter 6

Back at home, Rose poured herself a glass of wine and leashed Muffin and Cupcake, who had nearly expired with loneliness and hunger while she was gone, despite the fact that the neighbor kid looked in on them twice after school.

"He fed you earlier," she said, opening a cookie jar with treats. "You are not dying."

Their large, goggling eyeballs said, *We are seconds from death.*

A treat each did not fill them up, but despite the odds, they continued to live.

She sipped her wine, feeling the familiar pull she always felt when she was stressed or sad or longing for something more than a corner office at Integral Business Solutions. Her passion. Or maybe it was a fetish or a kink...or an emotional problem. One thing was for sure: It was a secret.

She went back inside and wandered slowly toward her bedroom closet. Way back. Hidden behind everything: a professional-grade camera and twenty-two-hundred-dollar microphone. A tripod. Light set.

A blend of peace and excitement filled her as she set up the equipment. The soft lights. The microphone so close to her lips she could kiss it. Then she looked in the fridge. Had she thought about this when she'd bought the five-pound bag of Granny Smith apples? She didn't like Granny Smith, but the skins were crisp and the sound of the peeler so satisfying.

She set it on the counter, reverently. Then she dug to the bottom of the deepest kitchen drawer and took out her apron. She put it on. She pressed her hands to her heart-center and turned on the camera, pointing it at the bowl of apples. She never showed her face.

"Hello, sweetheart," she whispered into the microphone.

She picked up the peeler and the first apple. She held the apple close to the microphone. Then she pressed the peeler to the apple and uncoiled a perfect ribbon of green, moving slowly so the microphone could pick up every droplet of sound. Her body relaxed. There was only the rhythm of her work and the sound of her breath, the apples, and her voice whispering to an audience she would never meet but was somehow still important.

"There's only this moment," she murmured. "This apple. Taste it. It's sweet like you are. You're safe with me." She lingered on the s's. "Ssssweet. Sssspecial."

Slowly the world faded away. She could feel every molecule in the apples. She worked until she'd peeled the whole bowl.

Finally, she signed off. "You are precious to me. You are precious to the world. This is Cherry Covered Apron. Good night, sweetheart."

Then she wiped her hands and powered down her camera. Five pounds of apple on the counter staring at her accusingly. *You don't like Granny Smith, and you can't make anyone a pie out of your kinky apples.* She shook some lemon juice over them so they wouldn't brown and put them back in the fridge. Maybe she could make dog treats out of them. She sent the video to her computer from the Wi-Fi camera then opened her video editing software.

It was well after midnight when she compiled the video, reduced the file size, and uploaded it to her website. The familiar flush of shame came back as she saw the status bar creep toward 100 percent. Why did she post them? Why wasn't it good enough to just make them and delete them or just to mindfully peel apples and not record it?

Muffin and Cupcake sat at her feet, staring up at her, their innocent brown eyes saying, *You're a pervert, but we love you, and you are our goddess, and give us a sausage.*

"Let's go pee," she told them wearily.

She picked up the glass of wine she hadn't finished and stepped outside. The pugs followed her. Rose sat down on her stoop and reeled out their leashes so they could pull this way and that like fat landlocked kites.

Her neighborhood was tucked between I-5 and Barbur Boulevard, but that strip of old oak trees reminded her of what she thought New England must be like. It was the closest she'd get to New England until pharmacists invented an uber-Ativan to save her from the terror of flight. She wouldn't move when she made partner, even though she'd have the money to buy a house on a hill. Who would she share the house with? Six more pugs? Another girlfriend who didn't make her heart skip?

She sighed, staring into the dark trees across the street. The videos. Why hadn't she told her sisters? Yes, the videos were creepily sensual. Yes, normal people had kinks like bondage and licking shoes. But her sisters wouldn't judge her. If they did, they'd still love her. But they'd ask questions. How long have you been doing this? (Years.) How many videos? (Hundreds.) Why don't you do something with your…hobby? (Ridiculous.) But there'd be a bigger truth hovering behind her answers. If Cassie, Ty, and Gigi weren't there loving her and needing her and living in a world where nothing was certain, Rose might just quit Integral Business Solutions. She'd live in a van and try to monetize her sensual squash videos. Okay, no. She would never live in a van, and she'd seen too many sushi and marijuana delivery businesses flop to think that you could monetize squash videos. But each time she posted a video, a voice in the back of her head whispered, *What would you do if you didn't have to be careful?* Who would she be if she could follow a wild passion down a rocky path that would lead nowhere but to the satisfaction of saying, *At least I tried?*

Yeah, right.

Cupcake nuzzled her hand, pleading with her not to make any choices that would interfere with the supply of designer dog food. Rose shook off her feelings of guilt. She wasn't hurting anyone. She was living her life, working a job, and having a small, private midlife crisis that a good night's sleep would cure. She'd just check her email one more time, then go to bed. She went inside, sat on the couch, and took out her phone.

There was the forwarded email from Emma at the film company. Rose had forgotten. Emma needed a nice let-down letter. She opened the message. *Stewart Productions.* She'd seen that name somewhere. She googled it, clicked, then stopped, her finger hovering over the screen.

The woman at the Pug Crawl with the hipster outfit and the nice sense of humor. She'd come out of a door labeled STEWART PRODUCTIONS. Rose's heart sped up as she clicked ABOUT. There the woman was: Ashlyn Stewart, owner of

Stewart Productions. She looked sexy and unpretentious in a black, multi-pocketed vest. In one hand she held a clapboard. It was obviously a professional photo, but they'd captured her about to call action. Stewart's bio listed a degree from USC and an impressive list of awards. Somehow Rose wasn't surprised, even though the woman who'd stumbled into the bright light of the Pug Crawl had looked confused by the presence of daylight…and a billion pugs. That was surprising if you weren't expecting it.

Rose copied Emma's email address into a new message and began to type. *Dear Ms. Gilman, Thank you for your interest in Integral Business Solutions. I'm afraid I do not have experience consulting in the arts.* She looked at Stewart's photo again. Stewart looked like the actually-cool person annoyingly cool people were trying to emulate. Natural. Focused. Open. Entirely herself.

Rose would never see her again. What were the chances that Stewart would be stepping out of her studio next year at the Pug Crawl? That Rose would even go? That the pug organizers would host it in the same random back alley?

My specialty is corporate restructures and supply chain.

Rose was curious. Stewart was attractive. Ty would say intersecting with Stewart's life, not once but twice, was a sign. Ty thought everything was a sign when it came to attractive women she would never talk to. Rose didn't believe in signs. And she didn't indulge her curiosity. The most fanciful thing in her life was the unicorn chew toy Cupcake and Muffin were slowly eviscerating at her feet. And soon she'd make partner, and then she wouldn't even have anything to strive for. She'd just be here, living this life, for the rest of her life. She'd probably die at the exact median age of women in her tax bracket.

"That's sad," she said to the dogs.

Not as sad as eating cotton unicorn, their eyes said.

Rose stared at her phone. There was no harm in being curious. *I don't think I'll be able to provide guidance in your industry,* Rose typed. *However, if you'd like I could do a free one-hour consult.*

chapter 7

The smell of fresh coffee filled Stewart Productions. Sunlight streamed through the wall of windows on one side of the high-ceilinged space. It made lighting sets challenging, but you didn't have to build a lot of sets to film commercials for car dealerships. Ash wasn't thinking about car dealerships as she stared through the glare on her computer screen at the last sex scene of her script. Seven years ago, when she'd penned the first draft, it'd seemed realistic. Now it dripped sweetness, like someone had taken real life and poured corn syrup over it.

Behind her, she heard the numbers on the keypad lock, then the door open. She turned. It was Emma and a prospective client. Ash flipped open her daily planner. She hadn't forgotten an appointment. Emma had probably charmed the woman in line at the coffee shop and brought her directly in. They didn't have time to do more ads if they were going to do a proof of concept in a month. But they couldn't afford to turn down work. Anxiety raced through her. Her heart sped up, perhaps thinking that if it beat faster she'd get more done. But the client was here, and she had to do something like stand up and look like she wasn't going to have a heart attack, and—

She stood and froze. The woman paused, too.

"Well, hello," she said in the same authoritative yet friendly tone she'd used at the Pug Crawl.

If she'd looked pulled-together before, now she looked like a Wikipedia definition of powerful professional. Her posture was upright. Her gray briefcase matched her gray pumps. Her navy suit held her full body with just the right amount of *You don't get to assess whether or not I'm attractive* and *I'm attractive.* She walked over. Her heels rang out on the concrete floor like this was her workspace.

"I'm Rose Josten."

Surprise rendered Ash speechless.

"Small world," Rose Josten said casually.

"How?" Ash asked. She ran her hand through her hair only to remember that she'd pulled it up in a messy knot on top of her head. "You," she added, making a good second impression. "What..."

"I've been thinking about pet sweaters," the woman said. "Cupcake and Muffin say they're calling PETA because I haven't knit them any." She held out her hand. "Nice to meet you when I'm not digging in the trash."

"Cupcake and Muffin?" Ash regained a little bit of poise. "I thought they'd be more Sotheby and Vanguard."

Emma's eyebrows had climbed. "You two know each other?"

"No," Ash said, just as the woman said, "Yes."

"Sort of," Rose Josten amended. "We met at the Pug Crawl."

"You went to the Pug Crawl?" A smile spread across Emma's face. "Ash never does anything fun."

"Ash spotted my dog's Gucci coat."

"That's great," Emma said, by which she meant, *You were talking to an attractive woman about something other than work. It's a miracle.*

"Dressing your pets in Target brand is so solidly middle class." Rose gave Ash a look that said, *I am so kidding.* "I mean, if it's not Armani, should you even have dogs?"

"I was shocked when I stepped out and there were all those pugs and not ten bespoke outfits in the whole bunch," Ash said.

"You looked like you had walked into an alternate reality." Rose's laugh was sweet and playful. "I've never seen someone look so confused by pugs."

"*One* is not confusing," Ash protested. "I'd been up all night."

"That's the problem," Emma said.

"So you make commercials?" Rose asked Ash conversationally, like they were meeting at a dinner party. "And you're working on a movie."

"Do you...need a commercial?"

What did Rose do? Attorney? Financial manager? They could film her striding across the marble floor of the Thomas Close Building lobby, then drawing up to the camera with a confident statement about her business. The image of Rose's pugs skittering across the floor behind her flitted through Ash's mind. She suppressed a smile.

"I don't need a commercial," Rose said, looking slightly surprised.

If Rose wasn't a prospective client...Ash looked at Emma. Ash didn't date, but that didn't stop Emma from occasionally trying to set her up. Had Emma been at the Pug Crawl? Seen Ash talk to Rose? Chased Rose down and told Rose she had to meet her friend. That meant Emma had told Rose a lot of good things about Ash, good things that it would quickly become apparent were not true or true but layered over with so much baggage, Rose should walk away immediately.

"Apparently, I'm here to help you not have a heart attack," Rose said.

Okay, Emma had led with the truth.

"Rose is a business consultant," Emma said. "She's Portland's best business consultant."

"Best west of the Rockies," Rose said with a shrug that managed to make the statement sound modest. "I've agreed to do a one-hour consult to help with your pitch."

Ash's mind reeled. Rose from the Pug Crawl was here to tell her how to pitch to Brentworth?

"How did Emma find you?" Ash asked.

"Google." Emma didn't wear the pretending-to-be-remorseful look that said she was up to something.

If anything...it was Rose whose slight shrug said, *Guilty as charged.* But that was impossible.

"The entertainment industry isn't my specialty," Rose said. "I mostly do manufacturing and supply chain. But I understand courting investors, and I am the best."

"Will you let her help you since her *job* is to help people?" Emma asked pointedly.

"I let people help me," Ash said.

"She doesn't," Emma said to Rose. "It's all *I am an island. Let me drown alone at sea.*"

Ash pretended to glare at Emma. "Islands don't drown."

"*Now* the great director forgets what a metaphor is?" Emma shook her mop of brown hair out of her eyes.

Even in Ash's darkest days, Emma had made her laugh.

"There's erosion," Rose said.

"Thank you," Ash said.

"So will you let me help?" Rose looked suddenly serious.

Ash's to-do list weighed on her shoulders like the barrels of water people wore on their backs when they hiked the

Pacific Crest Trail and then got eaten by bears. She felt the weight lift just a bit. The West's best business consultant would know what to do. Ash could spare an hour. Talking to Rose wasn't like leaning on her friends or her crew. She wasn't leaning on Rose the way she'd leaned on her ex. Ash was just getting advice.

"Would you like to sit down?" Ash asked.

Rose looked around. The studio equipment was packed in protective cases, everything inventoried and labeled. Ash's hand-drawn storyboards marched up and down the large worktable in the center of the studio in perfect lines. But there wasn't time to tidy everything else. Half-empty coffee cups and sad office chairs were scattered around the space. Ash got Rose the least shabby chair. She pulled her own chair up to the corner of the ten-by-ten table not occupied by her work.

Ash couldn't tell if it was for real or if Rose was teasing when she opened her briefcase, took out her laptop, and began, "Thank you for choosing Integral Business Solutions."

Emma hopped up onto one of the deep window ledges set in the concrete wall of the warehouse-turned-studio.

"I've done some research into the pitch process, but tell me in your own words," Rose said. "What's the situation?"

It's my last chance.

"Irene Brentworth is rich as shit," Emma said. "She gives people a ton of money to make films so she can hang around on set and tell people what to do."

"There's a little more to it than that," Ash said. "The producer oversees all the logistics from start to finish. Pre-production. What happens on set and when. Who's doing what where. We've heard Brentworth is actually a good producer, even though it does seem like a bit of a hobby for her. She's heir to a big oil distribution company. Then she moved the company to renewable power. She owns wind fields. And she invests in films she thinks are innovative, and then she gets to be on set and run the show.

"We've pitched to other people." Ash tried to keep the sigh out of her voice. "It's hard to get funding for a film like ours. There's room for a couple of queer romances a year in the mainstream, maybe one teenage coming-out story. But it's hard to get backing for a film like ours. It's a romance. But it deals with some serious issues, too. It's a hard sell." Especially when you'd personally ruined a twelve-million-dollar project. "But that's the kind of film we need," Ash went on. "These mainstream shows put up cute, perfect twenty-two-year-old actors living the dream. Or maybe if they care about the cause they'll make a *Boys Don't Cry* or remake *Torch Song Trilogy.* Everybody dies but we get enlightened. We need to show the world that *real* queer people find love in a way that's fun and true. They struggle and they survive. Everyone deserves love." If that was true, why was the ending so saccharine? Ash took a deep breath. "The only way to get funding for a film like that is if it's some rich person's pet project. Hence: Irene Brentworth."

And Brentworth was rich and eccentric enough to take on a blacklisted director.

"Is she queer?" Rose asked.

"No, but she set things on fire in the eighties," Emma said.

"Basically, the same thing," Rose said, one eyebrow cocked in amusement.

"Ash is the most brilliant director ever," Emma went on, "so Brentworth should totally pick her up, but—"

There were a lot of buts.

"But Ash doesn't know how to do all the logistical stuff they want to see. And she has to make the proof of concept."

"Which I should have had done before I sent Brentworth the logline." Rookie mistake. "But I'd..." *Given up.* "I didn't think there was any way she'd call back. I was throwing a coin in a fountain."

"And up came a mermaid," Rose said.

"Have you seen her movies?" Emma rattled off titles of Ash's films, a laundry list of Ash's past life. "When Ash directs, she helps people find the characters' souls."

Rose typed on her tablet without looking at the screen.

"You haven't lived a meaningful life if you haven't seen Ash's work," Emma finished.

Rose nodded, which was nice because Rose was obviously living a meaningful life without having seen Ash's films.

"That's why I'm still following her around," Emma added. "I was just a peon production assistant when we met, and Ash mentored me. Now I basically tell her what to do."

"And does she listen?" Rose asked.

"No, but she'll listen to you."

"They all do." Rose's lips quirked up in a half smile. "It's hard to say no to me when I know what's right for you."

"I bet you know what to do with a woman like me," Ash said, a second before she realized that sounded suggestive. "I mean, I'm very impressed by your credentials."

"So what do we need to do to get this rich, not-quite-lesbian's money?"

Rose had a lovely voice, not deep but not high or thin, either. A comforting, professional voice. What Apple wanted Siri to be but of course you could never program a voice like that. And Rose was sexy. Ash felt that little, irrational glow of *I like you* and *I'm having trouble concentrating because I'd like to touch your hair.* She hadn't felt that in years. Emma would be proud.

Ash refocused.

"We need to be ready to go into pre-production if she says yes." There was so much to do. Ash tried to take a breath. Where was the pink bunny when she needed it? "I need to give her a full proposal. Green-locked script. That means finished." The ending was still so wrong. "Fully realized characters. Locations. Cast. It'd be great if we could get someone known. There's something else." Ash hadn't talked about it with Emma, although surely Emma knew. "The whole industry watches who pitches to Brentworth. She picks hidden gems, the films no one thinks can turn a profit, but they do. But if Brentworth said no, it tells everyone, *You're not a gem.* You don't get investors after that."

"That's a lot of pressure," Rose said quietly.

Ash swept her hair back with both hands, but it was already up. The gesture made her look panicked. She took her hair out of its knot, shook it, and casually tossed it over her shoulder like a hair commercial. *I'm fine. Just fluffing my hair because I use Pantene.*

But the truth slipped out.

"If I don't make this happen, I won't make films again." Ash bit her lip. Saying it out loud made it real. The thought was almost too much to bear. *Never again.* "This is it." Ash's voice caught.

Rose sent her tablet to sleep and folded her hands on the table. "I don't think this is anything Integral Business Solutions' Twelve Point Success Metric can't address," she said, her voice so calm and melodic that Ash's heart slowed to a normal rate. "I'll have to get up to speed on your industry. It will take a few days for me to know absolutely everything." Rose's smile balanced between pride and an eyeroll. She stood and held out her hand.

Ash stood quickly and shook it.

"Wait," Ash said. "I thought you were only here for a consultation. We haven't even talked about payment."

"You can pay me when you get the deal. I don't usually work on contingency, but I'm interested in this project."

Was that a flirtatious glint in Rose's eyes? It was gone quickly; surely Ash had imagined it. Still, it was enough to leave Ash speechless for a second, mouth open, words stuck in her brain.

"It'll be a pleasure doing business with you, Ms. Stewart," Rose said.

"Ash."

"It's nice to meet you, Ash," Rose said, rolling Ash's name along her tongue like candy.

chapter 8

Rose sat with her back to her desk looking out her window. It'd be a corner office in a few months. She held her phone to her ear.

"So, you will be turning down a chance to meet the Cauliflower Baron in his natural environment?" the president of Beltliner International Dehydrated Foods asked.

Who would turn down a chance to spend a day with a man who referred to himself in the third person as the Cauliflower Baron?

"I would love to meet you in person," Rose said. "But my time is best utilized here. You understand as a company president, I'm sure, that the most important work must supersede those activities that would be more enjoyable."

Which would be more enjoyable: touring factories or running those facilities through the Twelve Point Success Metric? Actually, the factories would be interesting, even if the Cauliflower Baron had the ego of the Washington Monument. She'd never been to a factory although she'd consulted for dozens of manufacturing companies. But these factories were scattered across the Midwest and Southeast. Flight after flight after flight. The thought made her chest tighten. The street below her window receded farther and farther away. She glanced at the floor and tried not to think about the fact that no matter how solid it felt, it was just steel and Sheetrock standing because architects—who may or may not have cared about their jobs—designed it to (hopefully) stand up to whatever weather and earthquakes hit it.

"The Baron would love to meet you," the Baron said, "but your boss says you're the best. A man shouldn't interrupt a female's process."

Female's process? It sounded like menstruation. Rose put on her charming-professional voice.

"It is always a pleasure talking to you."

She hung up her phone and pressed two fingers to her forehead.

This is my life.

Chloe knocked on the glass door, and Rose beckoned her in.

"I see you've got SP on your calendar for this afternoon," Chloe said. "Who am I billing SP to?"

"Side project. The client wanted to stay anonymous. Doesn't want their shareholders to know they're getting a consultant. Just bill to SP and I'll get you the details later. Bill an associate's rate."

Chloe raised a perfectly shaped eyebrow. (Gigi gave her a discount at the salon.)

"Are you sure?"

It didn't matter what Rose billed. She wasn't going to collect from Ash. Billing Ash would be like stealing money from PFLAG. Ash had been so passionate about her film. Her dark-blue eyes had sparkled, as intense as a summer storm. She'd kept sweeping at her dark hair as though she couldn't stand to have a veil fall between her and her work even though her hair was pulled up. She'd looked at Rose like she was begging Rose to see something powerful and true. Rose had felt Ash's conviction in her body the way she felt the world existing around her when she filmed her own videos. She'd watched Ash across the large blond-wood table and suddenly the world was more real. Ash had said this was the kind of film they needed, and Rose felt the truth echo through her without even having heard the plot.

She saw Ash rising to shake her hand. She looked just like an indie filmmaker should, with a geometric design tattooed in dark greens and blues on her forearm and those skinny jeans and an elegantly threadbare T-shirt with the neck stretched out enough that Rose caught a glimpse of Ash's cleavage. An inadvertent glimpse. And Ash had that enviable hair that looked great messy, like she'd styled it by wrapping it into a bun on top of her head and then riding in a convertible. She rocked the look. And Rose wanted to unfurl Ash's hair, and she wanted to touch the velvet sides where Ash had shaved her head.

And she'd flirted with Ash, not that Ash had noticed or that Rose was the kind of woman Ash would notice (if Ash noticed women), but Rose had still flirted. *It'll be a pleasure doing business with you, Ms. Stewart.* Rose shook her head, an amused glow warming the general blah-ness of another day working for the Cauliflower Baron. She'd actually said that and held Ash's eye while she did. Okay, only for a split second, but still! Ty would assume Rose was desperately in love. Gigi would say, *That was it?* Cassie would scold them for hassling her. Maybe Rose wouldn't tell them. She'd keep that split second for herself.

"Rose?" Chloe prompted.

"What?"

"I asked if you'd like me to set up any regular meetings with your SP case? Your calendar is filling up for May and June."

Rose cleared her throat. "Save some seven p.m. slots for SP, maybe two a week."

"That's why you're making partner," Chloe said. "Those seven p.m. meetings."

Yeah. No. There were a million reasons why Rose was getting promoted. Taking on an indie film company for basically no money wasn't on the list. Integral Business Solutions frowned on pro bono work, although no one would stop her. A woman who was about to make partner could spend her evenings however she wanted. Not that Ash wanted to spend two evenings a week with her, but saving those time slots gave her a little thrill. Beautiful Ash Stewart with her sex-fern-human-suffering-healing-love queer rom-com was on her calendar.

Rose returned to her computer and googled Ash Stewart. The first hits were all movie-related. IMDb. Wikipedia. Ash had won best director at Sundance. Her second film had been an unexpected blockbuster. There were dozens of red-carpet shots, Ash—Ashlyn, as the reporters called her—dressed in fancier versions of her skinny jeans and T-shirts, usually with a leather jacket, occasionally in heels. She was almost always photographed next to a tall, blond woman listed as *wife and producer Victoria Crue.*

Victoria Crue was *always* described as *wife and producer.* Rose felt a moment of sympathy for her. She was obviously over-shadowed by Ash's talent. And on the red carpet next to Ash, she looked like a Barbie cutout. She was tall, skinny, blond, pretty, and whatever dress she was wearing was probably the look that season, but next to Ash she looked plastic, her smile too big, her teeth too white. Ash's smile was slightly lopsided, her dark hair messy even on the red carpet. Her clothes might have been designer, but they looked like she'd picked them up at a cool thrift store. She slouched casually when Victoria posed. Was this the ex who'd commission hand-knit sweaters for her cat?

Rose dug a little deeper. There was a BuzzFeed article titled "Ten Hollywood Breakups That Prove You Shouldn't Work with Your Wife." Ashlyn Stewart and wife and producer Victoria Crue were number eight because *artistic differences took their eleventh movie,* The Secret Song, *from a flight to a flop.* There was a candid shot of Ash sitting in a director's chair, head in her hands. Another article began *Sought-after director Ashlyn Stewart's recent divorce from wife and producer Victoria Crue killed* The Secret Song *a few weeks into production.*

The divorce seemed to have ended Ash's social media presence as well. There was her LinkedIn profile with no mention of Stewart Productions and an Instagram feed that ended on the set of *The Secret Song.* The URL for a personal website ended in a dead link.

Rose googled Victoria Crue. *Wife and producer* had become *producer.* She'd updated her Instagram an hour earlier with a photo of her and three other women toasting with tropical drinks. The caption read, *When you're voted the sexiest producer.*

No more sympathy for her.

Rose did a deeper dive into Brentworth, coming up with names of several people who'd pitched to her, some successful, most not. Usually, she'd send the list to Chloe. Today, she wrote her own email. *I wondered if you have twenty minutes to tell me about your experience pitching to Irene Brentworth.* She hit SEND on the last one and emerged in time for office happy hour. Then a quick trip home to change into yoga pants, an hour at Namaste Studio in the Pearl District, and on to the she-cave.

chapter 9

She let herself into Cassie's house. Delilah was at the kitchen table making a plague doctor mask out of papier-mâché.

"I hope that's for a school play," Rose said.

"They won't let us do anything fun," Delilah huffed. "We have to do *Brigadoon.*"

"So that's for…?"

"Prom."

"I love you," Rose said. "I fear you, but I love you."

Delilah muttered something into the cowl of her black cloak that sounded a lot like *I love you, too.*

Rose headed upstairs. Cassie and Ty were already there. Gigi arrived a few minutes later in a flurry of perfume and skin-care samples. She handed them around.

"We had three company reps come by today," she said. "Azalea Salon is on the map!"

They went around and shared their week. Ty wasn't *exactly* in love with a woman she saw reading on the TriMet, but the woman had been reading Audre Lorde and she had beautiful cheekbones. Cassie was worried about Delilah's eighth-grade field trip to DC.

"What if she gets there and starts protesting something? Chains herself to...I don't know, a bad senator?"

"We all want to say that won't happen," Gigi said in a way that said she absolutely did think it would happen.

"I'll talk to her about smart activism," Ty said. "You can't just go chaining yourself to people without a plan."

"Truth," Rose said, leaning back in her chair, cradling her skull goblet in both hands.

"Rose, what about your day?" Cassie asked.

"They have a guest instructor at Namaste. Cauliflower Baron is still talking about himself like he's his own biographer. Same old. Same old."

But it wasn't the same. She'd been looking into production costs for an indie film (about two to five million dollars, a lot more for a bigger production), pre-production schedule (two to three months), filming (as little as two weeks), marketing (a world of expensive, time-consuming opportunity). Rose pursed her lips and looked up toward the twinkle lights hung across the ceiling.

"I took on a pro bono client," she added.

"That's nice," Cassie said. "What do they do?"

"She's a filmmaker."

"She!" Ty said, eyes full of romantic speculation.

Rose's mind flashed to Ash's dark-blue eyes and tattooed arms. She pushed the thought away.

"There are a lot of women filmmakers," Rose chided.

"It's a disproportionately low number compared with men, which means that a lot of sexist stereotypes get perpetuated just by who controls the industry," Ty said.

"Thank you, Professor," Gigi said.

"But what's she like?" Ty's eyes sparkled.

Rose shrugged and looked away.

"She *is* interesting," Gigi said.

"Remember the woman I talked to at the Pug Crawl?"

"The one who saw you getting Muffin out of the trash," Gigi said.

"That one," Rose said ruefully.

"Are you in love?" Ty's eyes danced with emoji hearts. "What does that have to do with your client?"

"Weird coincidence. It's her."

"It's fate," Ty said.

"Of course I'm not in love. I got a message in the client portal from her friend. Have you heard of the movie *Under One Roof* or *The Memory Tree*?"

"I love *Under One Roof*," Ty said. "That was frickin' amazing."

"Ashlyn Stewart is the producer of *Under One Roof*...no, not the producer, the director. But now she makes advertisements, but she wants to get back into films. She's trying to get funding for a film. A queer love story."

Why not tell her sisters the truth? There was something about Ash that made the world feel bigger. When Chloe complained about SP's lack of tax ID number, Rose felt like a teenager happy for an excuse to say her crush's name. Not that she had a crush on Ash Stewart. Ash was just a glimpse into a life of passion and purpose, devoid of dehydrated vegetables...not that anyone's life was *really* devoid of dehydrated vegetables. They were in everything. Even things you wouldn't think about, like breakfast cereal.

Rose took a deep breath. The attic windows were open. The smell of flowers wafted in. Rose could hear the neighborhood breathing: the sound of a breeze, a dog barking, someone practicing the violin. It was spring, almost summer. When she was a teenager, before her parents got in the Cessna and said they'd call when they reached Colorado, spring nights had lasted forever. Back then she'd thought anything was possible on a night like this. Before she learned that anything *was* possible.

I'm so sorry. Your father was a good pilot.

"Ash has a big pitch coming up, and I'm going to consult for her. Just a few hours here and there." And then Ash would be gone. There'd be another Cauliflower Baron. More chats on Athena with women who were perfectly fine. It was all kind of sad if she said it out loud. "It's a way to support the queer community."

Rose didn't have a favorite sister. How could she when she loved them all so much? But if she did have a favorite, it'd be Ty for the way Ty nodded and said, "So it's *Ash* now. I see where this is going."

chapter 10

Ash paced the floor of the converted warehouse building that housed Stewart Productions, limping a little. The warehouse was always cold, even in the spring, even with the space heaters. Her bad leg wasn't that bad, considering the amount of titanium holding her together, but she felt the cold in every metal screw. But she wasn't thinking about that. She checked her phone: two minutes after seven p.m. Rose was the kind of person who'd be on time.

Her phone buzzed.

Rose: *I'm here.*

Ash could feel a smile spread across her face. She pressed her fingers to her lips to smooth it out. Rose wasn't excited about seeing her. Rose was just...nice. Maybe Rose was an optimist, thought they'd win the pitch, thought the film would gross millions and Rose would strike it big. But seeing Rose's name on her phone made Ash happy.

Ash opened that app connected to the building's security system, unlocked the door downstairs, and texted Rose to come up. Ash hurried to the studio door and propped it open. She slipped into the blazer she'd brought to dress up her Sex

Pistols T-shirt and ripped jeans. It was Armani, left over from her past life. She checked her face in a mirror in one of the makeshift dressing rooms set up for the actors in the shoots they did in-house. It'd been years since she'd thought about looking good for a woman. Did forty look good on her? Did the scars on her leg somehow register in her eyes? *Don't pick this one. This one's broken.* Maybe. But she didn't look all bad. She pressed her palms to her cheeks. Your wife leaving you in your time of need didn't mean your enviably high cheekbones deflated. Were her eyes still a blue so dark people mistook them for colored contacts? Yep. Still significantly blue. And the few threads of gray in her dark hair looked sophisticated. She shrugged. It was just a platonic meeting with a business consultant.

She slid into a chair at the large worktable and stared intently at her hand-drawn storyboards. Victoria had always said she spent too much time on the drawings. *We don't need art, Ash. We need stick figures that tell people where to stand.* But Ash needed to feel the characters' expressions emerge from her pen. Right now, though, she needed to look like she hadn't been watching her phone waiting for Rose.

A moment later, Rose's silky voice called from the open door. "Am I bothering you?"

It was the kind of voice that could silence a room with its calm. The kind of voice that could lull a lover to sleep. It fit with Rose's tailored suit and restrained haircut and at the same time it didn't. It was the voice of a goddess of business professionalism but with a murmur of something seductive.

"Of course not," Ash said, pushing her hair back except that it was already in a high ponytail.

Rose walked over, then stopped. "These drawings. You did those?"

"Waste of time."

"May I?" Rose hovered her hand over a picture showing the naked lovers as they lay down on a bed of moss.

There was nothing odd about sex scenes in Hollywood. Sex scenes were part of the business. But were they part of Rose's Integral Business Solutions' Twelve Point Success Metric? Ash felt herself blush.

"Nice detail in the ferns," Rose said.

Ash hazarded a glance at her. Rose seemed to be holding back a smile, like she knew Ash was blushing and was trying not to look amused.

"Emma warned me about the ferns," Rose said.

Ash frowned.

"It was in the trigger warning." Rose's smile opened up, but she didn't elaborate. She set her briefcase on the table. "Shall we get to work?" Rose sat down and opened her tablet to a document titled *Business Enhancement Plan: Stewart Productions. Focus: Pitch to Investor Irene Brentworth.* "Let's start with how you got Brentworth interested. What did you send her?"

Rose unfolded a Bluetooth keyboard and waited.

Ash got up and retrieved the notebook in which she'd printed her emails to and from Brentworth's office. She sat down next to Rose, not particularly close but the size of the table and the expanse of space around them made it feel intimate.

"Nirvana?" Rose looked at the faded band stickers on the notebook's cover. "Gin Blossoms. Garbage. Cat Power. You did like the nineties, didn't you?"

"Best music ever." Ash hummed a line of the Gin Blossoms' "Hey Jealousy."

To Ash's surprise, Rose picked up the song in that velvety voice. Funny how the mind stored megabits of song lyrics without you realizing it. Ash picked up the tune, and Rose smiled as they sang together. They both stopped before the line *I might be here with you.* And stopping seemed to say more than singing the line would have.

Rose didn't say anything. Ash was suddenly aware of the moment: the tall windows, the evening light, the industrial HVAC system humming in the background, Rose's half smile. Ash went whole days without breathing because she didn't have time to inhale, but she couldn't remember the last time her breath had caught like this. As though they realized simultaneously that the silence between them had stretched too long, they both laughed.

Ash opened the notebook to the initial Brentworth pitch and pushed it in Rose's direction.

Rose studied Ash's notes. "Your handwriting is like a font. You know when someone writes this neat, they're hiding something," she said in a dramatic whisper. She was joking, but Ash felt the weight of the things she didn't talk about anymore. Rose must have spotted some micro expression on her face. "Aren't we all," she concluded with a shake of her head. "You never know when one of your colleagues might be a serial killer."

"Have you picked out some potentials at Integral Business Solutions?"

"God, I wish they were that interesting. They'd all be the neighbor who said, *He seemed like such a nice guy.* No imagination." Rose turned back to the notebook.

Ash studied Rose. Her lip gloss was sensuous and wet. Pilot—their props, costumes, makeup, and sometimes set location manager—would say a woman in Rose's suit should wear a nude, matte lipstick.

"I see for your tagline, you've got '*Bridget Jones's Diary* meets *A River Runs Through It* with lesbians,'" Rose said.

Ash propped her elbows on the table, forehead resting on her fingertips. She looked through her fingers at Rose. Victoria had been great at taglines. How could Ash condense the script and everything she envisioned for the movie into two sentences?

"Give me the elevator speech," Rose prompted.

"It's about wanting things to be different and not knowing what to do to change them."

Ash stopped. Rose waited.

"That kind of describes *Frozen*," Rose said, not unkindly. "And *Star Wars*."

"I know. And the *Saw* franchise. Let me try again. It's a romantic comedy about a park ranger and a disabled firefighter who fall in love at a survivalist expo where they sell gear."

She could see the story, draw it, bring it to life in an actor's eyes. But to turn it into an elevator pitch . . .

The sun had gone behind the buildings across the street. Overhead lamps lit the high-ceilinged space.

"I'm not very good at summarizing it."

"I haven't helped anyone with a movie pitch," Rose said, "but I've worked on all sorts of sales pitches. You can prepare all the materials in the world, but if you're pitching to a single investor, they're going to want to see *you*. So, in your words, what's it about?"

Rose held Ash's eyes. Ash rolled up the cuffs of her blazer, then unrolled them. She'd written the script. When she'd directed movies, she'd known the stories through and through. If only the script didn't feel so unrealistic. Still, maybe unrealistic was okay. Fuck Hollywood and its lesbian-has-to-die tropes. Ash touched her fingertips to her lips, then rested her palms on the table.

"There's this woman who used to be a firefighter, and now

she's all into proving that she's still tough, but it's all to prove she's still worthy because she was in a fire where *she* had to be rescued," Ash said. "She's on leave and she feels like a failure. She meets a woman at a survivalist gear expo. The woman's been working in Fish and Wildlife way out in the wilderness, and she's bored and lonely. But the firefighter thinks the way to impress her is to ask her to do more and more physical things. Rock climb. Skydive."

Rose blanched. "No," she said quickly.

"We can cut the skydiving," Ash said. "It'd be expensive to film."

Rose nodded.

"So the park ranger thinks this is what the firefighter really wants, and goes along because she likes her," Ash went on. "The ranger wants to get back to a house with a gas fireplace and Netflix, but they go on all these adventures. They're both trying to be something they're not. But eventually they understand that the other one loves them because of their weaknesses, not despite them. It's corny, but America will love it. Everyone is worthy of love. Et cetera."

Rose's tablet had gone black. "It's not corny," she said.

But it's not true. Or maybe it was for someone. Maybe if Ash had had more grit…

"Did you write the script?"

"Yeah."

"I'll need to read it."

Obviously, Rose should read it. If Brentworth backed the movie millions of people would hear the actors speak the lines Ash had written, but Ash felt exposed. Would Rose read the script and see Ash's loneliness on the page? *I thought my wife would love me forever.*

"It's wish fulfillment," Ash said. "Rom-com sells."

"Don't worry," Rose said. "Send me the file. I already love it. Now let's talk budgets. Do you know roughly how much you need?"

And that was filmmaking. *Let's explore the tragedy of the human condition and now...do you think we could get a discount on that camera dolly?*

"Five million?"

"Too low." Rose turned her tablet, so it faced them both. "Here's my first estimate."

It wasn't *Lord of the Rings* money, but damn.

"We can't afford that." Ash sucked at her bottom lip.

"You can afford what you ask for," Rose said. "We're not going to ask like this is some small project. We're asking for blockbuster money. We're asking for what you're worth."

"But you don't know me." Ash hadn't meant to say it.

"I watched some of your movies before this meeting." Rose cocked her head. "I see you." She looked away and cleared her throat. "It's my job to assess the potential rate of return on a project." She wiped an invisible speck off her tablet screen. "Walk me through how many people you'll need."

"I'll be production designer. Director of course. I can help with the electrical work."

Rose rested her hand on the table between them, like a gentle stop sign. "Emma says you take on too much."

"I don't know when Emma decided to be my mother."

"That's what I do to my sisters," Rose said. "We meddle with the people we love. Now let's run through crew estimates *without* you doing everyone's job."

Rose gave her a surprisingly playful smile. And Ash had the urge to give Rose a friendly shove the way she'd shove Emma.

"You two are ganging up on me."

"We're ganging up *for* you."

After an hour of Ash realizing she knew less than she thought about personnel costs and insurance, Rose turned her tablet off.

"I want a coffee." Rose stood up. "Come on."

chapter 11

When they were outside on the street, Ash tried to think of a conversation starter. She used to make charming small talk at hundreds of parties. Now she drew a blank.

"So," Rose asked as though approaching a delicate subject, "this budget stuff isn't really your wheelhouse, is it?"

"Or the promotion stuff. Or writing a decent logline."

"Yeah. I'm not sure *with lesbians* is right. It sounds a little like you're adding fries to the order." There wasn't anything mean about the amusement in Rose's voice.

"I can't believe Brentworth went for that."

"I can. The script sounds beautiful."

"My ex handled all the budget and promotions and stuff."

Rose seemed like the kind of person who researched their clients. Had she read about *The Secret Song*'s spectacular fail?

Ash hesitated. "She needed me professionally, and I let her down."

Victoria had needed her in other ways, and Ash had failed her there, too. Ash's body—not her refurbished leg but the intimate parts—still hurt at the lightest touch. The innumerable MRIs and a strange nerve test that involved putting electrodes on her vulva had found nothing. *It's trauma,* a therapist finally told her. *It's your body saying your heart isn't ready.* Victoria didn't have patience for that.

They slowed their pace.

What if there was another universe in which she'd never met Victoria? Never taken that ride on the 101? A universe where an evening walk with Rose was the start of something special?

"I should have learned her side of the work," Ash said. "All I know is how to direct."

"What? You won't be doing the catering, too?" Rose said gently. "You don't have to be good at everything. That's where I come in." Rose bumped her shoulder against Ash's. "*I'm* good at everything."

"I don't expect you to do too much," Ash said. *I can't keep taking care of you, Ash.* She could hear Victoria deliver those words like an actor trying the line again and again, imbuing it with hurt one time, anger the next. "It's not fair to put that on another person."

"I'm your business consultant. It's my *job.*"

Ash let out a slow breath. Ash wouldn't let Rose down if the pitch failed. Sure, winning the pitch would be another line on Rose's vita, but it wasn't personal. And if Ash asked for too much, Rose wouldn't hate her. She'd just draw up a contract outlining what she would and wouldn't do for Stewart Productions.

"I'm serious," Rose said. "I help people reach their goals. It's what I do."

"Okay." Ash's voice came out rough.

Rose put her hand on Ash's arm. Overhead, a motion-sensitive streetlight flicked on with the same crackle Ash felt at Rose's touch, an electric blue spark. Rose let her hand linger. She held Ash's eyes. Then Rose withdrew her hand with a little shake of her head as if she'd just remembered a silly mistake she'd made and was shaking off the memory.

"So how did you get into filming?" she asked.

Film school, met a rich woman, directed her movies, won awards, got famous, lost everything.

Maybe Rose was changing the subject because she sensed Ash had issues, but Rose looked genuinely curious.

"I always loved movies," Ash said.

It had been a long time since anyone had asked why Ash had dedicated her life to twelve-hour days on set or why it still hurt that she wasn't there now.

"When I was a kid, I'd carry around a piece of cardboard with a square cut out and look at everything that way."

Did any of that matter now?

"And?" Rose prompted.

"We lived in this flat ranch home in a flat suburb in a flat part of Illinois. It was so normal. It could have been an ad for breakfast cereal, but I liked to find the moments when people were real. That look. That thing they said when they meant to tell a white lie. I love how film makes you really *look* at people, not just see them because your eyes are open. And film is artificial, but at its best it lets us see the human reality we miss because we're too busy."

"Trying to do too much," Rose said quietly enough that she didn't interrupt Ash's flow.

"And then when you've created that reality, you can tell stories and you can make them real. With the right camera-people and the right actors, you can show every layer of the character's truth."

Rose stopped on a corner beneath another streetlight. Across the street, an old factory building still bore the words

PORTLAND SUNDRIES painted on the brick. Rose turned to Ash. *"That's* the excitement investors want."

Ash looked at her. She couldn't tell what color Rose's eyes were. They hovered between blue and brown. Maybe gray. The blue of a sunny day reflected on the eternally gray waves of the Oregon coast. The rich mahogany brown of new chestnuts littering an autumn street.

Something zinged between them, making the air hum.

For a second, she thought Rose would kiss her. For a second, she thought she'd kiss Rose.

"That passion," Rose whispered, her voice breathy and commanding at the same time.

Rose touched her wrist.

All Ash's awareness focused on Rose's warm touch.

"What you said was beautiful. Not everyone has that passion."

Rose's voice sent shivers down Ash's back. They were standing close. The tingle that suffused Ash's body told her what it would be like to hear Rose whisper endearments while tracing her fingers across Ash's body. She wanted to hold on to the moment. When was the last time she'd wanted a woman? She'd lost that part of herself: desire and this silly glow of affection. But Rose had such beautiful skin and perfect curves and a lovely smile. She *wanted* Rose. And she thought she'd lost the ability to feel that. She wanted to tell Rose that Rose had given her a gift even though nothing would happen between them. Rose so obviously had her shit together, and it would be silly for Rose to sign on with damaged goods like Ash, but just wanting Rose was special. And then she realized she'd been staring at Rose for several beats too long. She turned away quickly, making it more obvious that she'd been staring.

"Has your pug eaten any napkins recently?" Ash mumbled in an amazing show of charming small talk.

Rose's laughter said, *It's okay that you were looking.* And if Ash hadn't known better, she would have thought there was a little note of, *I'm glad you were.*

"Well, let me tell you *all* about it because I am sure you want to hear it," Rose said.

They reached the coffee shop tucked in between two Victorian houses on the edge of the industrial district. Rose bought Ash a coffee.

Rose talked about Muffin and Cupcake all the way back, which was longer than Ash should have been interested in how Muffin got ahold of sponges, but somehow she still was.

They spent another hour going over expenses. Then Ash showed Rose around the equipment lockers, opening up a few of the cases to show Rose the cameras and lenses and the sad excuse for sound equipment she had to update.

"It just hasn't been a priority," she said. "You don't need a three-thousand-dollar shotgun mic to film a guy telling you to buy used cars."

Rose took the microphone from her hand and studied it.

"This has got to be ten years old," Rose said.

"Good guess. Ten exactly."

They walked back to the middle of the studio. It seemed like the end of the evening, but Rose lingered. Ash gestured to the sofa. Then they were sitting side by side, Rose telling a hilarious story about baking with her sisters. Ash reenacted Emma's gaming skills, miming Amphib the Destroyer's powers and her own demise. Somehow they moved on to favorite pens, then their feelings about jump ropes. Everything Rose said was witty and smart, and the way she laughed at Ash's jokes made Ash feel confident in a way she hadn't since the accident. She could have talked all night, but eventually, Rose said, "Getting back to business: I want to brainstorm marketing ideas. I thought maybe we could do a talk-and-walk. Get out of the studio, think things through outside."

Ash wanted to say, *How about tomorrow? How about right now? Let's find a lane with cherry blossoms.* She could see the shot perfectly. Ash didn't say anything as she studied the scene in her mind's eye.

Rose messed with something in her briefcase.

"I mean, I could come to the studio or we could do it over Teams," she added.

Ash came back to herself.

"No. Yes. I mean I want you." The slip! "I want *to*," Ash corrected quickly.

Back in the day, she hadn't been the kind of person who stumbled over her words. Maybe Rose hadn't noticed. Rose's bemused smile said she had. Ash pulled herself together.

"I don't want to do it on Teams." That still sounded dirty. "I want to brainstorm marketing ideas while walking somewhere with you. I want your business expertise." She did not need to use the word *want*. "I mean learn from. I want to learn from you." *Damn.*

Rose's eyes sparkled with laughter.

"Why thank you, Ms. Stewart. It's good to be wanted."

chapter 12

Rose kicked off her shoes and threw her jacket on her bed. Cupcake and Muffin were near death by starvation. They raced around her feet, then back to the top of the stairs that led down to the kitchen and their last chance of food and survival, then back to the bedroom.

"Live off your fat supplies for ten minutes." Rose knelt down and put her nose to Muffin's. He smelled like stale Cheetos. "I love you. Wait."

She changed into yoga pants and a soft, bamboo T-shirt. She glanced in the mirror. The fabric outlined her breasts, her nipples hard in the cool air. She hadn't thought about her body for a long time. It was a perfectly acceptable body. She had strong abs and curves. Would Ash think she was too thick? That she had a good body? She pushed the thought out of her mind.

Ash. Ashlyn. She was fascinating. All that artistic fire, that confidence of vision, her passion. But she seemed nervous, too, a little bumbling. Cute despite her intimidatingly cool style. Rose sighed.

"Tell me to forget it," she told the pugs.

Their eyes goggled with hunger. Rose gave in, went downstairs, and fed them. Then she set her tablet on the counter. Ash had emailed the script without a message. Rose downloaded the file. She'd stayed longer at the studio than she'd expected. She'd drawn out the visit with a coffee she didn't need. It was almost midnight. She should go to bed. She poured a glass of wine, curled up on the couch, and opened the script. It began, *Establishing shot: suburban neighborhood from above.* Ash would need drone footage. Rose would add that to the budget. *Close-up: Woman wakes to loud alarm set on her phone.* Muffin and Cupcake curled up at her feet.

Reading the script wasn't like reading a book. Descriptions of setting and action interrupted the dialogue. It was hard to picture the scenes. But slowly she eased into it. She saw the park ranger packing up her gear. She laughed as the two women emerged from a fun-run where they'd run through pools of mud. The characters were charming, their misunderstandings funny. When the two women finally made love on a blanket beside a waterfall, it was so right. It was the unconditional love anyone who had been hurt in the past longed for, love that accepted and healed, love that made the world a better place.

"I am not crying," she told the pugs.

They goggled at her with unconditional love and love for all the things currently in the refrigerator and the wrappers they came in.

Around ten the next morning, Rose set a cup of coffee on Chloe's desk.

"Morning meeting?" Chloe asked.

Rose was never late. Around her, the office purred with quiet phone calls and the occasional laughter.

"Something like that."

"Who should I bill it to?"

Muffin and Cupcake and not wanting to pull herself out from under her down comforter. She'd reread the end of the script three times. It warmed her heart. It made her want to squeeze her pillow and giggle with the simple happiness of the perfect ending.

"Put it on SP."

"Your secret project."

"Not a secret, just..." Rose gestured vaguely with her own coffee.

"Of course." Chloe respected hierarchies. Rose was her boss.

"What's on the docket?" Rose asked.

Chloe checked her computer. "Meeting with Mr. Cauliflower's CFO at ten thirty."

If Chloe saw the flash of shit-I-forgot cross Rose's face, she didn't acknowledge it.

"Eleven thirty Thomson-Graham Legal. Lunch with Arnold Faulk from First American Accounting." Chloe went on, finishing with the usual, "And your messages are in your inbox. There's two. Both from people calling about someone named Brentworth."

Hopefully one of them was the producer whose movie had gotten Brentworth's money. The fails would help, too, though. They'd had Brentworth's attention, but they hadn't sealed the deal. What did Ash have that they didn't? She saw Ash explaining the power of film, her eyes full of blue fire. Rose was cramming everything she could learn about the film industry like a student getting ready for a midterm, but she knew business and she knew people. That fire could win deals and change the world, but the people with that fire also missed deadlines and forgot appointments. They needed someone to manage the spreadsheets. They needed someone like Rose to be the boring one who remembered the details.

After many boring details, all handled with effortless efficiency, Rose packed up her briefcase and waved to the associates still in the office. She stopped in the single-stall bathroom and changed into her yoga gear. She usually waited until she got to Namaste Studios to change, but she didn't feel like walking downtown in heels. Did it matter if three junior associates saw her in her sexiest yoga pants?

Ty was already waiting for her in the lobby in sweatpants and a T-shirt that read GENDER IS A SOCIAL CONSTRUCTION. Together they strolled down Southwest Third Street on their way to the yoga studio.

"So how is she?" Ty asked.

Sunlight sparkled off shop windows. The air smelled of flowers, car exhaust, and coffee. The sound of a busker's saxophone mixed with Adele pouring out of a passing car.

"Who?"

"Really?" Ty nudged her with her yoga mat. "Kamala Harris. Beyoncé."

"Oh, you must mean the attorney I hired to check the shipping contracts for the Cauliflower Baron's Mississippi factory."

"I mean your *filmmaker*."

Rose grinned. Nothing would ever come of working with Ash Stewart except, hopefully, a big movie deal for Ash. Still, it was fun to string Ty along.

"Your filmmaker! What's she like?"

"She's..." *Exciting. Intense. Everything I'm not.* "She's talented but a bit head-in-the-clouds. Not irresponsible. She runs a business. But she's an artist. She's never had to handle a big film budget or a marketing plan."

Ty bounced in her secondhand Doc Martens.

"I mean, what did you talk about besides budgets? Was there sexual tension? Did you kiss her? I looked her up. She's super-hot."

Rose saw Ash's messy hair, her stylishly threadbare T-shirt, the geometric tattoo on her forearm. *We sang Gin Blossoms together.*

"You're smiling. Oh my gosh, this is the most exciting thing," Ty said.

"I talked to a filmmaker about budgets and *that's* the most exciting thing? You must really think my life is boring."

"Yes!" Ty said enthusiastically.

Rose gave Ty a friendly shove.

"She is objectively attractive."

Ty swung her mat at Rose's butt.

"Fine. Very attractive."

Ty hit her again.

Ty was right. She was smiling. She couldn't hide it. She didn't want to. Ash's attractiveness was more than her face, more than her straight nose and jawline—which was stronger than classically feminine—which all combined made her more beautiful. Beautiful in a way Rose wanted to watch. And she was so animated, swinging from passion to nervousness. Rose could see the energy tightening Ash's body. She was as exciting as a high-tension wire. But she was also easy to talk to. The kind of person Rose could spend all afternoon doing nothing with. And the script was gorgeous. You couldn't not fall a little bit in love with someone who'd written something so moving.

"She's kind of special." Rose ducked her head so Ty wouldn't see her blush. She described Ash's movie and their meeting. "Her friend says she works too much," Rose finished. "The pitch is what I'm hired for but I think what Emma really wants is for me to calm her down."

"Calm her down." Ty imbued the words with lube and a bed full of sex toys.

"Not like that."

"Can you do it?" Ty asked seriously. "Or is she like an artist who has to be on the edge to do her work?"

"I don't know. Someone has to be not-on-the-edge to do this pitch."

"She needs you," Ty said approvingly. "And what's that business with her ex-wife? I read about it in some online tabloid."

"She didn't talk about it." She didn't talk about it in a way that hinted at a larger story. Rose knew about those stories. "I'd like to know, but it's none of my business."

They arrived at the studio, the doors open to the sunshine, Tibetan bells playing on repeat inside. They took their seats in the large meditation room, and Rose took a centering breath. The room filled up. A few women chatted in the back, but mostly it was quiet.

"With a deep breath, you will clear your mind," their instructor began.

But Rose's thoughts bounced back and forth between Emma's instructions to save Ash from herself. And the script. And the way Ty teased her as though Rose might have a chance with someone like Ash. Of course, that was the point of meditation: to acknowledge errant thoughts and let them go. If meditation was weight lifting, each thought she let go was like one rep building up to a state of peace. Rose didn't want to push aside the vision of Ash messing with her hair as though she hadn't already put it up. The gesture was cute and nervous and sexy all at the same time.

"We honor our feelings, but they are not reality," the instructor intoned. "We examine our thoughts and we let them go."

Focus on your breath. Peace. Universe. How did the Namaste instructors stand hours of Tibetan bells? Even Tibet didn't play that many Tibetan bells. At least sub in some pan flutes. She'd complain about it to Ash when she saw her next. Ash would be amused. Rose liked the way Ash's smile had curled when she'd joked about her dogs and told stories about her sisters.

"Imagine peace radiating from your fingertips," the instructor said.

Rose pictured running her hands through Ash's hair. Would Ash sigh? What would Ash's face look like as she relaxed? Would her hair smell like perfume? Rose's own body grew languid as her thoughts drifted to Ash's lips. She should be embarrassed. Thinking about a client that way! Although they didn't have a contract. She didn't expect to get paid. That wasn't the usual client-consultant relationship. Maybe Rose was a patron of the arts. She couldn't create movies that changed the world, but she could help Ash do it. Did that make thinking about smelling Ash's hair less inappropriate?

It didn't matter. It was just a passing crush she'd never do anything about. And it wasn't her fault. Who could resist crushing on someone like Ash...dreaming about what it would be like to lounge on a tropic beach with Ash beside her. It was like glimpsing a tiny piece of someone else's life. A life that didn't include the Cauliflower Baron and the exact same coffee every morning...or if she did have the same coffee, in that alternate life she left all the cups out because she was too enthralled with her work to walk them to the trash can.

chapter 13

Rose arrived at the garden before Ash. She rolled down her windows and took out her phone. She really didn't have time to help a pro bono client brainstorm marketing ideas in the Japanese garden. She had four potential corporate clients waiting in her inbox. She began dictating a message.

"Dear Mr. Maynard, I am delighted you are interested in…twelve-point metric…believe you'll find…"

When she finished, she copied the message and pasted it into another email, changing the name for her next prospective client. And the next and next. She was just hitting SEND when a movement caught her eye. Ash had pulled in beside her in a sleek, silent Tesla. The door lifted like a wing, and she stepped out wearing ripped jeans, a leather jacket, and a black T-shirt with a faded band logo on it.

Rose got out of her Subaru Legacy, rated one of *Motor Trend*'s safest cars of 2021.

Ash made a minute gesture and the car door…wing… closed. She put on sunglasses. It was over the top. Ash might as well have stepped out of a sexy action movie. Rose shook her head.

"What?" Ash asked.

There was no point in pretending she could compete. Rose deliberately looked Ash up and down. "No one is actually this cool in real life."

Ash looked back at the car as though surprised that Rose had noticed, then gave an embarrassed snort. "My ex bought the car. And she left me with the payment." Something crossed Ash's face. "Victoria said I couldn't drive for shit."

Victoria Crue. She was the story Ash wasn't telling. Rose wanted to say, *Ten seconds on her Instagram page and I wanted to smack her.*

"I took lessons on a closed course," Ash added.

"And you car race."

"I didn't learn to *race*. I never went over a hundred and ten."

Rose chuckled "Come on, rock star." Rose motioned for Ash to follow her toward the garden's entrance.

The garden was on a hill. Trees obscured most of the sky-line, but Rose still felt like she was floating above the city.

"Am I taking up too much of your time?" Ash asked as they crossed the parking lot. "We could've met at your office."

Of course they could have met in her office. Rose didn't take the Cauliflower Baron to the Japanese garden. There was something distinctly date-like about this trip. Was she making Ash uncomfortable? Maybe Ash felt obliged to come because Rose was working pro bono. Still, there'd been something in the way Ash had stumbled over her words the last time they'd seen each other. *I want you.* No, it was a slip of the tongue, and Rose shouldn't think about it.

"We can go to the office if you like," Rose said.

Ash's sunglasses broadcast, *Nothing has ever unnerved me.* But her jaw tightened and she looked away. Was that dis-appointment?

"But I think this is better," Rose added.

"This has got to be boring for you compared with the big companies you work with." Ash pursed her lips.

I would watch you sort paper clips.

"This is my job, remember," Rose said.

They reached the garden entrance. Rose flashed her phone and her prepaid tickets at the attendant.

"Marketing isn't a science; it's an art. This setting will help you think."

Was that total bullshit? Had she just dragged Ash out here because she wanted to see Ash silhouetted against the iconic Japanese maple that graced the center of the garden?

"It's beautiful," Ash breathed.

Mounds of pink flowers surrounded a stone pagoda. A waterfall tumbled down mossy rocks. Ferns adorned the shade beneath Japanese maples. Yellow-green vine maples rose out of banks of rhododendrons. A hundred other plants Rose couldn't name surrounded a pool of koi. Nothing forced. Nothing cut with a straightedge.

Ash looked around slowly. "I can't believe I've never been."

"I try to come here every time it snows, I like listening to the garden when it's even quieter than now." That sounded dreamy. Rose cleared her throat. "I read your script."

Ash's shoulders tightened. She walked a few paces ahead on the softly curving path, then stopped.

"What did you think?"

"It was amazing."

Ash let out a long breath. "You don't have to say that to be nice."

"I read it in one sitting. It's funny. It's touching. I will not say that I cried at the end, but I cried at the end."

"You don't think the end is...unrealistic?" Ash stared

across the garden, but she seemed to be looking at something else.

"What's unrealistic about two people finding love?"

Ash shrugged.

How could Victoria Crue have earned Ash's love and then left her? Or had Ash left Victoria Crue? Rose glanced at Ash. Sunglasses. Leather jacket. Long legs in tight jeans. She was hot. She could have anyone she wanted. Was Rose inventing a personality for Ash? Maybe Ash had cheated on Victoria. Maybe Ash had used Victoria for money. Maybe the version of Ash she saw was a figment of Rose's imagination, a midlife crisis she'd never act on.

No.

The woman who wrote that script wouldn't say *forever* and not mean it.

Rose came back to herself. Ash had taken off her sunglasses and tucked them into the neck of her T-shirt. Rose opened her mouth to speak. Nothing came out. Ash bit her lip as though she was preparing to speak, too, but she didn't. The sunlight around them sparkled. Birds Rose hadn't noticed before sang out from every tree. The burble of water sounded sensual. Out of the corner of Rose's eye she caught the orange flash of a fish in the pool, but mostly she looked at Ash. There was a bone-deep longing in Ash's blue eyes. It couldn't be for Rose although it was Rose that Ash gazed at.

"I…" Rose didn't have another word.

"I…know. I…"

What did Ash know? She couldn't read Rose's thoughts. They were swirling too fast for Rose to read them. It was clear neither of them was going to finish their sentences.

Finally Rose said, "First, let's think about the film's iconic elements and how those create a brand image."

It would have sounded like a rejection, except the words came out in a lover's whisper. Rose felt herself blush. Ash smiled for the first time since she'd gotten out of the Tesla.

"Is that part of the Ten Point Success Metric?" she asked.

"Twelve points. Those last two points are very important," Rose said with exaggerated dignity.

They both laughed. Rose felt the nervous tension in her belly dissipate. Ash seemed to relax.

They walked on. It took Rose a few minutes to get Ash into brainstorming, but when Rose did Ash had dozens of ideas. She described the characters and scenes as though they were already on-screen, her voice at turns excited and reverent. Eventually, they took a seat on a stone bench beneath a weeping cherry tree.

"So what do you want the actual pitch to look like?" Rose asked. "In my world, it's a conference room with expensive pastries no one eats. What about yours?"

"It has to be in LA."

"Do we meet at Brentworth's office?"

Ash squinted. "I can't see showing the proof of concept in a boardroom. I mean, we can always send it to her in advance, but I'd like to be there the first time she sees it."

"If you could have anything you wanted, what would it be?"

"Anything?"

The insinuation in Ash's voice made Rose's heart flutter. That had to be flirtation.

"Sure, anything." Rose echoed Ash's tone.

"Hmm." Ash cocked her head pensively. "If I could have anything…" She chuckled, a hint of sadness behind her laugh. "But for the pitch, if I could have anything, I'd find some gorgeous vintage theater. Brentworth was a stage actor when she was younger. We'd show the proof of concept there. It'd be like the ghosts of audiences past were all around us, like we were part of all the great films that had come before, and what we did still mattered. It was still art. Even as everyone's trying to CGI it up and putting out *Fast and Furious 10*." She stopped. "I'm not throwing shade. I love *Fast and Furious*. But I want her to feel like Ingmar Bergman is sitting behind her with his hand on her shoulder. But I guess we'd have to take her back to the boardroom for the talk," Ash said. "There's a scouting challenge. Find a vintage theater with a modern boardroom attached."

"What if we made a boardroom onstage," Rose mused. "Brentworth would be back onstage playing the role of herself."

"Coming full circle. She was an actor and now she's a producer on the stage about to play this big role in the life of film."

"That's the brand image we want. We are the big role in the life of film."

We. Rose never said *we* to her clients.

"That'd be nice," Ash said.

"Do you really like the idea?"

"Of course."

"Do you have any neighborhoods you prefer?" Rose asked.

"For what?"

"For the theater."

"You're not actually going to get us a theater," Ash said. "We can't afford a rental like that."

Rose was not going to find a theater come hell or high water. She was not going to manufacture one out of thin air just to see the look on Ash's face when she showed her the pictures. She wouldn't pay the rental fee herself because she had more money than she needed and nothing to spend it on except her pugs.

Obviously, she wouldn't.

"I'll see what I can do."

chapter 14

Ash paused on an arched footbridge and looked down at the carp swimming below. She always wanted to be in the studio, and now that they had a proof of concept to film and a script that needed to be green-locked in less than a month, every minute outside the studio should kill her with anxiety, but she didn't want to leave the garden. Rose stood beside her.

The way Rose had looked at her...the complicated blue-brown of Rose's eyes, as though the two colors had mixed in equal parts without muddying each other. Entirely blue and entirely brown. An optical illusion that Ash could spend a long time considering.

And Ash had looked at Rose. And Rose hadn't turned away. She'd brought them back to business, but her voice had been low and rough. The words *brand image* had never sounded sexier. It was like they both knew they weren't saying something, and there was an intimacy in that. But what weren't they saying? *I like you? I want more than this? Nothing will come of this tremulous moment, but we were both here and we felt it?*

"I guess I should be getting back to the office." Rose stepped away from the railing.

"Yes." *No.* "I should get back to the studio."

They walked in silence to the exit, across the parking lot, and to their cars. There was the Tesla that Victoria had bought for herself and then pawned off on Ash in the divorce. *It'll help you get back into driving,* Victoria had said. It'd felt like a rebuke. Ash felt a twinge of pain between her legs. It had been a while since her body had clenched up at just the thought of Victoria and the accident. It was reminding her she was damaged goods. Just in case the look in Rose's eyes had made her forget.

Rose hesitated with her hand on her car door.

"I'll work on a marketing plan," she said. "We can go over the details, see what you like, see what you want to change."

Ash hated her body for reminding her that that confidence she had once possessed had ended on a curve on the 101. Why should one split second define everything?

"I know you're busy," Ash blurted, "but do you want to come back to the studio and see the sets?"

When they arrived at the studio, Pilot and Emma were applying a chalky substance to a plywood wall, Pilot painting in his usual velvet smoking jacket, the paint can held at arm's length, Emma in a spattered rugby jersey. It had been a long time since Ash had built anything resembling a set. Hollywood directors didn't build sets, and car commercials didn't need sets. But she and Emma had cleared space for the set, throwing away dead office chairs to make room. Jason had assembled three walls, and a cozy café had emerged from the two-by-fours and plywood.

Emma and Pilot both turned at the sound of the door opening. Emma whispered something to Pilot. His eyes widened.

"This is Pilot." Ash introduced him. "Pilot does set design, props, costumes."

"When Ash isn't jumping in and trying to do my job for me." He shot Ash a look.

"I'm helping," Ash said.

"Micromanager." Pilot flourished his bejeweled hand. "We love her, though." He turned to Rose.

"This is Rose," Ash said. "She's helping us with the pitch."

"And I'm helping Ash take things a little easier." Rose smiled at her. "I took her to the Japanese garden and we watched the carp."

Emma gave Ash a chummy slap on the back. "We've been worried about Ash for a long time. She never watches the carp."

"I don't think that means anything," Ash said, but Emma's teasing and Rose's smile made her feel warm inside.

Pilot shook Rose's hand. Emma had been talking about her. Ash could see it in the way Pilot looked Rose up and down. He wasn't checking her out for himself. He was assessing Ash's choices, like he assessed her choice of props. His slight nod said he approved.

"What are you working on?" Rose asked.

"I finally have a project worthy of my talents." Pilot gestured to the wall he was painting. "This will be a café and then we'll redesign it as a sporting goods store. I mean, we could find a real sporting goods store and a café but we'd have to get them to close for a couple of days and they have to have the wiring for the electricity we need to run the lights. It's easier to build a set."

"And the sound." Rose looked up, studying the sound-absorbing panels on the ceiling. "You'd have too much ambient

sound if you were in a real store. You'd have to rent the buildings beside the café and the store, and close off the street. And
there's the airplanes." She shuddered like she was talking about
snakes in a swimming pool. "They fly over all the time."

Pilot and Rose chatted for a few more minutes, then Emma
clasped Pilot's arm.

"We're done here," she said.

"We haven't finished the—"

Emma cut Pilot off. "Rose and Ash need to be alone. They've
got a lot of work to do."

Oh, the subtlety. Ash shot Emma a what-the-hell look.
Emma bugged her eyes at Ash and mouthed, *You're welcome.*
Ash felt her cheeks flush. Rose had the decency to pretend she
hadn't noticed the interchange.

"Give me the tour," Rose said as Emma and Pilot headed out.

Ash pointed to the breaks in the set walls. "I want to be
able to get a camera in here, here, and here. That's the other
thing about a set. You can shoot from wherever you like. For
the proof of concept, I want part of the scene where they're
in the sporting goods store and the firefighter is pulling out
all this equipment, trying to prove how tough she is. She's
going to go rappelling. Caving. Windsurfing."

"Sounds dangerous. Do you have to film those?"

"If we get the budget, it'd be awesome. For now Jason says
there's this gorgeous island in the San Juans where we can
film the fern scene. He's got a friend who can fly us out there
in one of those tiny planes people build out of kits."

Rose took a step back, pressing a hand to her throat, her
face suddenly pale.

"Are you okay?" Ash felt a flash of worry.

Rose nodded.

"Say something." That's what you were supposed to ask

when you thought someone might be choking, not that Rose
had anything to choke on.

"Sorry," Rose whispered.

Ash put her hand on Rose's back. Rose leaned toward her,
not touching but moving into Ash's space. Without thinking,
Ash wrapped her arm around Rose's waist. Her body was
soft. Ash could feel Rose's warmth despite her stiff blazer. She
wanted to pull her closer.

"You sure?" Ash asked.

What had happened?

"Just low blood sugar."

"Let me get you a—" Ash looked around the studio. "An old
Luna bar or some Montucky Cold Snack beer?"

She was obviously an excellent hostess.

"I'm fine." Rose stepped away.

Ash missed her warmth.

"Totally fine," Rose added, sweeping back her perfect hair
without mussing one strand.

Ash knew that gesture. *I'm fine. Look how fine I am. I've
fluffed my hair out because that's proof I've got my shit together.*
That wasn't low blood sugar.

"Tell me more," Rose said, putting on a smile that started
forced but mellowed into something real.

Ash felt a wave of tenderness wash over her. *What is it?*
She left a beat of silence in case Rose wanted to answer.
Rose didn't answer. She peered around the wall of the set,
then looked through the cutout that would become a café
window.

When Ash was sure Rose didn't want to talk, Ash said,
"For the sporting goods scene, we'll move this wall here." She
pointed. "I want to block a square with the women standing
here. The square shows how the firefighter feels locked in.

And the ranger is going to move over here." Ash reached over and grabbed one of the storyboard pages from the worktable. "See, she'll move here and that will create this circle." She stepped into the unfinished set. She could see the unbuilt walls finishing themselves in her mind. "It will give this feeling of opening up."

chapter 15

Ash had gone on for about thirty minutes before she realized maybe she was talking too much.

"Sorry, you didn't want to know that."

"I do." Rose pointed to the pile of plywood and two-by-fours. "Who's putting those together?"

"On a big production, there'd be a construction manager and crew. We've got me." Not a big asset given her bad leg. "And Jason, our sound guy, and Tucker, our grip. And a bunch of their friends who'll work for beer. This afternoon, I'll work on painting it."

"Do I get to watch you work?"

Rose's eyes flickered up and down Ash's body. Her earlier distress seemed to have melted away.

"I'd like that." In a move stolen from a B-grade, bad-boy movie, Ash took off her jacket and rolled up the short sleeves to reveal the tattoos that reached all the way to her shoulders. What was she doing? Rose watched, a wry smile playing at the corners of her lips. Did that smile say, *Please tell me you didn't just do that?* or *You got my attention?* Maybe both.

"Can I help?" Rose asked.

"You're not busy?"

"I'll die if I have to go to one more Zoom meeting." Rose took off her blazer and draped it over a box.

Now it was Ash whose gaze lingered on Rose. Her silk shirt strained ever so slightly against her large breasts. Ash had never seen her out of a blazer. Ash got it. Rose's body was luscious in a way tailored shirts would never quite hide. And those lovely curves were not part of Rose's brand image. The beauty of Rose's body hidden for the sake of her corporate image filled Ash with admiration that was both in her head and in her heart. Rose knew how to play the game with aplomb. And she was sick of Zoom meetings. Who wouldn't be? Ash got to be her respite from that life.

Ash tore her eyes away.

"This will be the shop floor." She'd already stenciled in the tiles and what would look like an inlaid image of the Columbia River. "It's basically paint by number. I can loan you a smock. But you don't have to. It's still messy, and you look so nice."

Hopefully that didn't sound lecherous.

"I won't spill a drop," Rose said ruefully. "I'm very careful."

Ash opened the paint cans and showed her where the colors went. She took her own place a few feet away. Rose was right. She painted without spilling a drop, meditatively stroking the tip of her brush along the lines on the floor.

"What's it like being a business consultant?" Ash asked after a few minutes of companionable silence.

Rose dabbed her brush in the can. "It's a lot of research, talking to people, and understanding how businesses succeed and fail. Businesses are like living things. They get sick. I get to be part of the cure." It sounded rehearsed. "It's good for the individual businesses, but it's good for the economy as well. People don't think about the cost of organizational inefficiencies."

"That sounds interesting."

"It's a romantic way to talk about maximizing cauliflower profits," Rose said ruefully. "You should be flattered. I should be working on the largest client Integral Business Solutions has ever had. It's a company that sells dehydrated foods to sixteen different countries."

"I rated higher than cauliflower."

"Dehydrated cauliflower." Rose looked up from her work and grinned. "Cauliflower is very important so that's a compliment."

Ash smiled into her can of paint.

"I have some good principles." Rose leaned down to check her lines. "I never bust unions." She touched an invisible flaw in her work. "If the company wants to save money by underpaying their people, abusing undocumented workers, I'm out. I mean... a lot of people get let go because of me. Being efficient often means fewer people. But not if that means cutting them without warning, or making everyone who's left do twice the work." Rose didn't look up from her flawless paint job. "I've had some conversations with some people."

Rose's tone had been mild until then. The way Rose said *conversations*, Ash was pretty sure she'd be terrified to be on the other end of those conversations.

"I don't know if I really believe in karma, but I've told some CEOs about it like I do. And I've told them not to call me back until they've worked a day on the factory floor."

"You're so fucking cool."

Rose looked up and beamed. "Nobody thinks that."

"I do."

As if on cue, Rose's phone rang. She rose gracefully and retrieved it from her purse.

"I have to take this. Sorry." She answered. "Good afternoon. What can I do for you? The Tennessee branch?" Rose paced with the casual gait of someone waiting for a movie theater to open. "Right. Yes. I hear you. The first thing you can do is not to hire the most expensive consulting firm west of the Rockies and then not take their advice." Her face was serene. "Think about it and get back to me. Yes, you can talk to my boss." She glanced at Ash and rolled her eyes. "I know you can take me off this project. *I* can take me off this project. Follow my recommendations." She hung up, tossed her phone on top of her purse, and smiled. "Where were we?"

Ash stared.

"That was the Cauliflower Baron. He's the biggest client we've ever had."

Rose sat back down.

"You just told your biggest client to fuck off?"

"He's fine." Rose picked up her paintbrush. "He's got an ego the size of Texas. He talks about himself as *the Baron*. It's like training a big dog. You have to assert calm dominance."

"That was..." *The sexiest thing I have ever seen.* "Epic. I feel like I just saw Luke Skywalker take down Darth Vader. You did that. Just like that." Ash gave a casual wave. "Like, *I'll quit the biggest case my company has ever had if you don't do what I say.*"

"I'm just talking his language."

"I'm impressed."

Rose shook her head and returned to her painting. "You're easily impressed."

Rose could make a CEO cower. And she was painting Ash's set floor like every molecule mattered. Ash held her fingers up in a square to frame Rose's face.

Rose frowned.

"Sorry," Ash said. "I was blocking the scene. Bad habit." Ash brushed her hair out of her face, feeling the smear of paint she had transferred to her cheek. "You must love your job."

Rose hesitated. "Truth?"

"Of course."

"I'm really good at my job. I'm going to make partner soon."

"Congratulations. That's great."

Rose's lips bunched in a frown. "I make a lot of money. I work with nice people."

Ash could tell there was a caveat. "But...?"

Rose didn't say anything for a moment, then she said, "I don't care about dehydrated cauliflower."

Ash didn't mean to laugh but Rose said it with an intensity dehydrated cauliflower couldn't possibly deserve. Rose didn't seem to mind Ash's laughter. She chuckled, too.

"It's in everything. I could tell you about cauliflower for hours. I've studied up. And I know a lot about test kits that test for acidity in agricultural irrigation systems and how to get a firm of high-powered lawyers to stop fighting with one another. I like learning new things..." She trailed off.

Ash would be happy to sit on the studio floor and listen to Rose talk about cauliflower. She liked the sound of Rose's voice. She liked her laugh. She liked the easy way they teased each other without it ever getting sharp, not like the way Victoria's teasing always cut close to the bone. But Rose didn't sound like she wanted to talk about cauliflower.

"If I live to the average age for a woman in America, I'm right on schedule for a midlife crisis." Rose sounded serious. "My sisters love what they do. They're like you. They all have this *thing* they love. Gigi owns Azalea Salon downtown. Cassie has four children. And she loves being a mother. Ty is getting her MFA and trying to write a novel, and she loves it. And here's the thing…can I tell you the truth? Cone of silence?" Rose looked around as though someone might be listening.

"I'll never tell."

Ash would hold any secret of Rose's close and safe in her heart.

"I'm jealous," Rose said. "I love my sisters so much. And every time they talk about their stuff, there's a little part of me that says, *I don't want to hear it,* because I don't have anything like that. I'm jealous of their passion. I suppose I'm jealous of yours, too. I'm terrible."

"It sounds human."

"Thanks." Rose gave a little snort. "The thing is, if I knew what I wanted to do, I'd do it. But I don't have a thing. Nothing I could build my life on."

"What do you like to do?" Ash asked.

"Spend time with my sisters. My dogs. I go to meditation class a few times a week. It's paying someone to tell you to breathe, but I like the way you turn off your mind and just exist. I try to be mindful as much as I can, although doing workflow optimization plans doesn't really say *Live in the moment.* They say that's when you *should* try to live in the moment."

Rose trailed her fingertips along a crack between plywood boards. Ash followed Rose's fingertips with her eyes. For a second, before she pushed the sensation away, Ash felt that touch drifting up her arm, along her collarbone, up her neck until Rose cupped her cheek.

"If I can stop my mind for a second and just *be,*" Rose said, her voice growing serious, "I feel like I'm air mixing with air or water mixing with water. I'm so much a part of everything that I don't have to carry the weight of being me. Not that I want to disappear or anything, but for a second I'm not my past or my future or what I have to get done the next day."

Ash could feel the sunlight moving across the floor.

"I could use a couple minutes when I wasn't my past," Ash said.

"I don't want to be that cliché," Rose said. "That woman who has it all and is looking for excitement when life isn't about being excited. It's about being a good person."

"You can do both."

For a second, Rose's expression filled with longing. Then the look was gone, and her corporate casual smile was back.

"Two point eight years and I can have a real midlife crisis."

It was unfair that this beautiful woman who smacked down CEOs before she let them abuse their employees should pine for meaning. And what had Rose said about Ash being cool? Ash was barely holding it together and wearing T-shirts she'd bought in high school. Rose was cool. Rose was epically cool. And she deserved a life filled with purpose.

"Come to a party with me," Ash blurted out.

Because going to a party was where people found purpose. But Rose wanted excitement, and the Aviary parties were always exciting.

"There'll be fire dancers and nude ice sculptures."

Rose's raised eyebrows said, *You need to read the policy on sexual harassment, don't you?* She shouldn't invite her business consultant to a party with nude ice sculptures. And when Emma had told her about the party, she hadn't specified that the fire dancers would be clothed, either. Ash had been to Aviary parties. It was fifty-fifty on the dancers' clothing.

"I'm sorry. That was inappropriate. I didn't mean to make you uncomfortable."

"It's *that* kind of party?" Rose's eyebrows climbed higher.

Did Rose think it was a sex party?

"Not a sex party," Ash said quickly.

Rose laughed. "I did not think you were inviting me to a sex party."

"Agh. Never mind." Ash put her hand over her face a second before she remembered she was covered in paint. She drew her sleeve across her face to assess the damage. Yep, she'd covered herself in burnt sienna.

Ash had had game. Once. Obviously, she'd lost it.

"Are you uninviting me?" Ash could hear the smile in Rose's voice.

"It's an artists' co-op. There might be burlesque. I shouldn't have mentioned it." Ash peeked at Rose.

"But will there be ferns?" Rose asked with a twinkle in her eyes.

It took Ash a moment to realize, Rose had just said yes.

chapter 16

Ash paced across the floor of the studio, notepad in hand. She stopped, jotted down the name of a park in Vancouver that might serve as a location if they could get a permit. Portland was generous with filming permits. Was Vancouver? She wrote *check Vancouver permit laws*. Emma popped out of the equipment locker.

"What are you doing?"

"Thinking."

She had to find actors, find a location, film twelve minutes so brilliant Brentworth fell in love with the project. They had a matter of weeks. If it weren't for Rose's help, she'd never make it. Rose was busy putting together the parts of the pitch Victoria had always handled. Ash could never have been the director she was without Victoria. Now she couldn't do it without Rose. But this was different. This was just a job for Rose.

Ash walked to the green screen set up in the corner and stared at the blank surface. Her heart raced in a rhythm that was either panic or excitement. She couldn't tell. Maybe it was fear and joy. And not about the film. Rose had said yes to the party with a flirtatious gleam in her eye. Rose cared. No matter how many times Ash reasoned with herself, the way Rose had looked at her, the way Rose stayed painting sets and talking said this wasn't just a job for Rose. Ash didn't want it to be. But what if she liked Rose more and more, until she was half in love, and Rose liked her, too, but she got sick of helping Ash? What if Ash shared all her baggage, and Rose looked into that emotional suitcase and said, *Wow, you've got a lot of stuff in there?*

"Ash." Emma had come up beside her. "Why are you staring at the green screen?"

"I'm not."

"Obviously you are."

"Maybe I'm asking too much of Rose. We haven't even drawn up a contract. What if I'm taking advantage of her being nice?"

"Does Rose Josten look like the kind of person who gets taken advantage of?"

The way Rose told off the Cauliflower Baron said no.

"I asked her to go to the Aviary party, but—"

Emma interrupted. "That's great!"

"I shouldn't have. You know how those parties are. What if some artist has made a giant vulva and naked women dance out of it?"

"That was last month," Emma said.

"Fuck." Ash rubbed her face. "I could tell her it's canceled."

"I'm kidding."

"I could tell her I don't have time. I've got too much to do."

"You have time to go on a date."

"It's not a date."

"I saw you two together when you came to the studio. She was looking at you like you made the sun shine."

Ash walked over to the worktable and sat down.

"Why are you making this difficult?" Emma followed her. "She seems cool. You had a moment at the Pug Crawl."

"I don't like her like that."

What a lie.

Emma raised an eyebrow. "Seriously? Cause you looked like you wanted to make sweet, sweet love to her in three-quarters of a fake café." She waved toward the set.

"That's inappropriate."

"It's your studio. As long as you lock the door, it's not that inappropriate."

"Talking about Rose like that is inappropriate." Ash hid her smile. Emma was incorrigible. "*Thinking* about Rose like that is inappropriate."

Emma didn't say anything in a way that said, *I'm not saying anything because now we're going to have real talk.*

"If I was someone else..." Ash said.

Emma knew Ash's story. She'd been by her side through all of it. Inexplicably. They hadn't even been that close, and yet Emma had stuck around.

"Sexual dysfunction is nothing to be ashamed of."

"I know." Ash picked at a bit of glue on the table. "But we work together. You saw how that ended with Victoria."

"Rose is consulting on one project. She has her own life that isn't wrapped up in yours. She's not depending on you to make her look like a genius filmmaker when really she's just good at organizing things."

"She's definitely good at organizing things."

"And that's her job, and after a few more weeks her job will have nothing to do with your job. But Rose wanting to go to a party with you, that is all about you."

But what happened if they went to bed together and Ash

sprang back like Rose had shocked her? God help her, she probably wouldn't cry but what if she did? Rose wanted excitement. She didn't want someone whom years of therapy hadn't fixed.

Emma placed her hands on the table and leaned in as though she were about to deliver a pep talk to her rugby team. "I am not going to let you overthink this. You're a great person. She's obviously into you. Do what normal people do. Go home, try on a hundred outfits, get drunk, and have a great time."

chapter 17

⌣

The industrial neighborhood that housed the Aviary, the across-the-river cousin to the neighborhood that housed Stewart Productions, would have looked abandoned except for the cars parked along every neighboring side street. Rose circled until she found a spot several blocks away. A few people in evening gowns passed her as she walked to the artists' co-op. She was obviously underdressed. Ash had said *Come as you are.* If Rose had asked Gigi, Gigi would have told Rose never to go to a party *as she was. As she was* meant 22 percent more formal than corporate casual. But Rose hadn't told her sisters about the party. She'd tell them about it afterward. Right now, she wanted it to be hers alone. And oddly, she didn't feel bad about her double-breasted blazer. (Gigi said double-breasted was where sexy died.) The air was cool. The night sky was bright with the ambient light of the city. Voices and classical music floated through the air. Ash had invited her, not some sexier version of her. Just her.

Rose looked up. From the ground, the Aviary looked a bit like the converted warehouse that housed Stewart Productions except that the tall windows were lit with a golden glow and pendants flew from their upper reaches. She looked for the entrance. The people in party dresses were heading for a long, metal staircase clinging to one side of the building. At the top of the staircase, a rectangle of light shone like a beacon.

It took Rose a second to recognize Ash leaning against the wall in the shadow of the building near the stairs. Ash stepped into the light. She looked gorgeously disheveled, her hair pulled in a messy knot on top of her head, a ripped My Life with the Thrill Kill Kult T-shirt hanging off one shoulder. Heavy eye makeup made deep circles of her eyes, making her look dangerous and fragile at the same time.

"Hey." Ash smiled down, not looking at Rose.

"You waited for me."

"It's…busy up there. I didn't want to miss you."

"In all the ferns."

Ash didn't laugh. She toed the ground, pushing a pebble back and forth. "Is it okay that I asked you? We work together and I don't know…"

She seemed genuinely worried, her eyes fixed on the ground, like she was waiting for Rose to scold her and hoping that Rose wouldn't.

"Of course it is."

"But you're consulting for us."

"People at Integral go out with their clients all the time."

Ash didn't look reassured.

"We buy them tickets to the opera. They buy us tickets to hockey games. Some of my co-workers have been working with the same clients for years. They're friends. Are you worried that you're a bad influence on an impressionable colleague?"

Ash's eye flew up. "I'm not, am I?"

"Ash," Rose protested. "Please." She smiled, trying to draw a smile from Ash. "You're not. And I need more bad influences. My sisters think I'm the most boring person alive."

"Your sisters don't say that?" Something protective flashed across Ash's face.

"Of course not. They *say* I'm lovely."

"You are."

Rose drew a breath. *Lovely.*

Ash bit her lip, like she realized the implications of what she'd said a second after she said it.

I don't mind.

Ash made a move like she was going to put her hair up, but it was already up.

"I just don't want...you know with us working together...if you felt like you had to be nice to me..."

Where did this hesitancy come from? Was Ash shy because she thought she'd asked Rose on a date and now she wasn't sure if Rose knew it was a date?

Ash opened and closed her mouth without saying anything, then gave an apologetic shrug as if to say, *I know I'm messing this up.*

It *was* a date.

This beautiful woman with her burning blue eyes and her art and her passion had asked Rose out. Rose's mind raced through an inventory of lackluster Athena dates and all the times—there weren't a lot but one was plenty—when Gigi had told her she'd die alone and be eaten by her pugs. She was racing toward middle-aged-before-her-time. She was a bored businesswoman with a closet full of low-heeled pumps, a forty-minute-on-average response time for all email, whose only interesting quirk was a secret penchant for fondling vegetables. She should be panicking. Flustered. This had to be a mistake. Ash would find out how dull she was. If this was a movie, she'd run away.

But that just wasn't her.

She realized in a flash, more a feeling than a thought, that she wasn't nervous, and she wasn't misreading the moment. She might be boring, but she wasn't making partner because she couldn't read people. And she wasn't making partner because she didn't go after what she wanted. She reached for Ash's hand, not taking it but touching her fingertips.

"I hope you don't think going to a party with a beautiful woman is a great burden on my time," Rose said softly. "A beautiful woman and one of the most interesting people I know." She slipped her fingers through Ash's. "And I'm not here because Integral Business Solutions consultants take their clients to hockey games because it's a good relationship-building strategy, so if you were hoping this evening would end with me giving you a bag of Integral swag and business cards to give to all your contacts..."

Ash beamed, and Rose had never felt so much joy fill her so fast.

"I don't even get an Integral Business Solutions mug?" Ash asked.

Rose leaned in. Her heart sang and her body tingled, but she felt perfectly calm. She kissed Ash's cheek.

"I suppose I could get you a mug."

Ash led her up the metal stairs. On a little fire-escape-like platform at the top, a man asked for their IDs, asked them if they had a designated driver or Uber on their phones, and showed them an infographic explaining consent.

"They're very responsible," Rose said as they stepped inside.

"The Aviary takes care of people," Ash said.

It also enchanted them. The ceilings soared. Enormous installations floated above their heads like jellyfish or angels. Artists had their stations set up so the guests could study their work. Through the open doors to a balcony, Rose could see a potter, sitting behind her wheel, talking to two men in evening gowns. Furniture in red brocades and gold rattan filled the center of the space, making rooms without walls. And there was an enormous ice sculpture of a naked man standing beside the bar, mist from a bed of dry ice rising around him.

"It's amazing." Rose gazed at the walls hung with paintings. "So much passion."

They walked over to the sculpture.

"It's very anatomical." Rose leaned forward.

The penis was remarkable for being made out of ice, but more impressively the striations of muscle in the figure's body were different colors of ice. A light beneath the sculpture illuminated their rainbow hues.

"And by the end of the night, it'll melt." Rose glanced at Ash, who was also examining the statue.

Ash held her hand over the mist rising from the dry ice. "But you'll remember it."

Yeah. Rose would.

Once they got signature Aviary drinks—a kind of Manhattan filled with pomegranate seeds, like a weird alcoholic bubble tea—and started to mingle, it became apparent that Ash knew everyone in the Portland art scene. Just because she was overworked didn't mean she was adrift in the world, with only Emma to keep her company. Ash was talented and charismatic, and had about a million fans, all of whom were here. Rose wasn't jealous. She hadn't built up an image of Ash alone in her studio longing for love. Well, maybe...But seeing Ash hug old friends and blush at their compliments made Rose happy. Ash deserved this.

Making her way through groups of friends, Ash led Rose to the expansive balcony, perhaps once an upper-story loading bay, strung with lights and filled with potted plants. There was another bar set up, although looking around it seemed that no one was drunk, not even tipsy. Maybe it was because you had to eat a cup of pomegranate seeds to get to the bottom of your drink. Maybe it was because the Aviary was intoxicating enough.

To make it all more magically surreal, a potter had set up a potter's wheel and was spinning a vase that had to be at least two feet tall. A small crowd had gathered around her, and as Rose watched, the potter pressed on the top of the vase, and it transformed into a widemouthed bowl. Rose was just about to draw Ash's attention to the potter when a woman stopped them.

"Ash Stewart?" A woman in a crimson bustier had come up behind them.

Ash turned.

"Someone told me you were here. I am such a fan of your work," the woman said.

Beside her stood a woman in gray slacks, a gray button-down, and a blazer.

Ha. A blazer. She'd tell Gigi, she wasn't the only one.

Recognition lit Ash's face. "And you must be Selena Mathis." She held out her hand. "I saw your exhibit at the Portland Art Museum."

The woman gave a modest shrug. "That was a lot of fun."

To Rose, Ash said, "Selena is the best portrait painter in America. I followed her work when I was down in LA. The way you bring people's reality onto the canvas. That's what I want to do on film."

"I saw *Under One Roof* when it first came out," Selena said. "I've never seen something like that. It was so real. And the use of cerulean blue. The way you turn the characters toward that color palette emotionally...perfect." She smiled at the woman standing next to her in a blazer. "Have you met my partner, Cade Elgin?"

The woman nodded. Rose studied the two. Their fingers were intertwined with casual closeness. Something magical radiated between them: ease and love and pleasure in each other's company.

They were an unusual pair. If Selena was in love with this unobtrusive woman in an outfit even more conservative than Rose's, maybe Ash could fall for a responsible, kindhearted, but possibly dull, business consultant.

To Rose, Ash said, "Cade runs the most influential debut-artist gallery in New York."

Okay...slacks-and-blazer was more exciting than she looked.

"This is Rose Josten," Ash said, "our amazing business consultant."

But even as she said *business consultant*, she touched Rose's back. Rose's body warmed. She didn't look at Ash. Rose's face would light up like a Christmas tree of happiness if she so much as glanced at Ash.

"She's one of the most powerful businesswomen in the Northwest."

"West of the Rockies," Rose said with affected modesty.

The women laughed.

"She's helping me with my latest project," Ash said. "I don't know what I'd do without her." The last words came out breathless.

Cade and Selena exchanged a glance. Rose liked it. It didn't say, *Why is the exciting filmmaker with this ordinary woman?*

Selena kissed Cade's forehead. "I know that story."

Maybe all artists needed a woman in a blazer.

Selena asked about the film. Ash gave an excited and muddled synopsis. They'd have to work on that.

"So what's the next challenge?" Cade asked.

"The proof of concept," Ash said.

Selena and Cade nodded. Apparently being in the art world, they didn't need to look up terms the way Rose had as she began prepping for their pitch... the pitch... Ash's pitch.

"I need actors. And I want an outdoor sex scene in the proof." Ash exhaled heavily. "I don't have time to put out a casting call, but where am I going to find two women who want to have sex on camera outside for almost no money just to help an unknown filmmaker?"

"Hardly unknown," Selena said.

A shadow crossed Ash's face. "Former filmmaker."

Rose glanced around. Inside, fire dancers were sparking flames at the end of long sticks, testing them with their fingers, and then blowing them out. A man tugged a length of silk that hung from the ceiling. Two drag kings waltzed to a string quartet. A woman in full bondage gear posed for a man with a lumberjack beard and a camera.

"I don't suppose there's anyone here who'd like to be part of pitching an amazing film about love and the queer community," Rose said.

"Someone who likes to perform? There's no one here like that." Selena chuckled. "I'll talk to my friend Jessica."

chapter 18

"So what's with the ferns?" Rose asked as they wandered toward the edge of the balcony and rested their elbows on the cool concrete wall that surrounded it. "Your script says something like *Note to props: Use synthetic ferns for intimate scenes.*"

"The ferns are..." Ash felt heat rise to her cheeks.

Rose laughed, but it was a gentle, loving laugh. "You're embarrassed! But you wrote it. It's going to be on film for everyone in the world to see."

"Optimist."

"Realist. Tell me about the ferns. We're both adults." Rose widened her eyes. "Now I'm thinking it's going to be really kinky."

"How *would* ferns be kinky?"

Ash felt the air between them crackle with desire and delight. It had been so long since she'd felt that. Had it ever felt like this with Victoria? Even at the beginning?

"You're the one who wrote the script."

"In the sex scene, the ranger touches the firefighter with fern fronds."

They were sexual, the way they curled in on themselves and then opened into their full glory. The nodules of pollen running up and down their underside. The sinewy stalks and delicate fronds.

"Touches her intimately?" The glint in Rose's eye said she knew exactly what Ash meant.

"I want to cut from when she's about to go down on her to a close-up of a fern when it's curled up on itself. Is there a word for that?"

"Fiddleheads."

"Being a business consultant really does mean that you know everything."

"My parents—" Rose stopped as though she'd just remembered that she'd left the stove on or her wallet on the seat of her car. "They liked camping. They cooked them to show us how there was so much bounty in the world without people even trying to create it."

"That's beautiful."

Rose tilted her face to the sky as though looking for a memory traced in the stars. Ash couldn't tell if it was happiness or sadness that flitted across Rose's face, as she said, "They were beautiful people."

Were?

Their hands rested side by side on the concrete wall. Ash placed her hand over Rose's, tuning in to any movement that said Rose didn't want that. Rose rested her head on Ash's shoulder. Ash rested her cheek on the top of Rose's head. Rose's hair was silky and not a bit like frozen-in-place-liberal-female-politician hair. Ash tried to think of a gentle way to prompt Rose to say more about her parents, but the potter interrupted.

"Do you want to throw a pot?" the woman called over.

Rose glanced back, seeming relieved by the interruption. "At what?" she called back, her cheer returning.

"Over here," the potter said. "Tonight is about experiencing art, not just looking at it." The woman held up two tent-size smocks.

"I'm wearing a blazer." Rose laughed.

"Not an insurmountable obstacle," Ash whispered into Rose's hair. "It's fun."

"Do *you* throw pots?"

"Not at people."

Rose elbowed her.

"Pottery was my thing in high school," Ash said.

"Not theater?"

"Definitely theater but that was pressure. That was achievement. Pottery was relaxing."

"Perfect." The potter ceded the wheel. "Do you want to show your partner?"

The sparkle of attraction between them didn't make Rose her partner. But Ash's protest was lost in the sound of party chatter, perhaps because she hadn't actually spoken. It'd be fun to see Rose at the potting wheel, just like it'd been fun to paint sets with her, to watch her hands, to see her out of her admittedly sexy-as-hell blazer.

"Sit behind her, like in *Ghost*. Ghost her but in the good way." The potter smiled, the creases deepening in her lined face. "If you want to, of course. It's consensual."

The woman cut a piece of clay with a wire and slapped it into the center of the wheel. "Have you done this before?" she asked Rose.

Rose shook her head, holding the smock away from her pristine outfit.

"It's consensual pot throwing," Ash said. "You don't have to."

Rose handed Ash her drink. "Throwing a pot at a cocktail party where we just asked a famous artist to solicit women to film a sex scene? How could I say no?"

"The inaugural pot," the woman said.

Rose donned the smock and took her seat at the wheel. Ash watched intently as Rose's hands closed around the clay. She could see the muscles in Rose's forearms.

"If you know how to center it, you can show her how," the potter said.

The lump of clay on the wheel threatened to spin out of Rose's hands. Rose giggled. It was a sweet, unexpected sound, so far from the woman who had hung up on the Cauliflower Baron.

"Are you going to show me?" Rose asked. "Like *Ghost*."

Ash fumbled for words and came up with, "Nineteen ninety. Directed by Jerry Zucker."

Rose was inviting Ash to wrap her legs around her hips, to press her breasts against Rose's back.

"I'd have to…" Ash mimed putting her arms around Rose's body.

Rose looked up at Ash, on her lips that bemused smile that was quickly becoming familiar and one of Ash's favorite things. "I've seen *Ghost*."

Rose scooted forward on the bench. Ash swung one leg over the seat. She felt the exact moment when her inner thigh touched the side of Rose's ass, and she felt desire. It would be followed by pain, her body tensing up in fear. She knew that, but she didn't care. Every other part of her body wanted this. Her heart wanted this. She could smell Rose's perfume, a complicated mix of burnt sugar, lemons, and lavender.

"Is this okay?" Ash breathed.

"Yeah." Rose sounded as breathless as Ash felt.

"And this?" Ash put her arms around Rose so she could reach the wheel, and she felt Rose lean back.

"Yes."

"Put your hands on the clay."

Ash covered Rose's hands with her own. Their forearms pressed together. The strength it took to move the clay into a perfect orbit pressed them closer together. Slowly the lump of clay grew symmetrical. Ash drew it up into the beginning of a bowl.

Rose let the clay slide under her fingers without moving.

"Can you slow the wheel down?"

Ash turned the dial on the side of the table.

"More," Rose said.

Ash slowed it another notch. Rose wet her fingers. Ash watched her hands. Rose seemed entirely focused on the lip of the bowl, her head cocked as though she were listening to it as much as feeling it. Her breathing slowed. Then she moved an inch down the inside of the bowl, stroking it upward, coaxing it to grow.

Need glowed between Ash's legs. To her surprise her body didn't ball up in a fist that said *no entry*. She felt the comfortable stretch of her legs around Rose's body, the warmth of Rose's body relaxing her. She felt desire, her body whispering that it needed more.

"I could do this all day," Rose said, growing the bowl taller and taller until it became a vase. "I'm obviously born to be a potter."

With that, the vase slumped over like a Dr. Seuss creation, the base spinning off center. Rose let out a big laugh.

"Can I take it home?" Rose asked the potter.

"Better yet. I'll fire it for you. I'll give you my card and you can call me to pick it up."

Rose leaned her head back against Ash's shoulder.

"It's better than an ice sculpture," she whispered. "It'll last."

Ash wished the party could last forever. She and Rose stayed until well after midnight, chatting only with each other. But the dreamy night had to end. They walked to their cars. Hope and happiness swirled in Ash's heart, turning the gray concrete warehouses into silver-screen castles.

They reached Rose's car first.

"Thank you for tonight." Rose didn't make a move to get in. The wind ruffled Rose's hair. She looked happy.

Every fiber of Ash's body wanted to press her lips into Rose's palm, run her lips up Rose's neck, drink her in.

"I'm glad you could come." The word *come* came out husky and seductive. "Came," Ash amended. Wrong again. "Were here."

"You know once you say it—" Rose leaned in, stroking Ash's cheek, then trailing her fingertips across the velvet nape of Ash's undercut. "—you can't get back out. The more you try to fix it, the sexier it sounds."

And Rose kissed her. Rose's lips were soft, and in Rose's hand on Ash's back, Ash sensed the same trembling excitement she felt. She parted her lips, and Rose's tongue brushed against hers. Their kiss deepened. Rose's hand tightened on her back.

Ash knew how to do this, knew how to kiss, how to make a woman want her, how to let a woman know she wanted her. She tightened her fist in Rose's hair. The other hand rested on Rose's jaw, gentle and commanding. *I know you. I want you.* She heard Rose moan, a low instinctual sound. With that moan, something shifted in Rose's kiss. Now it was messy, hard, needy. Rose was turned on. Rose needed her. It was so good and inevitable and right.

Rose pulled away but only enough to speak.

"Would you like to come back to my place?"

The two universes Ash lived in—the one where she was broken and the one where her real life was glittering with promise—pulled apart. Rose would touch her. She would flinch. The desire that felt so warm and right would disappear. The accident would flash back into her mind. Her body would go cold and dry. Rose's desire would turn to pity when she saw Ash's scars. Then she'd be to Rose the woman she'd been to Victoria: weak, fragile, like an exotic houseplant that kept dropping its leaves until you realized it wasn't worth the blooms you'd gotten it for.

"I can't," she whispered. "You're my consultant...I'm not looking for anything...I should...boundaries."

"We're not under contract." Rose's eyes were dark with desire and confusion. "I wouldn't ask you if I wasn't okay with this, but if you're not—"

"I'm not."

She wanted it so much. She wanted to be the kind of woman who stripped naked in front of her lover, confident in her own beauty, and then fucked passionately until they were spent.

The disappointment on Rose's face was almost enough to change Ash's mind. She couldn't let Rose go thinking she didn't love every second she'd spent with her. She just couldn't do *this*, and the words she needed to explain why evaded her.

"When I find the actors, I'm going to film on this island in the San Juans. Do you want to come with me?" Ash said it all in half a breath. The San Juans were beautiful, but not really what you offered a woman instead of sex. "We can camp there. There's a waterfall and porpoises." *I want you. I'm not ready.* "You can only get there by a little airplane, but Jason knows that guy who owns one."

"No!" Rose pulled back quickly. "Thank you," she amended in a calmer voice. "You'll do great out there. I've got to work on the Cauliflower Baron." She gave a forced laugh. "Do you know what would happen to the processed-food supply chain if we ran out of cauliflower?"

"I…no."

"Terrible things." Rose spoke with humorous melodrama, but her eyes were dark and hurt. She put a hand on Ash's cheek, tenderly, studying her as though she were saying fare-well. "Cauliflower is in everything." Then Rose got in her car, closing the door softly, and drove away, leaving Ash alone on the dark street.

chapter 19

≡

Five o'clock. Rose spun her chair around to face the window, her back to the glass office wall that looked out at her firm. She hadn't seen Ash for two days. They hadn't texted. Rose kept playing the night in the Aviary over in her mind. The feel of Ash's arms around her. The desire in Ash's kiss, as though all Ash's stress and passion had turned into sexual need. Rose wanted it so badly. And she could give Ash what she needed. Rose hadn't had exciting relationships, but she knew how to make love to a woman.

Love. The word stuck in her mind.

Sex. She knew how to fuck a woman.

What would Ash's face look like as she gave in to pleasure?

No. Rose grabbed a squeeze ball Chloe had picked up at the Accounting Oversight Excellence Conference in Houston (Rose hadn't attended) and squished it into a knot. Ash wasn't interested. Ash had said no. Clearly.

But Ash *was* interested. Rose didn't live a life of tumultuous affairs, not even a life of naked ice sculptures and parties with pop-up pottery studios, but she lived in the world with people who had emotions that you could discern by studying them. Or by being passionately kissed by them.

The trip to the San Juans wasn't a consolation prize for Ash not wanting to hook up. *Sorry, I don't want to have sex but would you like to see something that's kind of like a dolphin but not quite.* It was an invitation. *Adventure with me.* It was Rose and Ash sitting by a campfire, sparks snapping in the air, joining the Milky Way above.

Except they'd never make it. She squeezed the stress ball tighter. She could see the airplane in the supersize garage her father had built for it. So flimsy. So small. *We don't know what happened.* A tin can, smaller than her SUV, launched into the sky above the Rockies, that's what happened. And that's what would happen to Ash. Rose's stomach clenched. She took a deep breath.

Be in the moment. Hear the sounds around you. Breathe in. And out.

The phone rang.

"I have someone calling about Brentworth," Chloe said. "Should I take a message?"

It was one of the Brentworth hopefuls Rose had contacted. It was an excuse to call Ash and tell her what she'd learned. She picked up. The man had pitched a film about miners who form a community theater. Brentworth had turned him down.

"I'm working with a client who's pitching to Irene Brentworth," Rose said. "If there's anything you could share about your experience…"

Let him be a talker.

"Irene Brentworth," the man said. "She's old money. You get rich tech-boomers who want to be producers, throw their money around, mess up your film, and then complain that it didn't sell. But people say Brentworth is smart. Stays out of the way when she needs to, steps in when you think you're in trouble. If she'd taken my film..." He sighed. "I wouldn't be sitting in this office with no AC trying to sell an option. When her office called, I saw my name in lights."

Chloe stepped into view and gave Rose an *anything else?* look. Rose shook her head. On the other side of the glass wall, the office was emptying.

"Do you have any idea why she didn't take your film?"

Give me something I can work with. She needed this for Ash.

"She said it didn't have enough *vision.*"

"How can you tell if someone has vision?"

Who could answer that?

"Brentworth works by intuition. She's so rich she can do anything she wants."

Rose waved to an associate leaving the office, then took a sip of cold coffee. "My client hasn't decided on a director," she lied. "But she's got some people in mind. Have you heard anything about a woman named Ash Stewart?"

The man laughed. "I can help you here. Stewart is a trainwreck."

Rose squeezed the squeeze ball. Nothing about Ash was a trainwreck. A little out-of-her-depth, overworked, but not a trainwreck.

"What about her?"

"Your client isn't in Hollywood, are they?" the man asked.

"I'm not allowed to say."

"They're not," the man said decisively. "No one in Hollywood would touch Stewart."

You don't know. A cold feeling filled Rose's stomach. The guy had no reason to lie. If either of them knew, it was more likely him. But how could anyone blacklist Ash? Rose wanted to wrap her arms around Ash. *He's lying.*

"Why?" she asked.

"It wasn't a tabloid scandal," the man said, "so you wouldn't have heard about it if you're not in the industry. But Brent-worth would be an idiot to pick her up. And Brentworth is not an idiot. Stewart is, or she's just a fuckup."

How dare he? Rose wanted to smack the phone back in its cradle, but a person didn't get where she was by showing her emotions when it wasn't helpful.

"Interesting. Tell me more." She kept her voice neutral.

"Have you heard of the producer Victoria Crue?"

"No," Rose lied again.

"That's Stewart's ex-wife. They worked together. Victoria is a producer. Stewart was the director. They were good. I'll give you that. They'd gotten twelve million dollars for this film. They were in pre-production, about a month from film-ing, and Stewart bailed. She was there, and then she was gone. You'd think it'd be okay. Just get another director, but the investors wanted Stewart. Two of them pulled out, and then a third pulled because the first two did. Victoria tried to make it work. Victoria got Stewart to come back for maybe a week, but then Stewart was, like, *Fuck you, I'm out.* All her notes were on paper, too, and half of them disappeared with her. No one *really* knew what she saw for this film. But they had to film it. They'd attached some talent with fierce timeline clauses. If they didn't film, the talent walked away with a lot of money. It was a shitshow. The film's called *The Secret Song* if you want to waste two hours."

"Why?" The word left Rose's mouth on a gasp. She coughed and spoke louder. "Why did Ash bail?"

"Everyone says their marriage was on the rocks. This was a way to ruin Victoria's career. When Victoria fucked the film up, Stewart divorced her."

The cold feeling in Rose's stomach had turned to lead. "Is that gossip?"

"I know Victoria." He sounded protective. "She told me."

"Wouldn't that ruin Ash's career as well?"

"That's where the idiot part comes in. It did. Victoria is never going to be where she was before, but she's got a career. No one ever heard from Stewart again. Brentworth's not going to invest in a production with Stewart on the books, and even if she did, it's fifty-fifty whether Stewart would even show up."

Liar.

"Thank you." Rose hung up without the usual *your experience has been invaluable et cetera et cetera.*

Rose opened a browser. Search: *Ash Stewart "The Secret Song" scandal quit.*

A deeper dive. The guy was right. It hadn't made the tabloids, but buried ten screens deep in Google she found an online trade publication, a few blogs, and a court record for divorce. An obscure queer newspaper that had since gone out of business quoted Victoria saying, *"Of course I was devastated. I truly don't know why Ash did this, but I forgive her. Hate poisons the hater. I'm not that person."* Victoria's photo made Rose want to punch her. How dare she look sad and smug at the same time?

Ash hadn't bailed on a huge project to ruin her ex-wife. She couldn't have. That wasn't her. But Rose felt like someone had turned off the lights and left her in the glow of the emergency signs. How many times had she told Ty and Gigi that the way a person treated their ex was the way they'd eventually treat you? But it couldn't be like the man said. She *knew* Ash. Or did she? If Ash hadn't told her about this, what else had Ash left out? The feeling Rose had that every time they were together they grew closer was *her* feeling. And feelings were not reality. Maybe that's why Ash had offered a camping trip with porpoises instead of sex. She knew Rose liked her and she knew Rose knew nothing about her.

Rose opened her email. Maybe one of the other people she'd asked about Brentworth would have a different story. One of the people she'd contacted had written back a few seconds earlier saying she'd be happy to talk. Rose's hands hovered over the keyboard.

I was wondering if you'd heard of a director named Ash Stewart. My client has considered them for their project.

The woman's email came back with shotgun speed.

She's talented, but if you piss her off, she will screw you.

The woman included a link to the article Rose had just read. Victoria's face looked out at her with phony benevolence.

chapter 20

It was after seven. The windows reflected the studio back to Ash. She scrolled through the Instagram feed of Selena Mathis's friend Jessica, a member of a burlesque troupe called Fierce Lovely. Jessica had emailed to say she and her girlfriend, Raven, would love to be in the fern scene. Ash had to send them the script. She had to focus. She had so little time to shoot the proof of concept.

And she'd fucked it up with Rose.

She should care because it meant Rose might not send her the finalized supply budget and marketing plan. Fuck the marketing plan. She cared because she and Rose would never hold hands across the table in a cozy coffee shop. She cared because Rose wouldn't introduce her to her sisters. She cared because she wanted that other universe in which she'd gone to bed with Rose and made Rose sing with pleasure. Instead she'd offered to show her porpoises. And you weren't even guaranteed porpoises in the San Juans. There was just a chance you *might* see porpoises.

Ash jumped at the sound of her phone, almost dropping it in her rush to read the screen. It was Rose.

"Hi," Ash said breathlessly. *Be cool.* "Calling not texting, who loves the nineties now?"

It had been two days since she'd heard Rose's silky voice.

"Are you at work?" Tonight Rose's voice was flat.

Ash shouldn't have joked.

"I'd like to talk to you about the pitch," Rose said. "Mind if I come over?"

"Please."

Ash stood up and paced around the studio. She shoved a coffee cup into the overfull trash can and tucked a sticky paint can behind the set.

Rose appeared in the door in a pinstriped skirt suit half an hour later. Ash hurried over to greet her. She should hug her. No. Something was wrong. Rose's shoulders slumped. She glanced around the studio like she hadn't been there before. Ash opened her mouth to offer Rose a coffee, but they were out of Keurig pods. She motioned to the worktable instead. Rose sat opposite her, putting an expanse of table between them.

"I talked to some people who'd pitched to Brentworth before." Rose folded her hands on the table. She hadn't brought her briefcase. She'd said she wanted to talk about the pitch, but where was her tablet?

"I do image management," Rose went on. "It's not my specialty, but there isn't anything at Integral that I can't do. But I can't manage a scandal I don't know about."

Ash's heart sank. Of course Rose had found out.

"Victoria."

Her last days on set rushed back in a blur of painkillers and begging Victoria to see that she was trying. But she'd lost half her notes in the accident. She couldn't keep up with Victoria striding from trailer to set at double speed. Why hadn't Ash told Rose up front? *I ruined a multimillion-dollar film because I couldn't pull my shit together.*

"If you've got a reputation for leaving projects, I need to know." Rose's tone was more disappointed than angry.

Ash wished a fire alarm would go off to take her away from this stark moment. Rose's frown. The table expanding between them, until it felt like Rose was on the other side of the world. Ash had blown it. She'd had a brilliant consultant helping her. Instead of giving Rose the information she needed, she'd been dreaming like a teenager, pretending she was living those first days of a relationship before anything has happened when everything is possible. She'd been basking in Rose's smile, while reality stalked her like a Wes Craven movie.

"The people I talked to said you quit a movie you were working on." Rose winced. "They said you did it to hurt your ex. Is there another side to the story?"

Of course there was another side. Now was the time to tell it. The story was an ace in the pocket of pathos. If you were making excuses, you couldn't ask for a better story.

I was in an accident that I didn't cause. I spent ages in the hospital, then crawled out of my hospital bed to fulfill my obligations to my wife, my friends begging me not to go back to work. But I would not let my wife down until I exhausted every cell in my body. When I did, I fell into a deep depression, which she said was annoying. Then she took my hairless cat and sent me divorce terms her lawyer said were fair because I got a house in a city I didn't work in—after all, I obviously didn't want a career—and a car that looked like a Batmobile knockoff.

No one could hear that story and not melt.

Rose leaned forward. "Talk to me."

Ash jumped at the chime of a computer going to sleep. "I didn't do it to hurt her."

I need you.

"Then why did you do it?" Rose asked.

Rose would stay if Ash told her the truth. She'd stay and manage Ash's image because she felt sorry for her. And once again Ash would be a poor helpless soul who needed someone to save her. Ash didn't speak.

"I can't help you if you're not honest about the things that affect this pitch." Rose nudged the words across the table like she was coaxing Ash to give her the right answer.

I need you. She couldn't be a burden again. She could pull it together on her own. She had to.

"I appreciate everything you've done for me." Ash's heart ached with each word.

"Then trust me."

If only Ash could slow time or get ahold of her feelings. This wasn't the conversation she wanted to have. She felt a spasm as though someone had put their hand between her legs and twisted her delicate body in their fist. She didn't want to send Rose away, and she didn't want to relive the accident again as she laid the story out before Rose. She didn't want to see desire and admiration fade from Rose's eyes as Ash explained everything. Rose's pity would hurt more than the pain between her legs.

"I really like you," Ash said, staring down at her hands. "You're sexy and smart. You wear the hell out of a suit. I think I could walk around Portland with you all day, just talking about anything." She felt her heart break. "But I need you to go."

chapter 21

Rose sat in her car outside Ash's building, longing to run back inside and beg Ash to talk to her. If Ash had worn a sign saying I'M NOT TELLING YOU THE WHOLE STORY it wouldn't have been more obvious. Her blue eyes had gone dark, her face pale and anguished. But she didn't want to tell Rose the whole story, not as a friend and not as a business consultant. Rose wanted that intimacy; Ash didn't. Ash was charismatic. That blend of fire and vulnerability that Rose found so appealing it made her heart ache was on display for everyone. Rose thought they had a connection. Everyone probably thought they had a connection with Ash. That's what charisma was. Look at all her fans at the Aviary.

Rose started her car and drove home. At home, Muffin and Cupcake threw themselves at her feet.

"I'm an idiot," she told them.

But they loved her with the joy of every fan girl who had ever seen the One Direction tour bus, so they didn't concur. She jiggled their rolls of neck fat, leashed them, and walked around the block. Back inside, the house felt like a Pottery Barn store after midnight. Except for the pugs' toys, it was perfect, which meant the only thing that made it feel like home was a collection of eviscerated plush dolls. She went to her closet and took out her camera and her microphone, but they didn't call to her. What was she doing with this strange, tiny rebellion against her normal life?

In the kitchen, her phone rang from its charging pad. *Ash!* She leapt to get it. It wasn't the number she'd programmed in for Ash, but it was the same California area code.

"Yes," she said breathlessly. "This is Rose."

A person shouldn't be able to hear anger on a silent phone line, but Rose heard it.

After a pause a woman's voice said, "I'm surprised you picked up."

It wasn't Ash. Rose should hang up. It was spam or a hate-call from some employee who thought her consultation had led to their pink slip.

"Who is this?"

"Mia Estelle." She sounded too aristocratic to be a disgruntled employee. "Don't act like you're surprised someone found out."

"I don't know who you are. You called my personal phone at night. *Surprised* is one word for it."

The woman chuckled grudgingly.

Rose shouldn't engage. "I have four seconds to hear a legitimate reason you called."

It had to be a wrong number.

The woman snapped back to anger. "I know what you've been trying to do to Ashlyn Stewart."

It wasn't a wrong number.

"You have no right to get her off a Brentwood project by digging up dirt on her."

"What?"

"Gossip travels at the speed of light. You're a supply-chain consultant," the woman sneered. "What do you even know about the entertainment industry?"

Rose could have pointed out that she was Integral Business Solutions' rising star because she could learn an industry better than its CEOs. But that was not the conversation they were having.

"Ashlyn has been through enough without you trying to ruin this opportunity. If Brentworth wants Ashlyn, she wants Ashlyn. If your client thinks they can get in if they get Ashlyn out, it's not going to work."

"Ash hired me." Should she be talking to this woman? Maybe the woman was the one sniffing around for information so she could knock Ash out of the running with Brentworth. But no...the anger in the woman's voice said she was ready to throw down for Ash.

"Ashlyn did?" Confusion diluted the anger in the woman's voice.

"Technically her friend hired me." *Hired* was overstating it. "Emma Gilman."

"Damn, that hurts. Of all the people"—the woman gave a little laugh—"she kept Emma Gilman."

"What's wrong with Emma?"

"Nothing. Emma's great. But I'd have thought if she had room for Emma in her life, she'd have room for me."

The anger was gone, replaced by wistfulness. Was this an ex-lover? Ash's ex-wife? No, the ex-wife was Victoria. What had the woman said her name was? Mia?

"So Emma hired you. Why are you trying to get dirt on Ashlyn?"

"I'm trying to help her. Who are you anyway? And how do you have my number?"

Had Ash given it to her?

"You know everything is online," the woman said. "The only way to avoid a stalker is to live in a cave."

True that.

"Even that probably won't work," Rose said. "Are you stalking me?"

"How do you define stalking?" The woman gave a little laugh. "No. I was Ashlyn's friend. I still am if she'd return a phone call. People are saying she's got a chance to work on a film Brentworth is backing and that you're looking for a reason for Brentworth to dump her."

"No!" Even if everything people said about Ash was true, there was no way she would tell Brentworth. "I was looking into..." Should she tell this woman about the pitch? "Into an opportunity that Ash was interested in. I wanted to hear from folks who'd done the same thing. And everyone told the same story."

"Let me guess, she's the heartless bitch who tanked Victoria Crue's career because their marriage was on the rocks."

"That comes pretty close."

"Did anyone tell you about the accident?" Mia sounded bitter, but the bitterness wasn't directed at Rose.

Rose felt a familiar panic rising in her chest.

"What accident?"

Something had gone wrong. It was no one's fault. The wind was rough. Maybe the fuel gauge misread. They hit a bird. There was no way to know. She had to do something. But there was nothing to do. It was too late. They didn't make it. *I'm so sorry. Your father was a good pilot.*

"Ashlyn didn't tell you?"

"No."

"So damn proud. Or hurt. Or scared. I don't know. She

wouldn't talk about it. It was on the 101. Just bad luck, but it fucked her up. She didn't bail on Victoria, she was in the hospital. As soon as she got out, she tried to get back to the set. She wasn't ready, and Victoria hated her for it. They were the golden couple. Everything they did won. And while Ashlyn was in the hospital, it got clear that the golden touch was all her. Victoria's smart and organized, but Ashlyn was the genius. So Victoria left her. And I'm guessing Victoria didn't leave her because she was jealous or at least not *just* because she was jealous. From what I know about Victoria, she probably loved Ashlyn when Ashlyn was a shining star. Then Ashlyn wasn't, so Victoria didn't."

Rose wanted to grab Victoria by the collar and push her up against a wall. *How could you?*

"The shitty thing is," Mia went on, "people knew what happened, but Victoria kept telling her side of the story. And Ashlyn-the-heartless-villain makes good gossip, so people believed it. Her friends tried to set people straight, but we were her friends. We were biased." She spat the word out. "No one listened."

"And Ash got blacklisted."

"I can't even say she got blacklisted. She disappeared. She stopped calling us. The longer she was gone, the truer Victoria's story sounded. We miss her."

There was sadness in Mia's voice. It sounded like the same sadness Rose felt as Ash sent her out of the studio. *Don't push me away.*

Rose wasn't sure if she liked this woman, but she liked the idea that Ash had this angry fairy godmother fighting for her.

"Ash got a chance to pitch her own film to Irene Brentworth."

"That's the old Ashlyn. Go big or go home."

The affection in Mia's voice tipped Rose toward liking her.

"Do you think she'll get it?" Mia asked.

"She doesn't have a lot of time to film the proof of concept and get her pitch deck together. I'm helping her."

"She deserves this," Mia said with a vehemence that must have shaken the satellite her cell signal bounced off. "Make sure she does."

chapter 22

Half an hour later, Rose was in the car headed for Stewart Productions again. It was too late. Ash wouldn't be there. Rose just had to...make sure the studio was still there. It hadn't collapsed or caught fire. Ash was at home and fine and tomorrow—at a reasonable hour—Rose would call her. Rose just had to see because sometimes things happened.

She gripped the steering wheel at the intersection of Barbur and Terwilliger. In the chasm of infrastructure behind her, I-5 whizzed by, each driver a microsecond from death, surviving only by shared attention. A thousand eyes on the road. A thousand people not reaching for their phones and one reaching, right now, somewhere. Poor Ash. What had that moment been like when she knew what was coming and there was no way out? And how could Victoria leave her? Rose's heart raced like a car heading downhill without brakes.

A few minutes later, she was driving up Burnside, turning left on Northwest Twenty-Third, passing silent shops until she reached the edge of the industrial district. There was Ash's building. The wall of windows was dark except for two squares. One on the second floor where Stewart Productions rented its space. Rose turned the corner. Light spilled out from the downstairs doors and two men muscled a sofa through. Another woman walked in with a stack of boxes.

Rose parked and got out of the car.

"Moving in," the woman said cheerfully.

Rose approached. You didn't go in other people's buildings in the middle of the night because someone propped the door open. That was creepy and wrong. But Rose was still wearing her suit from work and a woman in a suit could walk in almost anywhere and not read creepy.

She went in, walking quietly up the concrete steps to the second floor. The studio door was ajar, as though someone thought they had closed it and it had stuck on the uneven floor. Just a crack open. A crack Rose should not look through. Ash had sent her away, and this was not her business. She looked inside. The space looked bright but lonely, like an airport in the middle of the night. And Ash sat at the table crying.

She wasn't wailing, but she wasn't holding back. She was crying like someone who didn't expect to be seen or comforted. Her elbows were propped on the table. One hand covered her eyes. Her shoulders rose and fell with each breath. And the sight broke Rose's heart.

Rose pushed the door open, raced over, and wrapped her arms around Ash, half standing, half kneeling before her in an awkward embrace. Ash felt feverish in Rose's arms. Without thinking, Rose pressed her lips to the top of Ash's head.

Ash drew back, wiping her eyes although her tears were still flowing. "You're here." Her voice shook.

Rose stood up, opening her arms in an invitation. Ash stood and slumped against her. She seemed to swallow back her tears. She rested her cheek against Rose's shoulder, her breath shallow.

"Oh, Ash," Rose said into Ash's hair. "Why didn't you tell me?"

"How are you here?"

"I'm sorry."

Ash felt limp in Rose's arms, as though every muscle in her body had given in to Rose's embrace.

"For letting myself into your building without permission for one thing."

Ash laughed and pulled away. She was wearing a sleeveless shirt with a deep V-neck and a breastplate of a silver necklace. She looked stylish, damp, and disheveled.

"And because I didn't believe what those people said about you," Rose added, "but I acted like I did."

"Why did you come back?"

"Do you know someone named Mia Estelle?"

Ash's swollen eyes brightened. "You talked to Mia?"

"Mia called me in the middle of the night and told me I was ruining your life, and I think the implication was she'd ruin mine, too. But she thought I was trying to stop you from getting the Brentworth deal. I told her it wasn't like that."

Rose wanted to touch Ash's face, wipe away her tears, hold her forever, but Ash was pulling herself together like a flower closing in reverse-time-lapse photography.

"And she told you about the accident?" Ash asked.

"Yeah."

Ash stared at the middle distance as though trying to figure something out. "I didn't."

"And you don't have to if you don't want to. But you could have told me something bad happened and you didn't want to talk about it, but that it explained everything."

"I was in a car accident," Ash said slowly.

Rose took her hand, gently leading Ash to a saggy sofa underneath one of the windows. They sat. Should Rose put her arm around her? Hold her? Give her space?

"I wasn't drunk or texting or anything like that."

Rose waited. With each word it seemed like Ash was wondering if she should say more.

"It was the 101. I was coming back from a weekend with friends in Santa Cruz." Ash gave a sad, little laugh. "Victoria was mad. We were behind schedule, and she didn't want me to take the night off, but we'd been going nonstop for weeks. I was nervous because she was mad. There was a curve. The other driver had the sun in his eyes." Ash's voice caught. "It wasn't anyone's fault."

Ash's breath was too fast. She looked pale. Rose put a hand on her back. *Breathe.* Rose put her arms around Ash and pulled her close.

"My Jeep rolled four times." Ash spoke into the lapel of Rose's blazer. "V and I were in the middle of a big project, and I was out for a long time. When it first happened, Victoria was sweet. But physical therapy took forever. I got depressed. She got frustrated. She said I wasn't the woman she'd married anymore. She begged me to come back to work. I tried. I couldn't handle it."

If only Rose could have been there with her, protected her, comforted her.

"Only tell me if you want to." Rose pressed her lips to Ash's forehead. "If you don't want to relive it…"

"I relive it all the time," Ash said bitterly.

Rose rocked her gently. "I want to hear the whole story then."

"When it was obvious I couldn't do the film, which didn't take long, Victoria told me to go back up to our Portland house to rest. I'd always liked Portland. She filed divorce papers a week later."

"What part of *till death do us part* did she not understand?!" That was too much. Rose tried to dial back her indignation. "How could she be so...wrong?"

"The woman she fell in love with was a star." Ash gave a sad laugh. "She didn't want me when I was weak. Why would she?"

"Oh, Ash." Rose wished she could hold Ash closer. If she could wrap her whole body around Ash, cradle her...kiss her...

"I should be over it," Ash said. "It's been years. Maybe Victoria saw that coming."

"You were in an accident. That's trauma. It stays with people. It's not your fault."

"That's what I'd say to anyone else," Ash whispered.

"Then why not to yourself?"

Ash didn't say anything.

Should she tell Ash what stayed with her? *My parents loved adventure. We all did. We were happy. But there was only room for two people in the Cessna, and you don't take your kids over the Rockies. And now I never fly, and I never risk, and I've spent my whole life trying to be safe, but you can never be safe.* But this wasn't about her; this was about Ash.

"Is that why you didn't tell me? You think this shouldn't affect you?"

"That." Ash sighed. "And I didn't want you to feel sorry for me."

Rose put her hand on Ash's cheek, cupping her face and turning it toward her so she could look in Ash's eyes. "You were in a terrible car accident and your wife left you and lied about you and destroyed your career. Of course I feel sorry for you. A stone would feel sorry for you. A sociopath would feel sorry for you. You have nothing to be ashamed of."

Ash gave a teary laugh.

"What can I do for you?" Rose asked.

"Find someplace that's still serving Thai food and take me out to dinner?"

The only place Rose could find was a food cart next to a dive bar called Rookies. They sat on a picnic table in the parking lot eating pad thai out of the same carton, listening to the strains of "Sweet Child O' Mine" coming from the bar. And it was perfect.

"The San Juans fell through," Ash said, crunching a mouthful of bean sprouts. "The guy with the airplane has to take his sister to horse camp in Idaho."

The noodles congealed on Rose's fork. She gulped. Poor girl. She pictured a tween in the back seat of a tiny airplane, her brother at the helm. She could see them landing on a dusty airstrip. Strange. The planes that crossed Rose's mind always crashed. Crossing Rose's mind was like going into the Bermuda Triangle. But the girl and her brother made it.

"Sounds like fun," Rose said. Horses were like giant, terrifying, stiff-legged dogs, but some people liked them. "I'm sorry about the island."

Ash shrugged. "That's part of the game." She sang a line of "You Can't Always Get What You Want."

It was good to hear her sing, no hint of pain in her smile. It was good like seeing the sun rise was good, good like spring, good like getting the text that said everyone had made it home safely.

"I got the Goose Hollow Mansion to rent us their grounds," Ash said, skewering a grilled shrimp. "It'll be tight getting the shoot in. There's a wedding in the garden after us, and we can't have naked women pretending to make love with ferns while some nice couple is trying to walk down the aisle."

"Naked women pretending to make love would be fine." Rose used her plastic fork to steal a shrimp from Ash's side of the tray. "But the ferns." She shook her head.

"It's going to be a beautiful scene," Ash said with mock indignation.

"Of course, it is. *You* are creating it."

Their eyes met the way they had outside the Aviary. Rose no longer needed oxygen or food or water. Just that look in Ash's blue eyes.

"I didn't really want you to go," Ash said. "Thank you for coming back."

"Always," Rose said before she could think of all the things that one word implied. She didn't try to fix it. That never worked. It just made it more obvious what you meant and hadn't meant to say.

chapter 23

On the day of the shoot at the Goose Hollow Mansion, Rose texted Ash at six a.m.

Rose: *How's it going.*

Ash texted back immediately.

Ash:

Concern made Rose sit bolt upright. It had been some days since they'd talked over Thai food, but they'd texted throughout the days and into the evenings. Ash texted Rose video clips from the proof-of-concept production. Rose texted pictures of Cupcake and Muffin and funny tidbits about her sisters. Ash had seemed fine. But things happened. Rose's heart sped up. She called Ash.

"Are you okay?" Rose said as soon as Ash picked up.

"The shotgun mic is dead."

Dead!

It took Rose a half second to untangle *dead* from the rest of the sentence. No one was dead or hurt. It was just equipment.

"Is there anything else?"

"Jason's going to kill me."

Cupcake and Muffin clambered from the foot of the bed up to Rose's lap.

"He's trying to be nice about it, but he's been on me to replace the old one for months. Maybe years."

Rose could almost hear Ash running her hand through her hair or trying to and realizing it was up.

"He was jamming time code, then it just went to static. It was like listening to a dial-up modem."

Rose resisted teasing Ash that Ash ought to like a dial-up modem.

"What else do you have on set?"

Rose had a shotgun mic in her closet. A three-thousand-dollar Schoeps. Total overkill for a secret video series no one ever saw except maybe a hacker living in his basement who ransomed URLs and sold them back to the owners. But the sound was gorgeous.

"Lavaliers."

Rose understood the problem.

Ash said, "Those are those mics they wire to people on set. A little pack on their belt, a mic clipped to their lapel. We're filming the fern scene. There's no belt in a sex scene. Jason's been trying to put the mics on the side, but there're crickets. Fucking crickets. Who has crickets in the morning?"

"They could be the spring peepers." Rose remembered some nature camp Cassie's kids had gone to.

"What are spring peepers?" Ash said with theatrical despair.

"No one knows. Frogs or bugs." She wasn't thinking about the peepers. "I guess the biologists know."

What no one knew was that she had the equipment Ash needed. Even her sisters who shared everything with her, from Cassie's pregnancy mucus plug (a concept Rose was still trying to unknow) to Ty's heartbreaks to Gigi's brief flirtation with cocaine and her tearful pleas for help. Everything but not this hint that Rose had another side, not always the responsible protector, that a life of creativity (and kind-of-weird sensuality) hovered at the edges of her vision.

"I'm so sorry," Rose said.

On Ash's end, Jason called out, "Dude, what are you doing?"

"We have to rent something," Ash said. "No one is renting film equipment at six in the morning. If we get something right at ten that gives us two hours." She exhaled heavily. "It'll never work."

"Can you stay longer?" Rose asked.

"There's that wedding," Ash said. "They barely fit us in. Fuck! Should I tell everyone to wrap up and look for another location? Would they catch us if we filmed in Forest Park? Help me. What do I do?" Ash hesitated. "No. You don't have to help me. This is my fuckup."

"Of course I'll help. Don't send everyone home yet."

Rose hurried out of bed. She caught her naked reflection in the mirror above the dresser. Curvy. Tall. She'd hooked up with women. She'd dated. She'd monogamized like a classic lesbian. Had she ever been excited enough about a woman to care if her butt looked big? It was hard to think about breast-to-hip ratio when a plane could crash on your house at any minute and you didn't know for *sure* there wasn't Ebola in Portland. She saw Ash's lanky body and delicate neck. Ash's collarbones could break a woman's heart with their beauty. This was what a real, Ty-style crush felt like. Full of insecurities and so exciting you could almost consider a Brazilian. (Rose's vulva said, *Don't you even think about it.*) But Ash did not want Rose with or without a Brazilian or if Ash did want her, she didn't want to want her. God! That was the kind of distinction Ty wasted hours on. *Did she want me to know that she wanted me but didn't want to want me?*

"Wait," Rose said again. "Work on what you can for another hour. Just try. I'll bring coffee."

Rose hung up and pulled an armload of carefully organized clothing out of her closet. She threw it on the bed. Cupcake and Muffin raced around her feet, panicked because there was a rhythm to the morning. This was not part of it, which meant Rose had forgotten to feed them, which meant she would never feed them again.

"Out of my way, you monsters. Live on your fat reserves."

There was her equipment, as organized as Ash's. Not just the shotgun mic but all the other mics and stands and cameras she'd tried over the years. She hesitated for a second, naked, the shotgun mic in her hand. If she did this, even if she didn't tell Ash how she acquired the perfect microphone at six in the morning, she would be showing Ash a part of herself she'd never shared with anyone...except the hacker living in his basement, stealing URLs.

chapter 24

Ash sat on a waterproof tarp, talking to the talent. They were being patient, sitting naked, wrapped in a silver energy blanket. Behind them the trees rose out of an early mist. In a moment, the sun would turn the mist golden. It was the perfect light for the scene. Too bad there'd be no sound. Could she cut the dialogue and layer over soundtrack instead?

Ash startled as Jason called out behind her.

"Holy fuckin' shit, dude!"

Ash turned. It was Rose, standing on the edge of the area they'd marked off for the shoot, wearing a tweed blazer that made it look like she'd just come from riding across the British countryside. Her hair was swept back, almost rakishly. A little hint of Gentleman Jack swagger mixed with her boardroom poise. Her cheeks glowed pink from the crisp air. She could not have been prettier if the best makeup artist in Hollywood had done her face. She carried a Starbucks Coffee Traveler.

Jason's "How did you get this? Where did you get this? You are, like, fuckin' Harry Potter magic. You're Matrix level" seemed a little over the top for coffee.

Ash hurried over. The mist swirled around Rose's feet. The

peepers or whatever they were fell silent for a minute—or
maybe Ash couldn't hear anything but the beat of her heart.
She wanted to hug Rose, to kiss her, to tell her that the
morning's fail stung less because Rose was there.

"You brought coffee," Ash said.

"And those little cake pop things."

"Forget the cake pops," Jason said. "Look at this."

Ash hadn't noticed the case in his hands. He set it down
on a folding table they'd set up for equipment and reverently
removed a slender shotgun mic.

"It's a Schoeps," he said. "Top of the line."

"I have a few more things in the car," Rose said. "Wind-
screen. Shockmount. Some cables."

Jason looked like he'd fallen in love with her. Emma
came over, the camera on her shoulder like an extension of
her body.

"Rose," she said with a smile that insinuated way too much.

"Rose brought coffee," Ash said.

"And five thousand dollars of sound stuff," Jason said.

Emma looked at Ash and then at Rose then at the mic in
Jason's hands. "Where did you get this?" she asked.

"I do supply chain. I know where to get things." Rose
casually poured herself a coffee from the coffee box on the
makeshift craft services table as though she had not worked
a miracle.

Ash stood close to her, breathing deeply to catch a hint of
her perfume. "How *did* you get this?"

"It's a long story."

Ash was going to say it couldn't be that long. It'd barely been
an hour since Rose called her, but there was a shyness in Rose's
eyes that stopped her. Ash touched Rose's back lightly.

"Can I show you around?"

Rose nodded quickly.

Ash introduced Rose to the tiny crew, all wearing their flannel, stocking caps, and multi-pocketed vests. "You met Emma and Jason, of course." She led Rose over to where Tucker, the grip, and Benjamin, the light tech, were tinkering with an LED panel.

"You like it?" Benjamin turned a dial and the panel lit with dawn light, brightened to day, faded to sunset, and glowed midnight blue. If the sun didn't rise in quite the right way, the LEDs fixed it.

"It creeps me out," Ash said.

"She hates LED," Benjamin said to Rose. "She'd like Edison bulbs and analog."

"LED is a necessary evil." Ash sighed.

"You know you love it," Benjamin said.

Ash huffed. "Anyway, come on, Rose. Let me introduce you to the talent."

"Does anyone film on real film anymore?" Rose asked.

"Occasionally. I'd love to do an analog film sometime, but it's expensive. And Ben is right, you can't make the sun rise with Edison bulbs."

"You and your vintage," Rose said, like she'd been teasing Ash about her nostalgia gear for years the way Emma teased her about her ASMR videos.

Ash went back to the craft services table and got coffee and cake pops for the actors, then led Rose to where Jessica and Raven were sitting, tucked close together. They were a couple in real life. Their affection would sparkle on-screen.

"You're the one who asked Cade and Selena to find actors," the woman named Raven said. "Thanks. We are so excited to do this." She kissed the other woman. "Jessica is a total exhibitionist. We can't wait."

"We're ready," Jason called out from behind them.

The last thing Ash wanted to do was send Rose away, but it was a closed set.

"I'm sorry. For sex scenes, we don't have people on set who aren't absolutely necessary. It's for the actors' privacy."

Raven laughed. "Jessica hoped you'd bring a hundred people."

"It should still be a closed set," Ash said. It was good practice.

"I don't mind," Rose said quietly. "I'll see you later?"

"We'll be filming some non-sex scenes after this. I could text you. You could come back and watch."

Ash wanted Rose to see her in her element, not puzzling over a budget or muddling through a synopsis she could visualize on film but could not articulate in words. Instead Ash would bring together lights and angles. She'd coach Jessica to turn her head and Raven to kneel down in just the right way, Ash's vision captured in second-long moments hidden in the sea of footage, like gold shining in a stream.

"I'd like that," Rose said.

Ash watched her as she strode away, her steps authoritative even as she crossed the damp grass, her tweed blazer flaring over her ass, even sexier than anything Ash had seen Rose wear before.

"Are we making a movie or are we..." Emma had appeared at her side. She elbowed Ash. "She's hot. She found a shotgun mic. I think you should marry her."

"I kissed her," Ash said almost under her breath. "Don't tell anyone. It'll make her feel weird."

"What?!" Emma looked like she was going to tackle her.

"Shh," Ash said. "Nothing happened. I'm not ready. I just told you because you're my friend and I know you'd kill me if I didn't tell you. Now we've got to work."

"I need to know everything." Emma elbowed her. "Why are

you just dropping that in like, *Oh, try the coffee. It's Sumatran. Also I kissed the first woman I've liked in years.*"

Ash deflected Emma by waving to the crew to come around.

Because I don't know what to think. I don't know how to talk about it. If you give me one more lecture on shameless sexual dysfunction, I'll pass out from embarrassment.

"How was it?" Emma asked, in what she might have thought was a whisper.

"Now, for take one"—Ash projected her voice—"I'm imagining a triangle. The tree here on the left, Jessica standing over there…"

The crew nodded. Emma shot her a look that said, *You are in so much trouble.*

And then they were making a movie. Ash's body hummed with excitement. She'd almost forgotten what it was like to be on set, outside, checking the sky for rain, ready to troubleshoot and improvise and make something that was more beautiful because of the challenges. Ash moved everyone in place and called action on the first take.

Raven and Jessica were easy to direct. They followed instructions with ease. Their real affection sparked on the screen and with a little coaching, they transformed it into the characters' love. The end of the script didn't feel as corny when they spoke the lines. Ash could almost believe in the redemptive love she'd written.

They ended up using the LEDs and the light was perfect although LED was witchcraft. When they were done with the sex scene, Ash texted Rose, and she came back. Rose spent most of the time following Jason around, asking him questions about the sound and watching him work. But when Ash called action, and everyone except the actors fell silent, Ash felt Rose's eyes on her.

*   *   *

They finished just in time, passing the wedding caterers on their way out.

"Pizza at Ash's house," Emma declared as they loaded the van.

"I'd love that," Ash said, "but I've got to edit what we have so far and tomorrow I have to go up to Tacoma to pick up the Steadicam we're getting repaired."

"Because she loves film and she hates sound," Jason said amiably. He gave Rose a bro-style slap on the back. "Rose cares about my work."

Rose beamed.

"Y'all go out," Ash said. "Put it on the studio card."

"Rose wants to see your house. Don't you, Rose?" Emma asked with the subtlety of a rugby coach yelling, *Go team!*

Ash felt her face flush despite the air that was still cool with morning dew.

"You don't have anything else going today, right?" Emma grinned at Rose.

Were they twelve? Was Emma going to pass Rose a note saying, *My friend likes you. Will you go out with her? Yes. No.* Ash had gone out with her on a date, and then Ash had checked the no box. There was so much in that box she'd have to explain before she could lie down naked with Rose, and there were so many reasons why a beautiful, cheerful, confident woman like Rose wouldn't want someone with so much baggage.

Ash gave Rose a look that couldn't possibly convey everything. *I like you. You're fabulous. You enchant me. If we were twenty, I'd take you in the woods on a bed of violets.*

"Rose has more important clients than us," Ash said.

Rose returned her look. "No. I don't."

chapter 25

The crew knew what to expect at Ash's house. They accepted the empty living room. Everyone liked the gorgeous view and the great gaming station. And all the pizza, beer, or wine they wanted, all on Ash. (And delivered because she didn't usually have food or beer on hand. Why bother when you could live on Red Bull?) She did have plates. Using disposable wasn't environmentally responsible.

Now Ash hovered near the open front door, nervously waiting for Rose to pull into the driveway. What would she think? When Emma described the house, she said Ash lived like a frat boy. But frat boys had more than one couch. They had posters and shelves of bongs. If she was a frat boy, she was a lonely, rich, minimalist frat boy. Too late to hit IKEA now. Rose pulled in. Ash stepped out and waved. Rose paused a few paces from the door and looked the house up and down. It was tall, with vaulted living room ceilings and ten-foot ceilings in the bedroom, which was empty except for a bed...not that she was going to show Rose upstairs.

"I'm trying to figure out if it's you," Rose said. "My sisters' houses are perfectly them. Cassie's is all family love. Gigi's got a condo in the Pearl and it somehow looks like a really high-end salon. And Ty lives in a box full of clitoris models and books by Judith Butler, which is totally her."

"Is it me?"

She'd loved the house when she and Victoria bought it.

"It's beautiful." Rose swept past her into the house as though she owned it, looking back over her shoulder coquettishly. "So I guess it is."

The crew waved as Rose walked in. Jason offered her a beer. Emma motioned to the pizzas. Emma had lined them up against the wall, a stack of plates and napkins at each end of the row. Rose didn't say anything about the lack of tables. She bent down and loaded three pieces onto her plate, looking far sexier than any skinny, kale-eating LA socialite.

The crew regaled Rose with stories about the commercials they'd worked on. Jason trounced Emma's Amphib the Destroyer with his half-snake-half-ninja-warrior. After most of the pizza was gone and before anyone had more beer than they should, Emma stood up and announced, "Time for us to go." She shot the crew a look and mouthed, *All of us.* The crew left with a chorus of thank-yous and implausible excuses. Benjamin had to update his voter registration. Jason had to help a friend build a Ping-Pong table.

"Should I...?" Rose asked as the crew left with Emma on their heels.

Rose looked beautiful, standing in Ash's empty living room, still flushed from the morning's chill or maybe the beer.

The answer was probably yes. Rose should go. Otherwise, Ash might kiss her again and then panic and then be one of those people who sends mixed signals and hurts people unintentionally or confuses them or just annoys them.

"Do you want to see the deck?" Ash asked. "The view is great."

Rose nodded like seeing the deck was a very important part of her plans for the day. Ash led her out. They leaned on the railing, their shoulders almost touching, looking out at the forest below the house and the city beyond that. She could feel Rose's presence like the sun. She wanted Rose to turn to her, take her in her arms, whisper, *I want you no matter what*, and kiss her. She wanted Rose to make everything okay in the bedroom, the way she seemed to have answers to all Ash's pitch problems. And she wanted to give Rose a few exquisite seconds of the passion Rose said she was missing. Ash hadn't wanted a woman in years; now she longed to kiss every inch of Rose's curvy body, to caress her, to make Rose feel better than Rose had ever felt before.

"Did you get a seismic assessment on the house?" Rose asked.

Ash momentarily forgot what *seismic* meant.

"What? Oh. Um…I think we did. I think we have an eighty percent chance of survival."

Rose looked over the railing, assessing the supports that held the deck above the steep slope. Her brow furrowed.

"You might be able to retrofit the supports."

That hadn't risen to the top of Ash's list of things to worry about.

"But you just moved in," Rose commented. "It takes a while to get all that stuff done."

Ash bit her lip. "Um."

"I know a good contractor who does disaster assessment. I had a limestone retaining wall put in to protect my house from landslides. It's on a slope below Barbur Boulevard. If the ground gets too wet…" She stopped. "I'm talking about retaining walls. Does that make me old?"

"I…um…I didn't just buy the house."

Rose cocked her head.

"I bought it about ten years ago."

"Not that I don't like what you've done with the décor."
Rose glanced back at the window. "But what happened to the
furniture?" She touched Ash's arm. "What happened?"

"Can I convince you I just hate upholstery?"

"If you want."

A pine-scented breeze blew up from the ravine.

"We had furniture. Victoria got it custom-made. This was a
vacation home because I like Portland. She took the furniture
in the divorce."

"She took your hairless cat *and* your furniture? The bitch!
Oh. Ty would kill me for using the female as a pejorative. The
asshole."

Rose's outrage felt like a warm blanket wrapped around
Ash's shoulders. Rose remembered Ash's cat.

"The whole point of custom-made is that it stays in the
place it was made for," Rose added.

Ash laughed. "I got the couch in college. Somehow Emma
found it in a storage unit my friend Mia had. I don't know how.
Emma and I didn't know each other in college, obviously. And
I'd lost touch with Mia by then. But Emma drove it up from
LA. Emma thought it would cheer me up. *She* cheered me up.
That couch belongs in a furniture graveyard. You must think
I'm a mess."

As clearly as Ash could envision a scene, she could imagine
what it would feel like to cuddle up on the couch with Rose,
tucking herself against the curve of Rose's hip. *I don't think it's
fucked up that you live in a Frank Lloyd Wright knockoff house with
less furniture than a frat boy*, imaginary Rose said.

It was kind of fucked up.

"In a really weird way," Rose said slowly, "I have the same

house." She looked at Ash, but her blue-brown eyes were farther away than the skyline. "I do have furniture. But when I bought my house...some stuff had happened with my family. I didn't have time to think about what I wanted my house to look like. I went to the Pottery Barn website. And I just bought each room. Everything in the living room. Everything in the bedroom. I ordered it all in beige. And I haven't changed *anything*."

"Do you like the look?"

"It's genetically impossible to not like Pottery Barn, but it's not me. It's...everything that happened."

"What happened?" Ash asked quietly.

Rose gave a quick shake of her head. "I am lucky to live in that house and afford that furniture. I shouldn't complain. I've got no excuse."

No excuse.

Ash knew that feeling and she understood changing the subject because you weren't ready to talk about it.

"The only thing that's personal is the dogs' toys," Rose said. "A dozen shredded unicorns. That's what makes my house a home."

Ash rested her hand palm-up on the railing beside Rose's, inviting Rose to place her hand in Ash's. When Rose did, Ash stroked the side of Rose's hand with her thumb, drawing a little sigh from Rose, and officially becoming one of those people who sent terribly mixed signals.

The moment should have gotten awkward, but somehow it didn't.

"I think it's cute you let your dogs shred unicorns all over your house," Ash said.

"You know how I got into pugs?" Rose said. "I went out with this woman who had one, and I think I dated her for four months just because of the pug."

"Then you got your own so you wouldn't have to break any more hearts."

"I don't think I've broken any hearts."

You could break mine.

"I doubt that. How could someone have you and then live without you?" Ash was still holding Rose's hand.

"Um, easily." Rose rolled her eyes. "No. Let me try that again. You're right. I leave a trail of broken hearts wherever I go. One awkward blind date with me and women don't recover." Rose withdrew her hand, but she caressed Ash's palm as she did, and the feeling tingled all the way to Ash's toes. "Ty says I just haven't met the right woman yet, and when I do, I'll fall ridiculously in love and do all the over-the-top stuff she does. She says I'll finally understand."

They were close enough to kiss. Rose's hip rested against hers. Ash felt like the filament of an Edison bulb, glowing and delicate. Rose turned to Ash, her eyes filled with desire and affection. The desire said Ash could take her to bed that moment. The affection said Rose would never make the first move. And Ash didn't quite have the courage even though the Edison bulb of her heart grew brighter and brighter as she traced Rose's lips with her eyes.

"I have to go up to Washington to pick up a camera," Ash said. "And there's so much to do, but maybe we could squeeze in a date to go thrift store shopping, and I'll buy you the tackiest, most personal couch we can find. It'll have stripes and elks embroidered on it, and tassels."

That was not the height of seduction. It wasn't even the baseline of seduction.

But Rose's smile grew bigger, amused but enthusiastic. "You do know how to woo a girl."

chapter 26

Ash jumped into the Tesla like she was training for *Fast and Furious*. She'd stayed up late editing the footage from the fern scene, but she wasn't tired. The footage was great, and she felt great. She'd been in the flow yesterday. There was no accident. There was no Victoria. Only the actors blossoming under her direction and her vision of the scene, so clear she felt like she was transcribing it not creating it. She was back!

And Rose. She'd felt such empathy for Rose. Whatever pain had manifested in Rose buying high-quality beige furniture, she wanted to comfort her. Even if Rose didn't want to talk about it, she'd leaned against Ash for a long time.

She didn't love driving to Tacoma to pick up the Steadicam, but they didn't have production assistants, so it wasn't anyone else's job. Anyway, it gave her time to think and crank up the radio.

Rain exploded somewhere around Vancouver. The last big storm before the sky cleared for the summer. She didn't mind. After she'd recovered enough from the accident to drive, she'd trained to drive without fear. Around and around the closed-course racetrack then up and down the freeway until she could drive without panicking when a semi passed her.

Before she knew it, Tacoma came into view. The camera was ready. She grabbed a sandwich and got back on the road, heading for the nowhere land between Centralia and Longview. The rain lashed the windshield. The sky was dark.

She turned off satellite radio and let the crackle of FM fill the car with its old-fashioned jumble of commercials and fading signals. Rose would tease her about it. So nineties. The DJ came back from a commercial for discount TVs.

"This one never gets old," the DJ said and the first notes of "Hey Jealousy" came on.

Ash hummed along, smiling at the rain and the road and her life. An old truck piled high with scrap metal pulled onto the freeway in front of her, and she smiled at it, too. She didn't even flinch. People got over things. She'd gotten over her fear of driving. She was going to get the deal with Brentworth. She'd get over the pain that seized the intimate parts of her body when touched, or she'd learn to handle it. She'd learn to love herself like all those therapists and self-help books told her to. Maybe she'd—

Something clattered. She heard it through the rain. She grabbed the wheel, scanning back and forth for cars coming in her lane or brake lights, for—

Wait! Suddenly her head knocked against the back of the headrest. Her seat belt squeezed her with monster force. The car flipped.

Over.

Over.

Over.

The highway flashed past her eyes. A cliff. A guardrail. She

was going over. This was it. *I want more time.* She was so close
to the life she wanted. She could taste it. But it was over.

Over.

Over.

From a great distance she heard sirens. She was fading
away. She would never see Rose again. She would never love
herself fully like a self-help book. She would never know
if Rose's touch would wake her body with pleasure. The
dashboard computer swam before her eyes, showing Rose's
most recent texts. Ash reached out instinctively. She had to
tell Rose. Panic strangled Ash's words but the speak-to-text
caught them anyway.

"Rose, I was in an accident. I wanted more…more…"

"Send?" the car asked.

"Send," she gasped.

Then everything went silent. She couldn't see. Everything
was orange. She wasn't breathing.

I want you, Rose.

Ash's vision came back. The radio was still playing. The
rain was still pounding. Had she died? Was heaven a stretch
of empty highway south of Centralia? That'd be a letdown.
Maybe it was purgatory. She didn't believe in purgatory. It
couldn't be hell, though. Suddenly she gulped in air like someone swimming up from a great depth. The exhale was a short,
sharp scream. Was that her last breath?

She drew in another. She was sitting upright in the driver's
seat, parked on the side of I-5 watching the windshield wipers
swish back and forth while the DJ embedded another ruthlessly catchy Dua Lipa tune in the heads of everyone in the
Centralia/Longview listening area. She rubbed her eyes. She
touched her leg. Nothing hurt. She was not in California. This
was not the 101. She was not flipping.

She had not died. The front of her car had sunk a few inches. In the rearview mirror, she saw something bouncing off the road. A piece of metal. She'd hit it. The truck with the scrap metal was a dot in the distance. She had a flat tire. Her driving lessons had paid off. She'd panicked, but she'd gotten safely to the side of the road. Her flashers were on. She was alive. She'd call a tow, fix up the car, and be back on the road.

Breathe. It was harder than the floating bunny made it sound. She saw her message to Rose on the screen.

"Text Rose." Her voice was still shaky. "Ignore my message. I'm fine. Butt dial. Sorry. Smile emoji. Smile emoji. Smile emoji."

"Send to Rose?" the computer asked when Ash paused for breath.

"Send."

Breathe.

Her phone rang through the car stereo, startling her with its volume. Rose.

Ash picked up her actual phone and texted Rose by hand.

Ash: *I'm fine. Don't worry*

Rose hung up and called again. Her text came through at the same time.

Rose: *PICK UP*

Ash looked at the dashboard. Text-to-speak had failed to translate the emojis and her text read, hysterically, *smile emoji smile emoji smile emoji.* She had to pick up. *Smile emoji* spelled out along with *I'm fine* didn't say *I'm fine.*

"Hi, Rose!" She tried to steady her breath.

"What happened?" Rose spoke slowly and deliberately, as if talking to someone who didn't understand the language. "Are you hurt?"

"It was a butt dial."

"Sweetheart," Rose said. "It's not a butt dial if you say my name."

The tenderness in her voice made a lump in Ash's throat. She looked at the texts. Yes. She'd called Rose by name.

"Is someone there?" Rose asked.

"I'm fine." Ash's voice wavered.

"Turn on your camera. Let me see you."

She wanted to see Rose. She needed Rose. If she could only press her face into Rose's chest, feel Rose's arms around her.

I can't keep taking care of you, Ash.

She shivered as the adrenaline ebbed from her body.

"I got a flat tire."

Ash put on her best smile. She switched to video call. Rose was in a kitchen. A woman—Ash guessed from her short hair that it was Ty—sat on the counter behind her. Ty waved.

"What happened? You look terrified. Where are you?" Rose said.

"Somewhere south of Centralia. I'm fine. I just hit something on the road." She looked in the rearview mirror. "It looks like part of…I don't know…a tractor. I'm sorry I texted you. You just have such a comforting presence." She'd meant to say the last bit like a joke, but it came out unbearably earnest.

"Oh, Ash."

Ash was going to cry if Rose kept being so kind. And she was *not* going to cry in front of Rose again. *Tell me to pull myself together. Tell me to suck it up. Don't be weak, Ash.*

"Here's what I'll do." Rose's face disappeared from view as she searched for something on her phone. "Send me a pin, and I'll get a tow truck out there. South of Centralia. There's not much south of Centralia. I'll get you a hotel, so you have someplace to wait."

"I have OnStar. I'm fine."

"I'm faster than OnStar. There's a McMenamins near there. Near-ish. I'll have them send a car to get you from the tire place."

McMenamins was a boutique hotel chain known for creepy art and naming their rooms after alt-rock bands.

"I don't think McMenamins sends cars."

"All hotels send cars for a price."

The authority in Rose's voice was sexy. Ash noticed, even though she was just a few minutes past thinking she was dying. It was *that* sexy.

"You really don't have to," Ash said.

Rose's face came back into view.

"I got you, Ash."

chapter 27

Ty hopped off the kitchen counter where she'd been flouting the threat of salmonella by eating raw cookie dough.

"Everything okay?"

Rose hung up, her hands shaking. Where was the crew? Why was Ash alone? Of course. She was getting the camera. Had she been driving all day? Was she going north or south?

"Ash was in an accident." Rose felt hollow inside.

"She looked okay."

"I need to see her."

"You just did."

"I mean in real life."

Things happened. The storm didn't show up on the radar. *Your father was a good pilot.* The world made sense and then it didn't. And every tragedy mattered, but Ash was special. She was kind and driven and tired and full of wild, bright energy. When she listened to Rose, Rose was more than a business consultant on the edge of a midlife crisis. And there was so much Rose didn't know about Ash yet. Her favorite foods. Did she have pets as a child. Was she cool in high school? Did she sleep curled up and motionless like a child or did she wake at the slightest sound.

"I have to go. I have to make sure she's okay."

Ty's brow furrowed. "To Centralia? Because she got a flat tire?"

She never wished her sisters weren't around, but now she wished Ty was somewhere else. Rose was overreacting. She knew it, but she'd seen the fear in Ash's eyes. She couldn't not go.

"She was in a bad accident years ago. What if she's re-traumatized?"

Rose looked around for her keys and wallet. Muffin and Cupcake hoped this meant a walk and began yodeling at the door.

"Fuck off, Muffin," she said. "She's on the side of the road. She could have a concussion. The trucks that go by won't see her. Sometimes people pretend to be police and abduct stranded motorists."

"Rose." Ty stepped in front of her. "Stop. Ash is not going to get abducted by someone pretending to be a police officer. She got a flat tire."

"But what if she's triggered? What if she...what if she..." There were so many things that could go wrong. So. Many. Things.

"Rose." Ty held Rose's shoulders. "Rose. Listen to me. She's not Mom and Dad. She's okay."

"I have to see her."

"Take a deep breath."

Rose took a breath.

"Another. Okay. Sit down with me on the sofa."

"I have to go."

"You have to calm down." Ty led her to the sofa. "Now,

let's think this through. You're going to meet her at the McMenamins?"

"Yes?"

"Just drive a couple of hours and surprise? Do you think that's maybe a little extra? What about calling her in half an hour and seeing how she's doing?"

Ty didn't have a right to wear that maternal expression. It was Rose who took care of things. It was Rose who knew the signs of appendicitis when Ty came home from high school sick. It was Rose who made sure Gigi got all the shots she needed to travel. It was Rose who drove Cassie to the hospital when her water broke the first time. Watched Delilah when her brother was born. Watched both of them when the twins were born. If that had earned Rose one thing, it had earned her the right to take care of Ash without Ty telling her she was being extra.

"Don't give me shit about it," Rose said.

"I'm not giving you shit. I know you really like her—" Ty held up her hand before Rose could protest. "I'm your sister, so I'm going to help you out here. There are two kinds of women: women who'd like a hot chick they just met rushing to their rescue because they got a flat and women who'd think that was creepy."

Rose rubbed her face. "I thought you didn't believe in binaries."

"I'm making an exception. You haven't liked someone for a long time, and so I can't let you rush up to Centralia if that's going to creep her out. It's like how I wouldn't let you drunk-dial her, either."

"When have I drunk-dialed someone?"

"Never. So maybe I would let you do it for the life experience." Ty put her arms around Rose, holding Rose's own arms to her sides. "You've got baggage. Everyone does. It's just...how soon do you want to open the suitcase and take the stuff out to show her?"

"Are you telling me not to do something crazy for love? *You*. Of all people."

Had she said *love*?

"I have experience." Ty released her. "And has it worked out for me?"

"Not so much."

"Right." Ty cocked her head, looking at Rose expectantly.

"Can you watch the dogs?"

"You're actually going to do it?"

"Yeah."

"That might be a terrible idea," Ty said. "Go for it."

It didn't seem like a terrible idea as Rose left Portland, maybe a little emotional, but not *terrible*. Even as she drove through Vancouver, the sun setting on her left, or when she stopped at Starbucks for a twenty-four-ounce coffee to calm her nerves, it seemed okay. It seemed like an almost good idea as she pulled off the freeway into the parking lot of the McMenamins, a large, red-roofed building with outside walkways and white railings that made it look like something from New Orleans. Behind it the Columbia River stretched out like a starless sky. There wasn't anything else around. Absolutely no reason why she might be in the area coincidentally. She parked at the far end of the lot and checked her phone.

Ash had texted. The tow had come. The tire center said she'd blown one tire and bent her axle. It'd take a day to get the parts to fix it. The lodge had sent a friendly busboy who drove Uber on the side and was happy to make two hundred dollars on his break. Ash was safe, working on her laptop at the hotel. She'd even sent a selfie with the caption *proof of life*.

Rose had to go home. When *Ty* said the grand gesture was a little extra, it was really extra.

Rose was going to turn around right now...except twenty-four ounces of coffee had caught up with her. She'd use the bathroom at the hotel and be on the road in six minutes.

Rose slipped into the hotel restaurant. It was a nice place. The restaurant took up the length of the building, a long stretch of windows looking out on the Columbia. Maybe Ash could relax a little while she was here. Enjoy the view. Get some sleep.

Rose peed and washed her hands quickly. She'd told Ash it was okay that Ash was still upset about everything that had happened to her in California. Rose had baggage, too. Like Ty said. That was nothing to be ashamed of, but it was not a reason to quasi-stalk Ash, either. Rose would forgive herself for overreacting. Maybe she'd think about seeing a therapist again. Ty wouldn't tease her about it. Rose would be back in Portland before midnight. Ash would never know.

Rose pushed the bathroom door open with a paper towel and tossed it in the trash can.

And there was Ash, looking relaxed in baggy cargo pants and a turtleneck sweater. Her hair was loose. Rose covered her mouth as though that might conceal her. Ash looked around like she might be hallucinating.

"What are you doing here?"

Dropping my baggage at your front door.

The world was full of infinite possibilities but none that could explain why Rose was there except the truth.

"I came to check on you."

"I texted you. I'm fine."

"I know."

Ash put two fingers to her forehead, then to her lips, then looked behind her. "You came all the way up here to see if I was all right?"

Rose stared up at the ceiling. "I want to tell you I was in Centralia anyway."

Only people in Centralia thought there was anything in Centralia.

"South of Centralia," Ash pointed out.

"South of Centralia." Rose sighed.

They looked at each other. A woman brushed past them. Somewhere in the restaurant a fork clattered on the floor.

"I'm sorry." Rose sighed. "Ty said it was extra."

Ash still looked perplexed. "I can't believe you came all the way up here for me."

Rose shrugged. "Sorry."

Suddenly Ash beamed. "That's the nicest thing...I have a table over there. The one with the laptop. I'll just—" Ash gestured to the bathroom. "Then I'll buy you a drink."

Ash had a booth by the window, her enormous laptop, an extra hard drive, and a set of headphones spread out in a makeshift workstation. Rose sat down. Ash joined her a moment later.

The waiter stopped by their table and handed Rose a menu. Rose's hands were shaky from twenty-four ounces of Sumatra and Ash's beauty, so she ordered a martini.

"Ty says there are two kinds of people," Rose said.

"I thought she didn't believe in binaries."

"She made an exception."

"What are the two kinds of people?"

"People who'd think it was creepy that I came up here and people who would probably think that...but in a good way." Rose fidgeted with a napkin on the table.

"God, Victoria would never have done that." Ash gazed out the window at the mile-wide river. "Sorry." Ash turned back to Rose. "It's creepy to compare people to your exes."

"It's fine if you tell me I'm nothing like her."

Rose didn't mean to look at Ash, but their eyes met, and Rose couldn't turn away from that dark, stormy blue. Time froze. The noise of the restaurant faded away.

"You're nothing like her."

Arguably, it was an ambiguous compliment. Victoria was successful, rich, pretty, connected, at least somewhat creative. But Ash wasn't talking about that; Rose was sure.

"I was worried about you," Rose said. "You'd been in that accident and that kind of thing stays with people. It's normal. I thought maybe you'd like company."

I thought maybe you were going to be hit by a semi right after being abducted by a serial killer posing as a policeman. Ash didn't need to know the specifics.

The waiter came back in record time. Rose didn't drink martinis. Now that she thought about it, she had *never* had a martini. (It wasn't good to drink too much hard alcohol. It increased the risk of various cancers.) She took a big sip and coughed.

"Oh my God, it's just cold vodka."

"Or gin. That's what a martini is," Ash said with an amused smile.

"I knew that."

Rose stared at the olive staring back at her. When Rose looked up, Ash was staring at her.

"It did freak me out," Ash said. "I thought I was back there on the 101."

Rose held her hand across the table, and Ash took it.

"I took driving lessons after the accident. I didn't want to be afraid of driving for the rest of my life."

Maybe Rose should have gotten on every plane she could. Maybe she should learn to fly.

"If something happened, I wanted to know what to do," Ash said. "And I did. I panicked, but I pulled over. I got my flashers on. I did everything the way you're supposed to." She pursed her lips. "I'm proud of that." Ash squeezed Rose's hand. "I'm really glad you're here. Otherwise it would have just been a shitty night. Now it's special."

No one else in the restaurant saw it, but every tree on the Columbia lit with twinkling fairy lights. A rainbow, like a black opal, stretched across the night sky.

chapter 28

Rose was here. Her presence made Ash's heart real. Rose had sensed how Ash had ached for comfort. And that meant that Rose saw something fragile and needy in Ash and yet Rose wasn't annoyed. She didn't act like a woman who'd had to drop everything to deal with a helpless friend who'd overreacted to a flat tire.

"Would you like to see the edits I've done on the fern scene?" Ash asked.

Rose's eyes shone with excitement as Ash turned her laptop toward her.

But she asked, "Is it okay? It was a closed set? When is it okay for just anyone to see it?"

"It's a good question. I wouldn't show the rough cut to just anyone, but I trust you."

Ash shouldn't be blushing. She wrote the ferns. Rose had read the fern scene. But still she felt exposed, probably more exposed than the cheerful, exhibitionist actors had felt. Rose was going to see her work—not the polished product of hundreds of people's work, but her tiny crew, her script, her editing. And there was no way to watch the scene and not think about the delicious tautness of the air between them. She handed Rose the headphones.

"You don't want everyone to hear?" Rose asked with a smirk.

"The soundtrack is very provocative."

"Right," Rose drawled. "The soundtrack." She put the headphones on and started the clip.

Ash couldn't see the screen, but she knew what Rose was seeing. Ash had been working on it all evening. The ranger and the firefighter bathed in soft LED light (that was only sinister if you knew it was LED). The ranger spread a blanket on a bed of moss. *Let me give you everything,* she whispered. She trailed wet ferns (silk ferns because Ash couldn't get a definitive answer on whether or not fern spores could cause unexpected allergic reactions) across her lover's breasts whispering, *We're part of nature.* The soundtrack soared. The firefighter threw her head back in ecstasy, calling out, *Yes. Yes. Yes!*

Rose's eyes widened as she got to the end of the clip.

Rose took off the headphones. "I definitely needed these."

Ash blushed hotter. "I wasn't embarrassed to film it."

"Are you embarrassed to show it to me?"

"No." Ash's cheeks flamed. "It's just...but...it's..." *When I think about ferns, I think about you.* "Something's off." Ash hadn't been able to put her finger on what. "I love the imagery. Raven and Jessica were great, but it's not quite what I wanted."

"It was hot." Rose touched the tip of her tongue to her lip, in an unconscious gesture so sexy Ash thought she might faint. "And sweet," she added.

"But?"

"It's great."

"What would you do if it was your scene?"

Rose looked startled. She turned the laptop back to Ash. "I don't know anything about film."

"You watch them."

"I advise cauliflower supply chains."

"But if you were a director, what would you say?"

"It's the sound," Rose said with casual certainty, like she was talking about supply chains or branding. Then she seemed to catch herself. "I mean...I have no idea. You're the artist."

"You do. Tell me. What do you hear?"

Rose hesitated then angled the laptop so they could both see.

"You have the music where you want ambient sound, and you have ambient sound where you want music. And you don't use the silence. I would fade out the music here, as Raven lays Jessica down." She started the clip again. "Right...there." She stopped the clip.

Two customers walked by and whispered something to each other.

"Shit." Rose closed the laptop quickly.

Rose and Ash looked at each other and laughed at the same time.

"Women arrested for playing pornography at a McMenamins south of Centralia," Rose said.

Without thinking, Ash scooted over and beckoned to her side of the booth.

"Sit here."

Then they were sitting side by side. Ash could smell Rose's perfume, feminine, sensual, but not girly. Like her voice it was rich and complicated.

Rose focused on the screen. She pressed one headphone to her ear. With the other hand, she marked time as the clip advanced.

"Here." Rose touched PAUSE. "I'd get really close to the sound of the ferns, and the wetness when she dips them in water, and Jessica's breath. When she gets closer to climax, fade out the music and bring in the crickets." Rose advanced to a frame. "And then here, I'd bring the sound up…is this the track for the ambient sound? And here." Rose sounded excited. "Can you bring the music—that's this track, right?—down between minute 2 and 3:35?"

Most people had no idea what they were looking at the first time they opened Avid Media Composer.

"Then here, after her body arches off the ground, I'd cut to her face, and I'd cut the sound, so it's totally silent as she climaxes."

"Wow."

Rose scrunched her nose in an adorable expression of embarrassment. "Sorry. I've been consulting too long. I can't do anything without giving people advice. You must hate that. Everyone thinks they can make a movie just because they've seen them."

"I don't mind hearing people's opinions, but this isn't an opinion. You're right."

Rose winced. "I can't be."

Ash could hear the scene the way Rose described it.

"You are. The silence represents the women finally finding peace and love," Ash said, "and the ambient sounds are their connection to the earth. It's perfect. It's what I was missing. I like the music I picked, but I couldn't…Emma would say I couldn't relax enough to just let the real sounds say what they needed to say."

Ash made a copy of the file and opened a new project window.

"You want to make it happen? I'll show you how the program works."

Rose's blue-brown eyes lit up. She had questions about the

interface, but not that many. Her hand moved back and forth between the keyboard, the mouse, and the touch screen. She didn't take her eyes off the screen, and Ash didn't take her eyes off Rose's hands.

Finally, Rose said, "There."

Ash put on the headphones. Some of the transitions were awkward. There were a few seconds of inadvertent silence when Rose hadn't linked the tracks properly. But overall, it was great. Listening to it, Ash felt the same peaceful tingle she felt when she watched Cherry Covered Apron. She almost told Rose, *I like to watch videos of a woman touching fruits and vegetables. Just thought you should know...in case it's a dealbreaker for you.* But Ash wasn't making that kind of a deal with Rose, at least not tonight. Tonight they were friends, and new friends didn't need to know about your weird vegetable thing.

"This is amazing," Ash said.

The waiter came by and asked if they'd like dinner. Rose looked at her phone.

"It's late. I should—"

The word "stay" leapt out of Ash's mouth. "I mean, you drove all the way up. Let me get your dinner."

It felt like more than friends having dinner. They were still sitting on the same side of the booth. Ash felt the other universe transposed over the real one, the universe in which this was a real date.

"Yes," Rose said.

They ordered and Ash closed the laptop. Rose moved back to her side of the table, and Ash felt her body cool at Rose's absence. But they didn't feel far apart. Conversation flowed freely. Rose told Ash about an insufferable co-worker. They compared shitty apartments they lived in during college. Ash ventured a few details about life in LA, like when they'd rented a helicopter for a scene and it ran low on gas and had to land in a field near a Costco. And after a second drink, she told Rose how Emma had set up an Athena profile for her without telling her.

"What?" Rose drew the word out. "That sounds like a rom-com."

The clouds made the sky outside darker than night. On the other side of the Columbia, far away, scattered house lights dotted the dark hills. The restaurant was cozy. The booth felt intimate.

"Can I see it?" Rose asked.

"I never used it."

Was that approval in Rose's smile?

"Is it still up?"

"I won't confirm or deny."

"What does it say?"

"I refused to look."

"You haven't looked? This is too good." Rose grinned. She took out her phone. "Let's see...what do I search for? Profession: entertainment industry."

"You're on Athena?"

Of course Rose would date. She probably had dozens of women interested in her. She hadn't been waiting around for Ash her whole life.

"I go on occasionally." Rose's shrug said, *Why lie?*

Was she talking about hookups? The thought made the cozy evening chill a bit. Rose would want sex even if she wasn't dating. Maybe she had friends with benefits. Maybe she was on Tinder. She probably did all the things Ash had once done without a second thought: bondage, fisting, sex in an airplane. (It was uncomfortable, but Victoria had insisted.) Ash couldn't give her that.

"Oh, here you are!" Rose said.

Ash groaned.

"*Profession,*" Rose read, "*production studio owner, producer, production design, director, workaholic. Hobbies: hiking, camping, long walks on the beach at sunset, and candlelit dinners.* Can candlelight dinners be a hobby?"

"And why are the beaches always sunset?" Ash asked. "Are people like, *Fuck no. I'm not walking at the beach until six forty-nine when the sun sets?* Emma could be more original."

"There's a place for childhood photos. Let's see if she uploaded any."

Ash reached for Rose's phone. Rose pretended to snatch it away, but she let Ash's hand catch hers.

"Let me see first," Ash said.

Emma hadn't uploaded photos, but that wasn't what Ash was looking for. She was looking for the dot that said Rose had messages. Fifty-three to be exact. All unread. Ash smiled.

"Let's read your astrology," Rose said when Ash handed the phone back.

They were both wiping the tears of laughter from their eyes when Rose read the last sentence.

"You sound fabulous," Rose said.

The waiter appeared at their table. "We'll be closing in half an hour. Do you mind if I close out your bill?"

Ash handed him her credit card.

"I should go," Rose said reluctantly.

"And drive all the way home? Why don't you stay." Had she just made an offer she couldn't fulfill? Rose's body would feel so good. Rose wouldn't judge her for her problems. But if she invited Rose to bed, she should do it when Rose could leave if Ash cried. Not during her tears. Rose would never do that. But afterward when it got awkward, Rose deserved an out.

"I mean you get a room, and I also have a room," Ash said. "Two rooms...neighbors...like in *Friends*...across the hall..."

A complicated look crossed Rose's blue-brown eyes, amusement, acceptance, and behind that disappointment. "Like friends."

chapter 29

Rose stood up and stepped away from the table to hide her disappointment. She *should* stay. She didn't feel tipsy from the martini, but women's bodies processed alcohol slowly and even below the legal limit your driving was impaired. And she'd barely eaten her dinner. How could she care about food when she was watching Ash's every expression as she told the story of the cheerleader she loved in high school. Anyway leaving would be weird, like she'd come for a hookup and if that wasn't happening it'd be better to drive home.

"That's probably a reasonable choice." Rose put on her business consultant voice.

Nothing to see here. Paperwork is done. Let's move on.

Ash lingered a few paces behind her as Rose approached the hotel's front desk, like she'd dropped Rose off at a dark house and was waiting to make sure she got in okay.

"I'm sorry, ma'am, we're actually all full," the clerk said.

Rose turned back to Ash. "I guess I'm off." She'd get a hotel in Centralia.

Ash toed the carpet. "It's late and...you could share my room."

"As friends."

If only Ash would say, *No, not as friends.*

Rose wished the front desk clerk wasn't watching them.

"Sure," Ash said, like *friends* was Rose's idea.

They didn't say anything as they rode the elevator to Ash's room. Inside, the room was paneled in vintage knotty pine. There was no overhead light. A lamp by the bed cast a romantic glow marred only by the life-size American primitive-style painting that hung above the bed: two ghostly women each holding the end of an enormous fork. Or maybe that didn't mar it. This was a McMenamins hotel. That's what people came for.

"I didn't bring anything to wear," Rose said, not looking at Ash. "I wasn't thinking I'd stay."

I just wasn't thinking.

"Me neither."

They laughed awkwardly.

"I'll just take off my blazer," Rose said.

"I'll sleep in this." Ash gestured to her cargo pants. "It'll be like camping. I'm just going to take a quick shower first."

"I'll catch up on a few emails."

Ash disappeared into the bathroom. Rose took off her shoes, socks, and blazer, sat with her back propped against the headrest, and opened her email on her phone. A Dutch company was investing in a lithium mine in eastern Oregon. A hearing aid manufacturer wanted to streamline exports. Rose's thoughts kept drifting to Ash in the shower, what it would be like to shampoo Ash's hair for her, to massage her scalp, run a bar of soap over her body with the same, slow attention Rose used in her videos. Caressing every molecule.

A few minutes later, Ash emerged from the bathroom,

dressed again and toweling off her hair. If they were a couple, Rose would see Ash like this every morning. They'd wake up next to each other. They'd read in bed together, cook together. Maybe Ash liked sports. Rose would kiss Ash's neck until Ash forgot the score.

"I don't know about consulting for a lithium miner." Rose refocused on her phone. Hopefully Ash hadn't seen her staring. "The mining is an environmental nightmare, but lithium batteries reduce fossil fuel use. You can't win."

Ash slid into bed, barely disturbing the covers.

"Enough lithium for tonight." Rose put her phone away and got under.

Ash turned out the light. "Good night." Her voice was rough in the darkness.

"Good night."

The inches between them were as slim as a piece of silk and as wide as the ocean.

"I don't want to make you uncomfortable." Ash rolled onto her side, facing Rose, her face blue in the dark room.

"You're not."

Outside a gust of wind whipped rain against the window. Ash wriggled deeper into her blankets.

"It would be wrong for me to…" Ash said.

It was adorable how she only finished half her sentences, but Rose needed Ash to finish this one.

"We're in a hotel," Ash said, "and there isn't another room…I wouldn't want you to feel trapped. I could leave. If one of us should leave, I will."

It seemed like Ash was going to go on. Rose stopped her.

"What are you talking about?"

Rose hoped she knew.

Ash hadn't asked the question, but Rose answered in her

mind. *Yes. Yes. Yes.* Yes to all of it. Yes to any of it. Yes to one night even if it was the only night and it broke Rose's heart into a million pieces. Now she understood Ty. Ty wasn't dumb. She didn't walk into these kinds of situations not knowing what could happen. She went in because she knew this moment was too magical to miss.

"I know I said friends, and I don't want to make you uncomfortable," Ash said.

Very slowly, as though she were touching a delicate orchid, Rose reached out and touched Ash's cheek. "We don't have to do anything *you* don't want to do. But for the record—" She stroked a lock of Ash's damp hair. "—you are not trapping me in a hotel in south Centralia."

Ash hesitated. Rose wanted to hold her like the most delicate egg. And she wanted to bury her face in Ash's cunt... vulva...lavender candy bag and suck her off until the guests next door complained about the moans. But more than that, she wanted to keep her safe.

Ash took a deep breath and squeezed her eyes closed. "I want to kiss you but I'm not ready to have sex." Ash said it like a confession she had to get out before she lost her nerve.

Rose contained her smile. Ash wanted to kiss her. The thought lit every synapse of her brain with delight and desire. But this was serious for Ash.

"That's okay." Rose slipped into the soothing voice of Cherry Covered Apron.

"I saw all those women who contacted you on Athena." Ash looked profoundly apologetic. "They'd be way more fun than me in bed. You probably want...more."

Sweet, precious woman. Ash thought Rose wouldn't want her if they didn't have sex.

"If you saw those notifications, you saw that I'd never

answered. And sweetheart—" Rose moved a little closer. "—there's nothing cooler than a woman who speaks up for what she does and doesn't want."

Rose's body said she'd like to devour Ash like an ice cream sundae, but her heart said she could wait for years.

Ash reached out and threaded her hand through Rose's hair. The touch made Rose's whole body shiver with pleasure. At first, only their lips touched. Rose held Ash's hand, their fingers interlaced. Then Ash drew her into a kiss that was half uncertain and half command and half fireworks. Three halves because it was more than any one thing could be. Rose let Ash take the lead. She didn't rush anything, but eventually Ash pulled her closer, a soft moan escaping Ash's lips as their hips touched. The sound made Rose's body throb. Rose felt Ash's lean body against her breasts. Ash ran her hand up Rose's back, across the band of her bra—which was, admittedly, uncomfortable to wear in bed, not that Rose cared.

"This is a lot of infrastructure," Ash whispered, the shyness gone from her voice.

"I have a lot of assets to support."

Large breasts were impractical, but they were a Josten women signature. Except for Ty, the skinny changeling.

"May I." Ash touched the clasp through Rose's shirt.

Ash could have flipped her onto her back, ripped her shirt off, and fucked her with any sex toy Ash might produce from her cargo pockets, and Rose would have gone for it enthusiastically. If they were already lovers, Rose would tell Ash to do whatever she wanted, but instead she said, "Only if that's okay for you."

Ash reached around Rose's back and slipped her hand under the edge of Rose's lace blouse. Rose thought Ash's touch through her clothing aroused her. Ash's hand on her bare skin was a match to tinder. Rose held still, lest the undulation of her hips frighten Ash away. Ash opened the six-eyelet clasp in one deft move. She had done this before. That was sexy as hell. If Rose was careful with her, maybe Ash would love doing it again.

"Should I take it off?" Rose asked.

"Sure."

Rose sat up and turned away. She slipped her shirt off, then her bra, then put her shirt back on although it would feel so good to take Ash's clothing off and feel their naked bodies pressed together. Rose slipped back under the covers. Still, when Ash drew Rose closer and their breasts touched through their shirts, her full breasts and Ash's small ones, the softness of their bodies melting together, Rose had to stifle a groan of pleasure and desire. She needed Ash. So. Damn. Much.

"You're beautiful," Ash whispered, although her lips were so close to Rose's she couldn't possibly be looking at her.

Rose ran her hand through Ash's hair the way she'd longed to. Ash purred with pleasure, then kissed Rose again, her movement urgent, her tongue commanding Rose's mouth. Rose felt like she would implode without release, but she didn't rush. And Ash didn't take it any further, and eventually, their kisses grew languid. Sweet exhaustion seemed to take them at the same moment.

Rose put a hand on Ash's shoulder. "Roll over."

Ash rolled with her back to Rose. Rose put her arm around her. They fit together perfectly. Rose's arm over Ash's waist. Her head against Ash's shoulder. Their knees folded together. Ash's ass pressed against Rose's hips. And although that was the most erotic thing Rose had ever felt, she wasn't thinking about that now. She was thinking about how natural it felt and how she wanted to hold Ash forever.

chapter 30

Ash woke to Rose touching her shoulder.

"I have to go," Rose said. "I have a meeting with the Cauliflower Baron, and I can't take it on my phone."

"What time is it?"

"Five. Will you be okay?"

"I'll be fine." For the first time in years, it felt true. "When do I get to see you again?"

"Soon." Rose leaned over and kissed Ash's forehead. "I'm almost done with your marketing plan, and I've got a guy who's going to review the budget." Rose stroked Ash's hair. Ash felt like she might purr with pleasure. "You'll need to finish the proof of concept, and I still want us to think about how the actual pitch will play out. Maybe keep thinking about that cool old theater."

Ash gazed up at Rose.

"But right now, you sleep," Rose said.

Ash called Emma from the road. Emma didn't let Ash get out a how's-it-going.

"You slept with Rose!"

"You jump to conclusions."

"I went by your house to drop off some stuff. You weren't there and you didn't text me back."

"Did it occur to you that I could have been kidnapped?"

"By your lover."

"Actually, I hit a piece of metal and got stranded on the highway."

"For real?" Emma's voice grew serious. "Are you okay?"

"I'm fine."

"Fine-fine? Or pretending to be fine?"

"Actually... fine. For real."

"So did you sleep with Rose?"

"How would I have slept with Rose if I got stranded on the highway?"

Because Rose cared about her. Because Rose had dropped what she was doing and driven hours to check on her. Because somehow, Rose didn't hate her for that.

Emma might write a terrible Athena profile, but she was also psychic.

"You did. Fuck yeah! I can hear it in your voice."

It was fun to string Emma along, even though Ash had called to tell her everything. And Emma played along because she cared. She wanted to know. She wanted Ash to be happy. Did Ash appreciate that enough? When they first met, Emma was an invisible production assistant. Then Ash had mentored her. Then Emma was just... there. In Portland. Taking a break from Hollywood and working at Stewart Productions. Did Ash ever say *Thank you for being there for me*?

"I love you," Ash said. "You're a really good friend. I don't tell you that enough."

"Are you dying? I love you, too. But we are not talking about that. We are talking about your sexy businesswoman."

"I didn't sleep with her like that."

"What's *not like that*?"

Ash told Emma about the accident. (She stayed in the slow lane drafting a safe distance behind a semi.) She told her about Rose arranging for a room and a car and then showing up at the hotel.

"She had a great idea for the sound in the fern scene. I had thought a crescendo in the music, but she—"

"We're not talking about the fern scene."

"We had dinner. It was wonderful. She's so easy to talk to. Then she was going to get a room as well, but the place was booked up, so I suggested she stay with me. We kissed."

She felt Rose's arms around her and how their bodies fit perfectly together. Nothing Rose had said made her feel like she deserved less or that she was wasting Rose's time.

"I told her I wasn't ready to have sex."

"And was that so hard?" Emma asked.

"Yeah."

"And what did she say?"

"It was fine."

chapter 31

Rose barely remembered what she said to the Cauliflower Baron, but her spreadsheets did the talking for her. Her plan for optimizing production was smart. Her plan for restructuring management was surprisingly easy. They'd do a climate survey of the factory workers to look for discrimination or bullying.

She wanted to talk to Ty. She hadn't used the group chat to tell her sisters about her night with Ash. Ash had been vulnerable, and she'd trusted Rose. It didn't seem right to put that in a string of text messages alongside memes of cats drinking margaritas and stories about Gigi's waxing adventures. But now it was five and she could walk to Ty's apartment on the Park Blocks.

She'd almost made it out when Howard caught her.

"Can I talk to you in my office?"

She had somewhere to be. A meeting. Very important. She couldn't think of a lie fast enough. Howard led her back to his office, closed the door, and gestured to her to sit.

"Of course, you don't know anything about getting promoted to partner," Howard said.

Howard reminded her of her father when her father bought her her first car. *You've got your driver's license. I wonder how you're going to get around town. Driver's license doesn't do much good without a car.* She hadn't thought about that day for years, and the memory startled her. She'd pushed the good memories away. They were too painful. She'd missed her parents too much. Then it had become a habit not to think about them. Then the memories had faded, until the only one left was that call. *Your father was a good pilot. Sometimes these things just happen.*

Perhaps reading Rose's momentary sadness, Howard added, "You are making partner. I'm just teasing."

He rested his hands on his table. "Now, you won't have been thinking about this because you haven't been thinking about making partner," he said, picking the ruse up again. "But if you did, there'd be the matter of the partner buy-in."

The partners took a percentage of the firm's profits. For this honor, they made an initial investment in the company. Partner was twenty thousand. Named partner was fifty.

"I just wanted to say *when* you get offered partner…" Howard grew serious. "And when you get offered named partner, I can help you with the buy-in money. I'm guessing you don't need it. But if you do…you're an amazing consultant. Whatever you need. I'll make it happen."

Partner. She'd almost forgotten. This was the big event her life was leading up to. Not pitching to Irene Brentworth. That was Ash's life. Her life was lithium mines and her name on the door.

"Thank you."

Fifty thousand. Rose could afford it. It felt like a dowry to a mate she didn't love.

*   *   *

"Sorry I'm late," she said as she sat down at the kitchen table in Ty's studio apartment.

"I was just grading papers." Ty closed her laptop. "Anything is better than one more paper that begins *ever since the dawn of time.* You didn't text us last night. You raced up there to save the woman you love, then nothing."

"Did you tell Gigi and Cas?"

"No. It's your story." Ty shrugged. "I'll make tea."

Rose scanned the eclectic mementos on Ty's shelves. She picked up a blown-glass model of the clitoris...or at least attempted clitoris. Whoever made it was not an expert glass-blower yet. Rose didn't have lumpy glass clitorises. She had a Pottery Barn pillar candle centerpiece.

The teakettle sang. Ty poured two cups.

"Outside?" Ty motioned to the window.

Rose ducked through the window onto Ty's fire escape. Ty handed her a cup of tea and followed her out. Two metal chairs looked out at one of PSU's campus buildings. Afternoon sun made the brick glow.

There was no getting away from Ty's questions, and she didn't want to. Rose told her the whole story.

"That is so wonderful!" Ty clasped her hands in the likeness of every Disney princess who'd ever fallen in love, the gesture a charming contrast with her sweatshirt, which read THE PATRIARCHY WON'T FUCK ITSELF in large block letters.

"What do I do now?"

Ty folded herself up cross-legged on her tiny bistro chair. "Call her. Tell her last night was special. Take her to dinner."

"What if she was just freaked out, and it was a onetime thing?"

It didn't feel like a onetime thing, but what if it was? Ty thought every woman she kissed (and a lot she didn't) was *the one*. They hadn't been. Not yet.

"Rose!" Ty protested. "She likes you. You're the kindest, sweetest person I know. How could she not love you?"

"I thought Cassie was the kindest person we know."

"Cassie's the nicest. You're the kindest one. You're the one who's there for everyone, who bails us out, who held us together when everything was falling apart. You're the one who tells us to listen to the birds and the wind. You take me meditating."

"You say you only go because we get to hang out."

"Exactly. And you remind Cassie how magic her kids are when she wants to kill them. You talk Gigi down when she's freaking out about the salon."

"But Ash is a cool indie filmmaker." Rose held her hands up to showcase her tan suit.

Ty gave her a look that said, *I don't know what you're getting at.*

"How long is she going to stay interested in me?" It was a real question, but it didn't touch Rose's heart. Everything felt certain. Ash *did* like her. They were wonderful together. "I remind Gigi to get her flu shots. I help you with your taxes. That's boring."

"You've told me to follow my passions ever since I was a kid. You've helped all of us do that. None of us would have the lives we have if it weren't for you. That's not boring."

But that's your *life.*

"And you're a kickass businesswoman. You're rich. You're hot. And she liked the way you edited her movie. How did you know how to do that anyways?" Ty teetered atop her chair, watching Rose intently. "Were you practicing so you could impress her?"

Rose mimed pushing Ty off her chair.

"And you have pugs," Ty added.

"Is that a selling point?"

"You make her laugh."

The way Ty described her, she didn't sound too boring.

"How long should I wait before I text her?"

"You haven't texted her? Text her *now*."

"But wouldn't that be too. I don't know...How long do people wait?"

"Are you asking me if there's an equation to tell you when you can text someone?" Ty's eyes sparkled with laughter. "Like thirty-six hours during the week, but if it's a weekend it's twelve if you know they like you and three days if you're not sure."

"Do I know she likes me or should I wait three days?"

"Don't you two have a pitch coming up that you need to work on?"

"Does that change the equation?"

"Agh! You know there's no equation. Just act like a normal person." Ty pulled her phone out of her pocket. "Don't overthink. Look, here's what you could text her." Ty mimed on her phone as though Rose might have forgotten how to text. "*How's it going? Did you get home safe? Want to go over some boring paperwork that I'm going to use as an excuse to see you again? Also, I want to kiss you or we could have sex or not. Your call. Also I'm in love with you.*"

"You are terrible," Rose said, laughing. She gave Ty a playful slap on the knee and took out her own phone. She stared at it. Ty was right. Rose had totally forgotten how to text. Then she came back to herself.

Rose: *How are the new tires?*

Ty peered over.

"You're getting a prize for the most romantic woman in the world," she said with a groan.

Ash texted back.

Ash: *Expensive AF*

"Ooh." Ty looked at the nonexistent watch on her wrist and grinned. "That was a three-second reply time. Anything between one and ten seconds means she's desperately in love with you. Everyone knows that."

chapter 32

Images of Ash filled Rose's mind that night as Rose set up her equipment on the kitchen counter. The soft lights. The black bulb of the microphone. She had to use an old one since Jason hadn't returned the Schoeps yet. She pulled a crimson stalk off the bunch of chard she had bought. The bottom was muddy. She set it on the counter, reverently. Then she dug through the kitchen drawer and took out the blue apron with the red cherries printed on it. She put it on and turned on her camera.

"Hello, it's Cherry Covered Apron."

She laid the chard in a bowl of water, bathing it slowly, rubbing the dirt with one fingertip, not removing it, more feeling it. Then she dipped her finger into the water and let one drop run down the length of the stalk, crisp and erect. She slowly rubbed her finger up and down, finding the juncture where the red stem met the green leaves.

"You are beautiful."

She imagined her words floating through space and curling up on Ash's pillow.

"You are safe with me."

Filming usually wasn't exactly sexual, but now a warm, urgent feeling suffused her body as she imagined sliding her fingers up the muscles of Ash's legs, down her neck, along the tight bands of her hip flexors. She imagined her tongue alighting on Ash's sex. She touched the edges of the chard leaf. She imagined drawing Ash's labia into her mouth, one side and then the other. She imagined Ash straining beneath her kiss.

She should have been embarrassed. She was stroking a leafy green vegetable while fantasizing about cunnilingus. She wasn't even handling a peach or some other sexy fruit. But when she put the equipment away, she searched her mind for the familiar residue of embarrassment; it wasn't there. All she could think about was seeing Ash.

And right now that meant strategizing for the pitch. Rose had better put the chard away and work on the plan. The pitch had to be spectacular. They couldn't send Brentworth a massive video file and meet her in a boardroom. They needed Brentworth to leave the pitch transformed.

She glanced at her phone to check the time. DO NOT DISTURB was on, but a silent dot announced new messages: her sisters checking in, carrying on the four-way conversation they'd kept up for years. Ups and downs. Highs and lows. Deals they'd seen at the grocery store. Rose wished she could text *I just finished a new video. It's gorgeous.* Instead, she sent a picture of Muffin and Cupcake asleep on the sofa, then opened the text she really wanted to read.

Ash: How was work today?

Rose: I was brilliant. It was boring.

Ash: How was Mr. Cauliflower?

Rose: On Zoom with a giant cauliflower in his background. Except photo looked like a brain.

She sorted through files in the cloud, found the meeting records, and sent Ash a screenshot of the Cauliflower Baron with a giant cauliflower growing out of his head.

Ash: 😂 🥦

Rose: *This is my life* 😳

She could never make a Cherry Covered Apron video about cauliflower. Mr. Baron had ruined Cruciferae for her.

Ash: You're so much more 😌

Rose wanted to text, *I'm dreaming of your kiss.*

Rose: *I've been thinking about how we want to show Brentworth your scene.*

Ash: Me too. She's got a big personality. We gotta do more than just a PowerPoint

Rose: *Was thinking about your cool old theater idea.*

Ash's number appeared on the screen and Rose answered. Rose loved the way Ash started in without preamble, like they were used to switching back and forth between texts and calls.

"Where do we get a theater?"

"I've been thinking about that. I can look around. It's LA. There's got to be something we can rent, but also...your friend Mia."

"Mia?"

"I looked her up. She's in real estate now."

"She always said she wanted to go into real estate." Ash sounded delighted. "Her mom was a real estate agent. She grew up seeing all these beautiful houses in LA."

"From what I saw online, she owns a ton of stuff. Why don't we ask her if she can hook us up?"

There was a long silence on Ash's end.

"Did something happen between you two?"

Had they been lovers? Had Mia sided with Victoria? The

venom Mia had brought to the conversation when she thought Rose was trying to blacklist Ash said no.

"No...I just...we lost touch."

"She said she'd be willing to help you if she could."

"Oh." It came out as a sigh.

"Do you want to ask for her help?" Rose asked.

Another long silence.

"I shouldn't," Ash said finally.

"Then can I?"

Rose considered calling Mia in the middle of the night. It would serve her right for calling Rose after midnight, but a good business consultant knew when to ask for a favor. She called at two fifteen p.m. the next day. If Mia had been out late, she'd be up by now. If she had a day job, she wouldn't be thinking about quitting time yet.

"It's Rose Josten," she said.

"Rose, I have your number programmed in." Mia's voice was as warm as it had been cold when she'd called before. "What do you need?"

"A theater."

Rose texted Ash as soon as she got off the phone.

Rose: Mia has a theater in West Hollywood she'll let us use free. She wants us to come down and see it before the pitch. Get everything set up.

Three dots appeared on Rose's screen for a long time while Ash failed to finish her text sentence. But finally, she did.

Ash: Will you come with me?

Rose googled the drive to LA. It was fifteen hours if you drove straight through with no traffic jams. They had mere days to get ready. How would she explain to Ash that with everything Ash wanted on the line, Rose had to spend one precious day driving? Or two? Was it safe to drive fifteen hours in one day? Maybe if they split up the drive. Would Ash be okay after the flat tire in Centralia? Yes, Ash had taken driving lessons. Ash had overcome that fear while Rose had avoided IKEA for years because the store was under the PDX flight path. But fifteen hours on the road? But she didn't want to be afraid. She wanted to catch a commuter flight like a normal person.

Rose: Of course.

Rose texted the sisters' group chat.

Rose: I'm going to die.

But she didn't feel like she was going to die. She felt like she'd just grown wings to fly.

chapter 33

Howard stood in Rose's office door.

"I heard you put in for a vacation?"

Rose turned from the window. It was coming up on the longest day of the year. She wanted to take Ash to the beach (there wouldn't be a tsunami, there really wouldn't) or out to Sauvie Island (hell, they could go to the nude beach, Rose was all in). But this was a working "vacation."

"Just a couple of days," she said.

"But you're in the middle of Beltliner."

Dehydrated vegetables. Rose concealed her sigh behind a sip of coffee. "I'm interviewing their upper management, and I'll compile those interviews while I'm away."

"Okay." Howard didn't look convinced. "But if anything goes wrong with Beltliner...you sure you don't want to wait a couple of months for your trip?"

"I'm helping my friend plan a wedding."

What was Rose supposed to say? *I'm in love with my pro bono client, and I will risk certain death by crash or panic attack—it's one or the other—to fly on an airplane if it means I get to spend another day with her.*

No. She wasn't in love. Ty was the one who fell in love overnight. But the chance to spend another night in a hotel with Ash...the unscripted time after they talked to Mia. Rose pictured a high-rise looking over the city at night, Ash lounging on four-thousand-thread-count sheets. *Can I kiss you?*

"My friend will kill me if I don't help out, but I'll stay on top of everything." Rose put on her professional smile. "Have you *ever* seen me drop the ball?"

"No, I haven't, Ms. Rose Josten."

Howard gave the wall beside her door a jovial slap. It sounded like a gavel. Rose wasn't going to fuck up Beltliner. The partnership technically depended on a vote by the senior partners, but they would vote yes. She'd pay the fifty thousand for a named partnership. Go big or go home. But it didn't feel big. She closed the door behind Howard, and for a moment she couldn't catch her breath. This was it. One exciting interlude, then her name on the door of Integral Business Solutions. This was her life. Ash's face flashed before her eyes, but Ash wasn't the answer. Another person couldn't be the answer to the question swirling in her mind. *Is this who I am?*

Rose had been very brave when Ash said she'd make the reservations. There was no reason the plane was more likely to crash if Ash chose the carrier. Rose had been fine when she packed and repacked her roller bag. But her pulse pounded in her ears as she got in the Uber.

"PDX?" the driver confirmed.

Sorry. I mistyped. IKEA. IKEA wasn't open at seven in the morning. *A diner. Burnside. A drug drop. Never mind, I don't need a ride.*

"Yeah. PDX."

She was three breaths away from a heart attack as she

walked toward Gate F. Something the size of a house was going to launch itself into the sky using a questionable law of physics. Things went wrong. Birds flew into engines. The control tower missed a dot on their radar. The pilot was drunk. And she hadn't seen Ash since their night together. What if Ash arrived and it was clear the night hadn't meant anything to her? Ash got all wistful when Rose mentioned Mia. Maybe Ash was dreaming of Mia. That sort of thing happened to Ty all the time. Rose was risking certain death (was it a risk if it was certain?) to spend time with a woman who—

She stopped for a moment, picturing Ash gazing up at her from the bed they'd shared, sighing as Rose stroked her hair.

You're overthinking.

It was two hours until takeoff. Too early but Rose wanted to be at the gate before Ash so that she could stage herself casually reading on her tablet. She checked her phone as she walked. Gigi and Cassie had already texted.

Cassie: *Have a great trip. I'm proud of you. New experiences!!!*

Gigi: *You must be in love.*

Gigi: *What happens in LA stays in LA* ☺

Cassie: *Don't pressure her.*

Ty chimed in, which meant she was up at seven a.m. and hell had frozen over.

Ty: *You got this big sister*

Gigi: *What are you wearing? Not a suit!*

Rose: *Jeans and a white blazer.*

Gigi: *Aghhhhhhhhh. No.*

Rose: *It's more ecru. That make it better?*

Should she wear something different? Gigi had been teasing her about her blazers for years, but it'd been a joke. Now it was advice.

Gigi: No!

Ty: She's a professional

Rose dodged a man vacuuming the iconic green and pink PDX carpet. The airport was starting to fill up with morning travelers who didn't know about their impending doom.

Gigi: She's seducing a movie producer in LA.

Cassie: Don't drink anything unless you pour it yourself.

Ty: Call me if you want advice . . . 🐚 🐚 🐚

Gigi: About her jewel box

Ty: VULVA

Gigi: Sounds rubbery

Ty texted an anatomical drawing of the vulva with the parts labeled that she just happened to have on her camera roll because she was Ty.

Gigi: Won't be labeled in real life

Rose: I sleep with women. I know about the jewel box. 🎁

Cassie: If you get nervous on the plane, just meditate.

That would not erase the fact that she was ten thousand feet up in a four-hundred-ton metal tube that lifted off the ground by magic and, if the passengers didn't clap three times and say they believed in fairies, would fall out of the sky.

Gigi: Ativan & Dewar's

Cassie: Don't mix drugs and alcohol.

Gigi: Better living through chemistry

Ty: Ash will protect you

Gigi: 🍆 + 🍑 *Do it*

Cassie: Are you telling her to have sex in the airplane???

Gigi: Yes.

They were trying to distract her, to make this feel normal, to forget that she hadn't been on a plane since she'd flown home from her year abroad. *It wasn't anyone's fault. Sometimes these things just happen. Your father was a good pilot.*

Ty: *Love you big sis*

Cassie: *You got this.*

Gigi: *I'm serious* 🏃 + ⏰ 🐛 🐛 🐛

Rose smiled. Maybe if she could string all the love gifs together in one message, she could tell her sisters how much she loved them.

Rose: *Miss me when I'm gone :)*

Cassie: *Text when you get to your hotel room.*

Rose was about to walk past her gate when Ash's voice stopped her.

"Going somewhere else?" Ash asked.

Ash looked tired but happy. She stood up. Rose hurried over, then stopped. She'd had all night to think about this moment, and she hadn't come up with anything to say. Ash stepped forward. Rose turned away and put her bag down, realizing in that split second that Ash was coming in to hug her. Rose opened her arms. Ash held back. They touched shoulders like co-workers pretending to like each other. When they pulled away, Ash's face had fallen like she thought Rose was brushing her off.

How? If anyone should be worried about being rejected it was Rose in her ecru jacket, not this beautiful woman wearing goldenrod jeans, a My Life with the Thrill Kill Kult T-shirt, and a leather jacket that was almost certainly a designer piece left over from her Hollywood life. Ash smelled divine, too. An unnamable scent. If a perfumer took what skyscrapers looked like the first time a country girl visited the city and turned that moment into eau de toilette, this was it. And she looked crestfallen and like she was trying not to. Rose caught Ash's hand and held it up to her lips and pressed her lips to Ash's knuckles.

"It's good to see you." Damn, she sounded formal, and

awkwardly kissing the back of Ash's hand said, *I got my seduction skills playing a knight in the eighth-grade play.*

Ash beamed.

"You too." Ash picked up a coffee and held it out to Rose. "Black for the serious businesswoman. I guessed. I can get you cream and sugar if you want."

She wanted whatever Ash had brought her.

They sat down. On the other side of the gate a pack of women in T-shirts reading BACHELORETTE BOSS BABES giggled and passed around travel-size bottles of hand lotion that almost certainly did not contain hand lotion.

"Are you going to hit all the clubs in LA?" Ash asked with a grin.

"Because I'm such a partier?"

Ash touched the cuff of Rose's blazer. Rose felt the touch travel through the fabric to her skin to her core to her heart. She was ridiculous.

"It's the buttoned-up ones who are wild inside," Ash said.

"Are *you* going clubbing?"

"I used to." Ash gave a rueful laugh. "I used to go to all the clubs. I had a lot of money, and I knew a lot of people."

Rose loved the cocky turn of Ash's lips. There was so much Rose had yet to know about her, and she wanted to know all of her.

"Did you like it?"

"I did." Ash pursed her lips. "Mostly. It would have been more fun if you were there."

The compliment glowed in Rose's heart.

"You know what I don't like about clubbing," Ash said. "It's the drink mugs with LED in them. They're so glaring. I hate that we have to use LED sometimes. Do we even know what LED is?"

"I think someone does."

"But should it be in your drink? Are we sure it doesn't change your DNA?"

"You're worried about LED lights in your drinks," Rose said. "Have you thought about *that*?" She gestured toward the plane waiting outside. She'd almost forgotten herself, but it came rushing back. She hid her panic behind a joke. "I mean, how are people freaking out about BPA and 5G when those are flying overhead? Really, how do they stay up? It's terrifying."

"As the plane speeds up, the air flows over the wings. That pushes the air down," Ash said. "The downward movement creates the lift. Weight pushes down. Drag pulls it back. And thrust drives the plane, metaphorically speaking. Four parts." She looked satisfied. "Simple."

"How do you know that?"

"I almost majored in physics."

"It was physics or film?"

"Bodies in motion. Angles of light. Basically the same thing."

The clerk at the counter called priority boarding, then Business Premier boarding, then advanced boarding for anyone with the airline's credit card. A couple of bachelorettes jumped up and hurried to the line.

chapter 34

Rose was going to die. That part sucked. But this normal banter, like she and Ash were...a couple. It was almost worth dying for. No, apparently it *was* worth dying for because Rose was here.

Finally they called their group. Seats 24 D and F. There was no one in E. Just the two of them on an early-morning flight like they were going for a weekend getaway, Ash by the window, Rose by the aisle.

Rose's heart dropped into her stomach as the engine kicked on. The flight attendant explained the seat belt as though anyone left on the planet did not know how to fasten a seat belt. The plane rumbled, pulling slowly away from the gate. The plane had headphone jacks. No one had wired head-phones anymore. That meant the plane was probably twenty years old.

The plane sped up.

Ash played a game on her phone.

The front wheels lifted with a sickening lurch. Ash showed Rose her phone. "I got a hedge for my castle."

She was adorable. This woman who filmed forest sex scenes,

who'd flipped her car four times and survived, who'd kissed Rose like Rose had never been kissed before...she was grinning at the screen because she'd won a make-believe hedge.

"I thought I'd lose points because I haven't played for months."

She was the most fascinating person Rose had ever met, and now they were going to die.

The plane listed to the left.

She tried to remember every point in Integral Business Solutions' Twelve Point Success Metric. The plane dropped sickeningly.

"Always makes you think it's going to fall out of the sky," Ash said. "Ooh, look. I got a birdbath."

Breathe. Meditate. Why hadn't she taken Ativan?

Ash looked over.

"You all right?" Ash asked.

"Fine."

Rose didn't realize she was gripping the armrest until Ash touched her hand.

"I'm so sorry," Ash said. "You were serious about being scared."

Rose released the armrest and tried to sound calm. "It's just the *metaphorical* part. Thrust drives it, *metaphorically.*"

"Don't listen to me. It isn't metaphorical. They fly. They really do. Would it help to look out the window?"

"Why would that help?" Rose squeaked.

"Right." Ash pulled down the shade and scooted into the empty seat between them. "I got you."

She took Rose's hand. Rose tried not to death-grip it like the armrest.

"I used to fly all the time," Ash said, "when I was beautiful and famous. Everywhere. Every kind of turbulence. I'll tell you if we're going to crash. If I don't say anything, you know we're fine."

Rose turned to Ash. She wanted to bury her face in Ash's shoulder. She could tell her. *Eighteen years ago, my parents died in a plane crash, and I haven't flown since. Or done anything since.* Ash had trusted Rose with her story. She would sympathize. She would let Rose hide under her leather jacket. But Rose didn't want this to be about eighteen-years-ago and the Cessna and the Rockies. She was going to LA with Ash Stewart. Ash stroked the back of Rose's hand in a slow, soothing motion. Rose felt the touch ripple through her body. Her fear ebbed.

I want this.

Ash held her hand until the captain turned off the FASTEN SEAT BELT sign.

"Flying is more trustworthy than LED," Ash whispered. "Think about how long we've been flying, and then think about how long people have been drinking stuff out of those LED glasses." Ash tucked her phone into the seat pocket. "Let's pretend we're going to a bachelorette party." Ash was trying to take her mind off the flight. "What's the first thing we do when we land?"

"Get massively drunk?"

"Have you ever been to a bachelorette party? We got massively drunk before we left for the airport."

"At six a.m.?"

"We were a little behind schedule, but yeah, we were lit by six. Now how do we know each other?"

The plane rattled. Rose couldn't think of anything.

"The bride is your sister," Ash supplied. "The groom is my brother. We didn't know we'd be flying together, but I'm glad. I've been watching you at parties. I'm always waiting for my brother to introduce us, but you never stay long enough.

You're a high-profile lawyer, and you don't have time for
fucking around, so I'm fascinated to see if you're going to go
clubbing with the bachelorettes. I've always wanted to see you
let loose."

Rose's breath hitched. This was a new side of Ash, confident
and flirtatious. She wasn't accidentally insinuating something
she hadn't meant to say; she was biting off the words like
chocolate.

"What do you do?"

Ash considered. "I'm a big-time contractor. I build LEED-
certified mansions. I'm very tough. The bride wants us to wear
T-shirts that say KISS ME, I'M WITH THE BRIDE. But if any guys
get close to you, I'm going to step to them and they'll back
down so fast."

"I'll be impressed."

"That's the idea."

Rose wanted to ask what the lawyer and contractor would
do after scaring off men and—if they were going to be
efficient about the whole not-being-hassled thing—taking off
their T-shirts. But the FASTEN SEAT BELT sign chimed on. The
plane shook. Rose couldn't breathe. Ash reached for Rose's
hand again.

"It's okay," Ash said. "And it's okay to be scared."

chapter 35

LAX was bustling. They caught a taxi to their motel. Rose felt her anxiety ebbing away, replaced by the excitement of LA with Ash. Rose had driven to Seattle, San Francisco, and once to Reno, but she hadn't been to LA. Ever. It was so warm and bright. The cab let them out in front of a motel on a busy, dusty street. The Executive Comfort Suites. Ash had made the hotel reservations. Now she looked back and forth between Rose and the motel and the disappearing cab. There was nothing *executive* about the Executive Comfort Suites.

"It looked better online," Ash said. "I was trying to economize."

"I think you succeeded."

"I'm sorry. I'll find another place."

Ash looked like a model standing in front of the low-slung motel. A passing truck gusted a swirl of grit around her feet. Ash would have a wonderful Instagram presence as soon as they settled on the exact branding. Rose wished there was a reason to take Ash's photo now. She'd print it. She'd keep it in a hardback book and look at it when she was old.

"I don't need anything fancy." Rose looked up at the faded sign above the hotel. "They have phones and free breakfast."

"I love a good landline," Ash said.

Rose bumped Ash's shoulder with her own. "You would."

The Executive Comfort Suites was not booked full, and the man behind the counter had no problem with early check-ins. They dropped their bags in their rooms. Ash had booked two rooms, which was appropriate even if it was disappointing. Rose would share a twin-size bed with Ash. To see Ash naked. To touch her. To learn how Ash cried out in climax... The images flashed across her mind before she could stop them.

They called an Uber, Rose gave him the GPS for the theater, and they headed down the dry, dusty road.

"Have you been to LA?" Ash asked.

Rose shook her head. "Will I like it?"

"Love-hate."

They got on a highway and then off. Traffic got heavier. Ash looked out the window. She was looking at her old life. Did she miss it?

The theater was on a side street off a boulevard lined with bistros and rainbow flags. They followed an alley to the back of the building as Mia had instructed.

"Mia said to call when we got here," Rose said.

Ash leaned the back of her head against the brick wall. "I haven't talked to her in years."

"Do you have history?"

"So much," Ash said.

"I'll call." Rose took out her phone.

"Rose," Mia sang out as though they were old friends. "One sec."

Mia swept out as though she'd been standing on the other

side of the door, black hair cascading over her shoulders. She froze, staring at Ash. Ash looked at her with the same awestruck expression. Then Mia exclaimed, "Ashlyn," and threw her arms around Ash. "You're here." Mia squeezed her, then held Ash at arm's length. "It's still you." She pulled Ash back in, putting both hands around Ash's waist with easy intimacy.

What had they been to each other? Ash talked about Victoria, but she must have had other partners. They'd be beautiful together. Mia was six feet tall before the spike heels. Her skin glowed a luminous light brown. Jeans and a green silk T-shirt showcased the musculature of a dancer. She made other human beings look like they'd grown up without essential nutrients, a panther among pugs.

Mia released Ash and held out her arms to Rose. "Do you hug?"

Apparently Rose did because a second later Mia had her arms around Rose with the same down-to-earth squeeze of one of Cassie's hugs.

"I am so glad you brought her here. Thank you, Rose." She gave Rose one more squeeze. "Thank you. So. Frickin'. Much." She released Rose and returned her attention to Ash, kissing her on the cheek. "You managed to get more beautiful. Come. I'll show you the theater and then we'll talk. I want to know everything."

Ash looked happy and abashed, like she was embarrassed to admit how much she liked the attention. Rose liked the joy on Ash's face. She liked Mia's doting on Ash less. Rose trailed behind them.

"Ash, you're going to rock this," Mia said. "Brentworth *has* to take you on. You want coffee? Vodka tonic? It's three a.m. somewhere. Harry would say it's *gin or Georgia*."

It was obviously an in-joke.

"Poor Harry." Ash laughed. "Our southern gentleman. Fine. Lead me astray."

Mia led them down a hallway papered with playbills and lit with sconces. At the end of the hall, she pushed open a door marked STAGE EXIT—CAST AND CREW ONLY. Twilight enveloped them as they stepped into the backstage area. Mia bounded forward on her death-defying heels and opened a micro fridge by the wall. She poured Ash's drink.

"And you, Rose?" Mia called out. "Vodka tonic?"

Vodka before noon? Obviously not.

"I can't let Ash drink alone."

"Me neither." Mia gave a musical laugh.

Beautiful flutes played when Mia Estelle laughed.

Rose's eyes adjusted to the dark. Mia had tucked her arm through Ash's and was pouring vodka tonics with one hand.

"Did you know Brendon got his PhD in media studies?" Mia said. "And Gus asks about you all the time. And don't think I haven't been following you. The tulip farm commercial your studio did. That was so sweet." Mia raised her drink to her forehead. "I faded away without you."

Ash rattled the ice cubes in her glass, then took a nervous swig.

"You're the one we all loved," Mia added.

"You're too much. Show me this theater," Ash said.

Mia disappeared behind the stage curtains. Ash followed. Rose made her way slowly. They emerged on a dim stage.

"The Elsinore," Mia said. "Cue houselights."

At her command, soft chandeliers lit like dawn. Light filled the theater. It could have been 1932, some era so unimaginably elegant that even its ghost left Rose breathless.

Ash turned around slowly, mouth open, eyes shining. "It's all Edison bulbs, isn't it?" she asked.

Mia laughed her flute-quartet laugh.

"Ashlyn Stewart." Mia affected a sultry drawl. "Would I give you LED and drop ceilings? Now let me tell you the history," she went on in a deep voice. She must have been imitating someone, because they both laughed again. Mia rattled off the theater specs ending with the state-of-the-art sound system she'd had installed last year.

"You always wanted to get into real estate," Ash said.

Mia gave them a tour of the space, pointing out architectural features and the accessibility renovations she'd done. Then she led them to the front row and gestured for them to sit. "So, Rose, what's the plan? You said you want the pitch to be special."

The plan didn't include Mia being a goddess, but Rose had to go with what she had. She pulled out her tablet.

"Brentworth is a true patron of the arts, and she's a big ego." Rose recited what she'd learned about the producer. "She wants to feel like she's starting something epic, like she's discovered the Holy Grail of filmmaking. We want to give her an experience, not just a pitch."

"In my theater, fully catered, liquor, peacocks in the aisle."

"I don't think—" Ash said.

"Don't rule out peacocks. I know a guy who's trained some not to poop indoors."

Mia kissed Ash on the cheek again. "Let me do everything you need."

Let her not do *everything* Ash needed.

"By the way, I've got a burlesque show here tonight," Mia said. "It's sold out, but I'll put you on will-call. I always save a few seats for VIPs."

Ash and Mia tried to include Rose as they talked, but every comment was an in-joke. The warmth in Mia's eyes told Rose that Mia had been longing to share these jokes, that she loved Ash, that behind the jokes was relief. *You're here. You're okay.*

The excitement Rose had felt pulling up to their hotel turned into a knot in her stomach. Ash and Mia could easily enjoy tender reunion sex. Ash wouldn't have planned it, but she'd be comfortable with Mia in a way she wasn't with Rose. It was like the closer Ash got to LA, the more her nervous energy mellowed into confidence. The way she wrapped her arm in Mia's made it hard to remember that Rose had ever seen Ash without Mia. Ash wouldn't mean to lead Rose on, but now, in the heat and sparkle of LA, who would pick their dutiful business consultant over this goddess who was also clearly a beloved friend?

Did Gigi know anyone who could...not kill Mia...but convince her to move to Costa Rica?

Rose swigged her vodka.

"Let's get a tourist heart attack brunch," Mia said. "I know a place that serves eggs Benedict on top of French toast."

Go and watch Mia and Ash bask in their reminiscence or go back to the hotel and fret about Mia and Ash basking in reminiscence? Which was better?

"I have to spend time thinking about dehydrated cauliflower," Rose said.

"Ouch. Are we that boring?" Mia said.

"She really does have to think about dehydrated cauliflower," Ash said. "She's consulting for this multibillion-dollar dehydrated food company. It's amazing the things she knows. CEOs talk to her and they're, like, *Yes, Ms. Josten. I'll do whatever you say.*"

"Sexy." Mia nodded approvingly. "Very boss. Ash and I will drink a Volcano Bowl for you."

Ash thought she was amazing, but Ash and Mia were going to share a Volcano Bowl. Their straws would touch. Who wouldn't want to move to Costa Rica? It was a beautiful country.

chapter 36

Mia kicked off her heels and gestured for Ash to follow her up the steep, narrow staircase that led to the light and sound booth.

"I finished my MBA," she said as they climbed. "Emphasis on real estate. I just started investing in Boise. And don't laugh. Boise is the new Portland."

"I'm not laughing. I'm impressed."

They reached the top. Mia's head barely cleared the ceiling. "And so am I. Your own studio. Pitching to Brentworth."

Mia sat down on a rolling chair and motioned for Ash to take another. They sat in the blue light of the sound panel. Maybe Ash could get one of the techs to show Rose around. She wanted to show Rose other things as well. Her old neighborhood. Her favorite taco place.

"So talk to me." Mia grew serious. "I know you got hurt. I know about Victoria. But what happened? You were in the hospital. Then you were back on set for a few weeks and then you disappeared."

Ash had called her friends, talking in stilted bursts. Mia was doing a full-length film in Cartagena. Another friend had signed a two-year contract with a studio in Bollywood. Ash was in pain. She read a lot. Victoria left. *The Secret Song* failed. Ash started answering calls with texts.

"I'm sorry I lost touch. I'm ashamed of that."

"You don't have to be ashamed." Mia put a hand on Ash's knee. "I just want you to come back."

For the first time it struck Ash: If she returned to her life in LA, she'd leave Rose. If she got her old life back, she got her *old life* back. But there was this other life, this *real* other life, where she was tiptoeing toward something sweet with Rose, and Rose was patiently waiting.

"I missed you." Mia's voice drew Ash out of her thoughts.

"I missed you, too."

"We picked you in the divorce, you know. No one from the old set hangs out with Victoria. No one ever got you two. I mean, we got why Victoria wanted you, but why you wanted her... If it wasn't you, we'd have said you were in it for Victoria's money. But you aren't like that." Mia gave a little I'm-not-judging shrug. "Even if you were, you could have had a dozen producers lined up to make your films. You didn't need Victoria. Every time you two showed up at a party, people were surprised, like, *Oh, Ash hasn't dumped her yet?*"

Ash's mind raced through the parties she'd thrown with Victoria, their trips, their late nights fucking in glamorous hotel rooms, their fights, and the rare nights when they stayed home. They hadn't had anything to talk about on those nights. She could always talk to Rose. She could say, *What do you think of measuring spoons?* Rose would say something dry and funny, and they'd talk about measuring spoons.

Mia scooted her chair over and flung her arms around Ash in a big, guileless hug. "I like Rose for you."

"We're not together... exactly."

Mia gave her a don't-even-play look. "Why not?"

"I'm damaged goods." Ash shrugged.

"She looks like she wants to eat you alive." Mia pushed Ash's chair so it spun. "And like she'd fight me for you if I got in the way. And probably win."

chapter 37

Rose flopped onto her hotel bed, letting the air-conditioning cool the sweat on her brow. She should work. She lay on her bed watching the sun crawl across the popcorn ceiling. Then she took a dip in the kidney-shaped pool, hoping Ash would appear in a bathing suit and towel. *I was looking for you, Rose.* She didn't. Rose picked a lounger under a faded umbrella and googled Mia's burlesque show. If Mia wasn't comping them tickets, they'd be paying five hundred apiece. The price didn't intimidate her; the outfits in the photo gallery did.

She went back to her room and opened her laptop.

Cauliflower.

Production chain.

Ten new clients in the portal. Chloe said they were all winners.

How could that matter when Mia's arm was around Ash's waist?

She opened the four-way chat. The last message was from Gigi.

Gigi: 🥨🥐🍊🍒🤩?

Gigi had discovered emojis later in life and was making up for lost time.

Rose: Whatever that was: inappropriate!

Gigi: What are you up to then?

Mia was tasting Ash's French toast. Mia had wiped a crumb off Ash's lip. She'd bought her a peacock. They might be having sex.

Rose: She's with an old friend who's gorgeous.

Her sisters' texts flew in instantly.

Cassie: Not as gorgeous as you.

Gigi: We'll kill her

Ty: What are they doing?

Rose: They went to brunch.

Rose: They're licking French toast off each other 🫠

Hyperbole was a foreign language to Rose. Ty text-wept over women she'd just met. Gigi threatened to kill the distributor who'd messed up her wax order. Even Cassie lamented sometimes. But Rose wrote full sentences with punctuation.

Cassie: At a restaurant?

Gigi: text a pic

Ty: get consent

Gigi: they're in public, you don't need it

After decades of sober, factual texts, her sisters thought she was serious.

Rose: They're not actually on a table.

Ty: In the bathroom?

Rose: They're not actually having sex.

Probably.

Rose: But Mia is a goddess.

A stream of gifs and emojis threatened to break her phone.

Rose: She got us two hotel rooms.

Ty: So you wouldn't feel pressured

Ty: *Ash is in love with YOU*

Rose: *She can pressure me.*

Rose: *We're going to a burlesque show.*

Gigi: 🐦 🐦 🐦 *What are you going to wear*

Gigi: *Say blazer and I will disown you*

Rose: *Blazer*

Gigi texted a link.

Gigi: *Marianna Villard. There's a store in the Michael Dallas* hotel. Buy one.

Rose clicked the link.

Rose: *$3000!?!*

Gigi: *What else do you spend your money on?*

Rose: *Pugs.*

Gigi: *They will eat you when you die alone*

Cassie: *They won't.*

Gigi: *They might. Buy a dress!!!*

Rose waited for Ty to text something about capitalism and the beauty industry.

Ty: *Buy the dress*

At least buying the most expensive dress she'd ever handled—let alone bought—and spending another three hundred dollars on tailoring (with an extra charge because she needed it that day) kept her mind off Ash. Well...not off but at least to the side of. When the courier brought the tailored dress to her hotel room, she tried it on and studied herself in the mirror. It was almost worth what she'd paid. Mia was gorgeous for whatever Amazonian species she belonged to, but Rose was hot as hell for a human being.

Back in her hotel room, Ash turned up the AC. Her second-floor window afforded her a view of a pawnshop advertising DVDs, a salon called Skin by Serina, a prom and quinceañera rental, and, in the distance, a sun-bleached highway. She'd always liked places like this, places that could be anywhere...anywhere dry at least. Compton. New Mexico. Mexico. It made the world feel bigger. Victoria would have sacrificed a kidney before she stayed at a place like this. Rose didn't mind.

Rose.

Ash wanted to unbutton Rose's blazer, peel off her silk shirt, hold Rose's breasts in her hands. Was Rose wearing a lace bra or something more practical like the bra she'd worn the night they kissed? Ash lay down on the bed. Tentatively she unbuttoned her jeans. She slipped her hand inside and touched her underwear. She thought about Rose's arms wrapped around her and Rose's lips on hers and Rose's curves beneath her conservative suits. Ash rubbed a small circle over her clit.

She didn't feel a rush of arousal, but it felt good. It felt natural. And as she kept touching herself it felt more instinctual. She wasn't poking around with her fingers to see if she was still numb, to see if arousal turned into pain. Her body was saying, *Touch here and here, a little harder.* She stopped before she got close to coming in case her body tensed up in pain instead of release. But she kept her hand over her vulva for a long time, staring up at the ceiling. She'd felt pleasure. Mild, ordinary, uncomplicated pleasure, like someone who hadn't been broken. She felt like someone who was going to a world-famous burlesque show with a beautiful woman who was probably working at the little hotel desk on the other side of the wall but maybe was lying in bed thinking about her.

Ash dozed in the warm room. When she woke, the sun had taken on an orange cast. She took out her phone and texted Rose.

Ash: *Get dinner before the show?*

Rose texted an immediate yes.

Rose: *What are you wearing to the show?*

What was she wearing? Jeans and a T-shirt? She stood up and looked in the mirror. The shaved sides of her head were growing out. She looked like a hedgehog with a mullet. She would see people she'd known. They'd look at her with pity. *That's Ash Stewart. She used to be a great director. Now she can't even find a barber.* Fuck them. Half the guys she'd known forgot to shave. Most of the actors stayed in sweats until it was time for costuming. Rose would be underdressed, too, but she'd look sexy and confident. *I have way more important things to do than dress up for all you wannabe influencers. Billion-dollar companies are waiting for me to smack them into submission like a dominatrix of the Fortune 500. I don't do that in a cocktail dress.*

Ash: *Don't know. You?*

Rose texted a picture of the most beautiful dress Ash had seen since she'd last walked a red carpet.

chapter 38

Rose hurried down the walkway to the shaky stairs leading to the parking lot at the front of the hotel, carrying the ridiculously priced clutch she'd bought along with the dress. She stopped when she reached the bottom. Ash stood with her back to the hotel. When she heard Rose's footsteps she turned. And Rose knew that no matter what happened, even if she never saw Ash after this week, Ash would always remain the brightest star. The warmth of the sun. The expanse of the ocean. The heartbreak of first love. Lust for mind and body together.

Ash held out her hands in a this-is-all-I-got gesture.

"Oh," Rose breathed.

The suit fit Ash perfectly. She looked taller. The sleeves rolled up to show her tattoos and a large, gold watch, like a gangster in an old movie. And she'd tightened up the sides of her hair. She wore lipstick and dark eyeshadow. And when Ash spread her arms, Rose saw the edge of a black bra. No shirt. The deep V of the jacket showed just a hint, but if Ash unbuttoned her jacket, she'd be topless.

"I didn't have time to buy a blouse." She touched the jacket's lapels with a cocky smile.

"A blouse?"

The word struck Rose as funny. If Ash's outfit needed anything it would be a camisole made of twilight and a vest made of rose petals.

"I could put on a T-shirt," Ash amended, looking suddenly embarrassed.

"No." Rose hurried over. "You are so fucking gorgeous." She stared at Ash. "Do not put on a blouse." She caught another glimpse of the bra, a sheer material with serpents stitched in a pattern that just barely hid Ash's nipples. Rose looked away quickly, blushing.

"Do you like it?" Ash's flirtatious smile said she'd seen Rose looking.

"A blouse would definitely be too much." Rose stood close to Ash, tilting her face up.

Kiss me.

"Why are you saying *blouse* in quotation marks?" Ash asked.

"Because you're too beautiful for blouses. Target sells blouses. People wear blouses when they work at a bank."

Ash didn't say anything, but her eyes traveled up and down Rose's body, her smile shifting from flirtatious to something dark and honeyed.

"You look amazing." Ash reached out, almost putting her hands on Rose's hips but not quite. "Absolutely amazing."

"Gigi told me I couldn't go to a burlesque show with a gorgeous woman and wear a blazer."

"A blazer would have been fine."

Rose felt Ash's eyes settle on the neck of her dress, her gaze a luxurious touch.

"But this is better. Did you tuck this in your carry-on because you're always ready to make the world drop at your feet?"

"Marianna Villard hooked me up."

"An investment," Ash said knowingly.

"And you?"

Ash's honeyed gaze turned into her self-deprecating smile. Rose wanted to wake up to that smile as much as she wanted Ash to seduce her like a lover from a burlesque show. Ash pointed her thumb to the shops across the street.

"I'm wearing a teenage boy's prom suit. It still smells like Axe."

Rose leaned in to smell her. Then it felt totally natural to throw her arms around Ash's neck like a teenage girl with her prom date.

"I love that so much."

The crowd at the theater was dressed in enough glitter to rival the lights of a slot machine. Ash bought them both glasses of peach Bellini, and they moved to the side of the lobby to watch the crowd.

"I hate Bellini." Ash clinked her glass against Rose's.

"Why did you get it?"

"Because it matches your outfit." Ash brushed her cheek against Rose's as she whispered, "And we look fabulous."

Maybe Rose was Cinderella. Maybe tomorrow it would all have been a dream. But for tonight, they were magnificent.

Eventually, Mia appeared in a cocktail dress slit to the hip. She led them to a narrow staircase, then to one of the boxes.

"For my VIPs," she said and because the universe was a just place and God loved Rose, Mia did not stay.

The houselights dimmed. The master of ceremonies appeared in a metallic silver tailcoat, top hat, and bustier. The first act was a fire dancer who could not possibly be abiding by LA fire codes, which Rose would have pointed out—maybe left the building to be careful—except that Ash had draped an arm over Rose's shoulders and was absently caressing Rose's arm, as though she had no idea how her touch made Rose tremble...or she did and was going to keep doing it all night. Ash leaned in as one of the dancers spit a column of fire from her mouth.

"I could do that," Ash whispered, grinning. "I just haven't tried."

Ash was so fucking cute. It wasn't fair that someone could be that sexy and that adorable. Rose would never recover. She never wanted to.

chapter 39

After the intermission, the master of ceremonies ambled out to the edge of the stage. "Now we'll need a few participants from the audience."

Hands went up. Rose shook her head. "Never," she said. Playfully, Ash pointed to Rose. Rose slapped her arm down.

"Anything might happen," Ash whispered.

Rose had spent her whole life afraid of *anything* happening. Hunker down. Stay put. Life was one long shelter-in-place drill.

"Fine," Rose said, pretending to glare at Ash. "Raise your hand. You get what you deserve."

To soften her words, she gave Ash a kiss on the cheek. They hadn't talked about the night south of Centralia, but the air between them was charged with an energy that made Rose giddy.

The houselights came up. The master of ceremonies looked around the audience. "You," he said, pointing to a couple in the front row.

"You put him up to this," the woman protested to her partner.

"Are you dating?" the master of ceremonies asked.

They nodded.

"Then up you come. It's couples only tonight. Sorry, you lonely singles. Freedom comes at a cost."

When the couple was standing on the stage, the master of ceremonies eyed them up and down.

"Well, you'll do. Now I need two more couples." He picked a pair of older men. "Now I will pick the last couple, but first let me tell you about the prize." The master of ceremonies spread his arms. "Sponsorship moment!"

A screen lowered from the ceiling. A projector produced a photograph of a tropical beach and the words LIFE IS JUST AN ESCAPE AWAY: NEW DESTINATION RESORT, CANCÚN, MEXICO.

"The winners of this little competition will win a four-night stay at the magical New Destination Resort." He slipped into a television advertising voice. "Where love and adventure bring you new horizons."

"Sounds like a rest home," Ash whispered.

The projector showed a montage of ocean sunsets.

"I remember vacations," Ash added a little wistfully. "They'll probably try to sell you a timeshare."

When was the last time Ash had taken a vacation? Ash needed a few nights in a tropical paradise.

"I'll retire to New Destination with you," Rose teased. "We'll buy a timeshare and wear visors."

"I'd like that." Ash laughed. "How many pugs do we have to have?"

Rose leaned closer. "Eight."

Ash opened her eyes in mock horror.

"Now, the New Destination Resort is not the only prize." The master of ceremonies scanned the crowd. "The lucky couple will also win a one-night stay—tonight as it turns out—in a Benson-Lux Hotel Honeymoon Suite. Of course, we all know what that means. Some rock star canceled at the last minute and no one—even in LA—is crazy enough to pay Benson-Lux prices, soooo...surprise. The couple that wins this game isn't staying in that seedy little hotel you rented. City view, champagne, your own private rooftop pool and Jacuzzi." The master of ceremonies fanned his face. "Now, who do I want?"

Rose looked at the people on the floor trying to guess who the master of ceremonies would pick.

"Don't look away," he said.

Rose looked at Ash.

"Don't look at her, either."

Ash laughed deep in her throat. She curled her arm around Rose's shoulder. With the other hand, she pointed to the master of ceremonies.

"I've made my decision," the master of ceremonies said. "The beautiful couple in the box."

Were they a couple? Ash looked at Rose. They froze. The theater disappeared. Rose saw her own desire reflected in Ash's eyes. *Yes.*

"We'll win," Rose whispered.

Rose stood and held out her hand to Ash. Ash took Rose's hand. Rose wanted the moment to last forever, Ash's hand in hers, Ash's desire naked in her eyes.

I want you.

Rose's heart raced as they walked down the steps and out to the stage.

The game was a kind of dating game. Ushers had the audience write questions for the couples. They had to guess their partners' answers. Ash and Rose sat on opposite sides of the stage. Ash raised her eyebrows in a look that said, *We got in deep, didn't we?*

Rose mouthed, *We got this,* although, of course, they didn't.

The master of ceremonies started with the gay couple, reading off questions. They lost on *What would your most romantic date be?* The man and woman fared a little better but lost on the boyfriend's happiest childhood memory.

"Now for my favorites," the master of ceremonies said. "I know. A father shouldn't have favorites, but, darlings, no one can prove you're mine." He turned. "What are your names, my lovelies?"

"Rose."

"Ash."

"I don't believe those names for a second, but fine, Rose and Ash. Your first question goes to Ash: If you had to guess Rose's passwords, where would you start? If you get this right, she'll have to change her passwords, but it'll be worth it."

Ash scribbled down her answer. The assistant gave it to the master of ceremonies.

"Ash thinks Rose uses the *super-long passwords her computer generates for her*," the master of ceremonies said. He unfolded Rose's answer. "Rose writes *totally random characters, numbers, and symbols.* Should we give it to them?"

The crowd cheered their *yes.* The master of ceremonies opened the next question. Rose won the round with Ash's least favorite thing about LA: LED lights. Ash won with the thing Rose loved most in the world: her sisters.

"If you keep getting these right, we'll actually have to give someone the prize. Okay, one more question. Describe one thing you'll do when you are old and gray."

Dream about you. Rose looked at Ash filling out her slip of paper. *Watch your films. Remember these nights as the brightest of my life.*

The master of ceremonies collected their answers.

"Well, shit," he said. "We're going to have to give it to them, folks. They both wrote *Have eight pugs.*"

A puff of confetti floated down.

"Stand up," the master of ceremonies said. "You may now kiss the bride."

Rose's thoughts swirled faster than the confetti as Ash walked toward her. Rose stood and nodded. Then Ash's lips were on hers. Soft. Hot. Rose's body pulsed. Her heart filled with the lights of LA. Her knees melted, but Ash held her up, pulling their bodies together, their hips touching. In that strong embrace Rose felt the confidence that had made Ash a star. Yes, Ash stumbled over her words. Yes, bad things had happened to her. But *this* was who Ash was. The crowd cheered and, as if the sound released Ash's inhibitions, she pulled Rose tighter. Heat seared through Rose's core...or clitoris or vulva or whatever word Ty would insist she use, but it was more than those parts. Her whole body was alight with her desire for Ash.

Then Ash released her quickly as though Ash had lost track of herself, as though she felt the same way, and had just remembered where they were. But she looked proud and mischievous, like she knew exactly what she did to Rose, and wanted Rose to know she knew.

"Another round of applause for our winning couple," the master of ceremonies said.

Rose felt like they deserved it, not for guessing eight pugs but for being who they were.

chapter 40

Ash stepped into their suite at the Benson-Lux Hotel. The floor-to-ceiling windows showed the city pulsing beneath them. She wasn't looking at the city, though. She was looking at Rose's reflection in the glass. The asymmetrical, peach-colored gown accentuated the languid grace Rose's suits hid. The billowy, taffeta skirt shone with a hint of gold that wasn't thread and wasn't glitter but an inner iridescence, like Rose had swirled the desert sunset up in her skirts. The fabric fell off Rose's creamy shoulder. Ash wanted to kiss that shoulder, gently bite it, or bite hard if that was what Rose liked. She wanted to know everything Rose liked and do it for her again and again.

"Breathtaking," Ash said.

Ash wished she were behind a camera so she could capture every second, although Rose didn't need Ash to direct her. Rose was perfect without instruction.

"The Executive Comfort Suites had free local calls," Ash said. "I don't know if this really compares."

Ash joined Rose at the window.

"I can live without a landline," Rose said, and for the first time in human history, those words sounded seductive. But she turned to Ash and added, "You know we don't have to do anything."

Ash felt like the glass window disappeared. Ash stood at the edge of the sky.

"We can make love, or we can just drink champagne and watch the city. It's all cool," Rose added, but her eyes were dark with desire.

Ash couldn't remember the last time a woman looked at her like this, like she was all that mattered. Not her connections, not her next film, not the red carpet she was about to walk down. Everything felt right. Ash wanted to touch Rose, taste her, feel Rose's hips lift with pleasure. Before the accident, Ash had loved sex. She'd loved the power and delight of bringing a woman to climax. She wanted to give that to Rose, over and over until Rose was exhausted and wanting and begged for just one more time.

Her heart trembled with the certainty of what came next.

Love.

No. Sex. After all this time.

But the word *love* kept creeping into her mind, like sunlight creeping around the curtains in the studio. Rose ran her hands up Ash's back and up her neck until she held Ash's face in her hands. But really, Rose held Ash's heart in her hands. Ash could feel Rose's restraint, as though Rose was taut with need but holding back.

"I'm nervous." Who was Ash kidding? She wasn't going to wreck Rose with orgasm after orgasm. She'd probably fumble the whole thing like a teenager.

"That's okay." Rose brushed her thumbs over Ash's cheeks. "I am, too. Gigi keeps texting me emojis that I think mean I should've had sex with you in the airplane. Ty sent me an anatomical drawing of the clitoris."

"You do know what it looks like?" Ash opened her eyes wide with pretend shock. "Should we look at that drawing?"

Rose nipped Ash's lip with the gentlest touch of her teeth. "Yes. I know perfectly well. My sisters are just trying to be helpful because they know I like you."

"You talked to your sisters about me?" The pleasure at that thought dispelled a little of Ash's nervousness.

"How could I go to LA with you and not tell my sisters?"

"About your business trip?"

"Yes," Rose said with mock formality, "about the business trip my company doesn't know I'm taking with the brilliant filmmaker who I'm starting to...adore."

"Adore?" Ash savored the word. "I don't think anyone has ever adored me."

"Of course they have."

Not like this.

"I adore you, too," Ash said and meant it with every cell in her body. "Would you like to go to the bedroom and adore each other there?"

"Well, since you asked so nicely," Rose said with a grin, and she took Ash's hand and led her to the arched doorway that led to the grand hall that led to the bedroom. The chandelier overhead was the size of a small car. An enormous bed faced another wall of windows. About a thousand pillows graced its brocade cover.

"I would throw you on this bed, but I couldn't do that to a Marianna Villard dress."

"I had to seduce you"—Rose kissed Ash lightly—"because I don't think I can get out of it on my own."

Ash unbuttoned the one button that held her suit jacket closed and let it fall open. The accident had left her arms and chest unmarked.

"You are lovely," Rose murmured.

From the waist up.

Before she lost her nerve, Ash ran her hands down Rose's sides and then her back, looking for zippers. The dress fell open in the back and slid off Rose's shoulder. Ash caught it before it touched the floor, and Rose stepped out. Her lace bra and panties matched the peach color of the dress. She stood before Ash, hands on her hips, her full beautiful body poised to be admired. And Ash did. Rose's body was all the luscious things in one: peaches and buttercream frosting and sweet vanilla liquor. She had large, natural breasts, hanging a little lower because, like Ash, she wasn't nineteen anymore. She was more beautiful than nineteen.

And in the back of Ash's mind, she waited for the moment when her body would tense up in fear, but the moment didn't come. Not when she led Rose to the bed. Not when she lay down on her side and Rose trailed her fingers along her ribs. Not when Rose caressed her nipples through the thin fabric of her bra. They lay side by side, facing each other, taking up about one-eighth of the swimming-pool-sized bed.

"May I take off your pants?" Rose asked.

Ash's heart hung between beats.

"I'm not perfect."

"That's a problem since I'm *completely* perfect," Rose teased. She traced Ash's sternum, leaving traces of heat on Ash's skin.

"I have scars."

"From the accident." Rose propped up on one elbow, suddenly serious. "You know that's okay." She stroked Ash's cheek.

"Okay." Ash closed her eyes. "Okay," she said again, helping Rose help her out of her pants. They slid off the end of the bed. Ash lay flat on her back, her eyes closed.

Rose gasped. "Oh, Ash."

She stiffened as she imagined Rose surveying the damage. Ash would have felt less exposed if she had walked through downtown Portland topless.

"I can get under the covers." Ash didn't open her eyes. "You don't have to look."

She felt Rose's breath on her face, then Rose's kiss on her forehead.

"May I touch you?"

Victoria had never touched Ash's scars. Victoria had researched laser scar removal.

"Yes." Ash tried to relax. People had surgeries. It wasn't a big deal.

Rose traced the surgical scar on Ash's hip, her touch soft but not reluctant, not the touch of someone overcoming distaste but the touch of a woman exploring her lover's body for the first time. Ash's throat tightened, not with pain but with how much she needed to be touched like this, like her body was worthy, like she was enough.

"I don't know how you did it," Rose said.

Ash opened her eyes. "What?"

"Survived. Came out so talented and beautiful. I don't want to hurt you."

"You won't."

You might. Her body. Her heart. All of her laid out for Rose.

Rose knelt on the bed beside Ash and kissed the scar on Ash's ankle, then moved upward, kissing each line as though this was the most precious part of Ash.

"You're perfect," she said again. "And you don't have to be."

Ash waited for memories of the accident to flood her mind. Rolling over and over. But they didn't. And she loved the way Rose tenderly kissed her leg. She liked Rose's fingers stroking the underside of her knee. But were other things Ash wanted even more.

She trailed her fingernails down Rose's back. "I have plans for you."

"Tell me."

When Rose looked at her again, she looked hungry. Ash rolled Rose onto her back. She cupped one of Rose's breasts in her hand. Then she rolled Rose's nipple between her lips, sucked, and nipped at her until Rose clutched at her shoulder. Rose's hips writhed beautifully in her peach underwear. Ash stroked her once. She was wet. Rose let out a frustrated groan when Ash returned her hand to Rose's waist and her kisses to Rose's breasts. Ash kissed her chest, her neck, her lips, occasionally letting her hand stray across Rose's underwear.

When Ash began kissing the delicate skin of Rose's inner elbow, Rose moaned, "Oh God, Ash. You're doing this on purpose."

Ash drew back. "What?" she asked innocently.

Rose closed her eyes. "Please."

Ash had forgotten—and in another way she could never forget—what it felt like to tease a woman to distraction. Rose's chest was flushed. Her lips swollen. Slowly Ash kissed down Rose's belly. She pulled off Rose's underwear. She kissed Rose's soft, golden curls.

"Yes?" Ash murmured.

Rose rose up slightly to look at Ash poised above her sex. "Yes," she said with delightful irritation. "Fuck. Yes. Right now."

Ash parted Rose's legs and offered Rose one long, slow sweep of her tongue. Rose cried out in pleasure. "Yes!" She gripped Ash's shoulders.

Ash felt nervous and delighted as she trailed her tongue lazily around Rose's sex. She licked Rose's opening and circled Rose's clit without touching it until Rose's hips bucked. With the heel of her hand, Ash massaged the soft flesh of Rose's mons. Rose, the dignified businesswoman, was delightfully loquacious in bed.

"Oh, God, Ash. There. The way you...just like that...that's going to make me scream."

But her cries of pleasure weren't totally out of character for the best consultant west of the Rockies. She did like to give advice.

"A little harder. Harder. I'm more sensitive on the right side—oh! There!"

It was a lovely gift to Ash. It was easy to be a rock star lover with such specific instructions. Ash's heart soared with Rose's every cry. But finally, Rose's cries became fluttery and desperate. Rose was too taut. Too close. Rose lifted her hips, clutching the sheets.

"Breathe," Ash whispered.

Rose took a shaky breath. Ash pressed her lips to Rose's vulva, breathing slowly herself. She felt Rose relax. Then she drew Rose's hand to the place where her tongue worshiped, licking around Rose's fingers as Rose touched herself. Rose pressed herself hard, moving her fingers only a fraction of an inch and keening in pleasure. It took her only a second. When Rose had stopped moaning, Ash drew away, wiping her face on Rose's thigh. She crawled up the bed.

Rose draped her arm over her eyes, laughing. "I'm not always that loud...never that loud."

"I like it." It was the most beautiful, sexy, exciting thing Ash had ever heard.

Rose withdrew her arm and looked at Ash. "Don't be smug."

If Ash didn't know better, she'd have thought she saw love in Rose's eyes. Ash grinned.

"You are. I can see it," Rose said.

Ash tried to suppress her smirk, but the thought of giving Rose pleasure just made her smile more. "A good director knows how to work with the talent." Really, Rose had been the director, but Ash didn't point it out. She smoothed her hand down Rose's side, then gave her ass a firm squeeze.

Rose gave her a playful swat on the ass, the movement rolling their bodies together. "Now what can I do for you?" Rose asked.

Ash's clit throbbed with desire, but there was still the chance her body would betray her. Rose would slip a finger inside her and Ash would cry out in pain, not pleasure. And Ash would ruin this perfect moment.

"Hold me like you did before," she said, realizing how needy the words sounded the second they left her lips. "Sorry." Ash buried her face in Rose's chest. "That sounds like I'm coming with the U-Haul. I just mean..."

"Shh." Rose wrapped her arms around Ash, pulling her close. "You won't need a U-Haul. You don't have any furniture."

chapter 41

Rose woke slowly, cocooned in the soft sheets of the ten-plus-star hotel. When she opened her eyes, Ash was sitting in bed beside her fully dressed...or as fully dressed as last night's outfit allowed.

"Good morning, lovely." Ash had her laptop in her lap.

"Are you working already?" Rose asked sleepily.

"I was earlier."

"What time is it?"

"Eleven."

"Eleven?" Rose checked her phone on the bedside table.

Ash grinned the same self-satisfied grin she'd given Rose the night before.

"You're cocky." Rose beamed.

"I didn't say anything," Ash said.

"You were thinking."

Rose looked around. Ash followed her gaze. The bed was a mess, and there were throw pillows everywhere. Their eyes met, and they both laughed.

"We did that," Ash said.

"I loved it," Rose said.

Too much? Should she have said *I liked it* or *You were great?* Had she used the words *make love* last night? Endorphins excused that. Ash was lucky Rose hadn't screamed *Marry me and have my babies!*

"Me too." Ash pushed her laptop aside and flopped next to Rose.

Rose couldn't stop smiling. She stretched out, arms above her head, feet reaching to the foot of the bed. Ash looked at her appreciatively.

"So," Ash said, "our flight out isn't until this evening. We could go look at those peacocks Mia talked about."

"I do like housebroken peacocks."

Ash crinkled her nose adorably. "Mia says they're *somewhat* housebroken."

"Hmm, how somewhat?"

"I think it's a no on the peacocks, so I was thinking, instead, what about a picnic?"

"You mean skip out on work? Shouldn't we both be..."

"Editing and managing cauliflower? Yes." Ash pushed her laptop aside and snuggled up beside her. It felt perfect and perfectly natural, like they'd been together forever or like they should be. "I didn't used to be a workaholic." Ash trailed her fingers down Rose's stomach. "No, I guess I was always a workaholic, but I was a workaholic because Victoria was. She was rich but she wasn't lazy. I gave a hundred percent for me," Ash said thoughtfully. "But she wanted a hundred and twenty. That last twenty was for her."

"You shouldn't have to give more than you have."

Rose slipped her arm around Ash and cuddled her closer. Ash was happy. Rose could tell in the way Ash relaxed against her. And Rose was happy. And they made each other happy.

The thought was almost too big to hold. This moment felt like a blissful dream, but it was Rose's real life.

An hour later, a valet pulled up to the front of the hotel in a Cadillac SUV. Ash and Rose were still dressed in the clothes they'd worn to the burlesque show. Even in the glitz and flash of the Benson-Lux Hotel people looked at them. At her and Ash Stewart. Holding hands. Dressed in eveningwear at noon. Ash opened the SUV door for her, then swung into the driver's seat. They changed into regular clothes at the Executive Comfort Suites and packed their luggage in the SUV. Ash stopped at a caterer on their way out of town, then hit the highway.

Rose couldn't stop staring at Ash. Ash looked gorgeous in rose-tinted aviator glasses and a black tank top that showcased her lean body. And Rose had touched her and kissed her and perhaps tonight or at least soon, she would taste her, and she would taste better than any peach or fortune cookie or jewel box.

The drive took them out of the crush of the city, onto a desert highway, and then down a long drive. A sign on the side of the road read ELEANOR ASHTON BOTANICAL GARDEN.

"What is this place?" Rose asked.

Ahead of them was what looked like a stucco mansion, all soft curves and terra-cotta colors. Around the house was desert but not the scrub seen alongside the highway. As they drew closer, Rose saw palm trees, flashes of pink flowers, and luminescent cactuses.

"The house is a museum. Art from all over. And the grounds are amazing. Ten acres. I guess the woman who created it loved desert gardening. She said she hated the way people tried to grow lawns in Southern California instead of appreciating what makes it beautiful naturally."

They parked. Ash opened the trunk and took out the picnic basket from the caterer, a blanket, and a cooler bag.

"Let's find a spot," she said.

The air was hot, but the garden had little pockets of shade. They walked until they found a place under a madrone tree on a little rise. Ash tossed the blanket down and pulled a wine bottle out of the cooler. She had brought stemless glasses, conveniently weighted to stay upright on uneven ground. She'd brought everything else, too—a dozen cheeses, crackers with flecks of rosemary, mangoes, chocolates with an ice pack to keep them cool. Suddenly Rose was starving. It was heaven, eating the food and sipping the wine. The air held just the right amount of heat. The madrone tree shaded their skin.

"That theater really is beautiful," Rose said as she sucked on the sweetest strawberry she'd ever tasted. "Brentworth is going to fall in love with the movie and you. You're going to get this."

Ash lay down, twirling a dry madrone leaf in her fingers. "The only thing I've wanted since Victoria left was to be a director again."

"Why did all the people in Hollywood believe what Victoria said about you bailing on the film? Why couldn't your friends clear your name?"

Ash held the leaf up to the sky, perhaps imagining a camera angle. She turned it flat, then sideways. Then she crushed it in her hand and let the pieces fall on her chest. "I could have cleared my name."

Rose gazed down at Ash lying on the blanket beside her.

"All I had to do was pull out some pictures of the crash. Wear shorts. Show everyone the X-ray of my titanium shin. I didn't want to tell them a sob story. Victoria made it clear how unattractive that was." Ash sighed. "Victoria wasn't going to produce my films, and I didn't want people to produce them because they felt sorry for me."

"People don't produce movies because they feel sorry for someone."

How could Ash have been that talented and thought no one would want to work with her except Victoria?

"You'd be surprised why people produce movies," Ash said.

"But you were at the top of your game."

"I guess when Victoria said she didn't want me, I thought no one would. It was a long recovery. I was depressed. Then it was too late." Ash felt around for another leaf and began breaking it into even halves. "How could I go back to my friends, who I'd lost touch with, and say, *Could you help me?* Who would want to help that person?"

"Mia would help you," Rose said. "I would. Emma would. And I imagine there are dozens of producers who would want to work with you if they knew that you hadn't bailed on *The Secret Song*. They'll be sorry that Brentworth got to you first."

Rose lay down on her side next to Ash. "When I was a kid, my father always used to say that asking for help was a present you gave the other person because when you asked for help, they knew they could ask you."

Her father's face smiled out from the memory. Dancing eyes. Uneven beard. The wildly printed shirts he wore to entertain and embarrass his daughters. The one with rainbow frogs he'd bought when Rose came out. The one with smile emojis. He wasn't just the minutes it took for the Cessna to fall out of the sky. Suddenly tears welled up in Rose's eyes, not tears for her parents' deaths but tears for their goodness. "If you let them know that you were tired or confused," she said hurriedly, blinking her tears away, "then they knew they could tell you, too. Admitting you're vulnerable isn't weakness."

"Thank you." Ash moved closer and kissed her tenderly, murmuring through their kiss, "How are you so wonderful? So kind. Beautiful. Smart. Funny. You make me so happy."

Then Ash stopped talking and just kissed her. It was a perfect kiss, soft but hungry, but a tear slid down Rose's nose onto her lip. As though Ash had tasted the salt, Ash pulled away and looked at Rose with concern.

"What is it?"

It was easy to say vulnerability wasn't weakness, but when you'd had to be the strong one for everyone else...vulnerability was a luxury. Rose listened for the sound of birds or insects, but there was just a faint breeze crinkling the leaves.

Ash took Rose's fingers in her hand and kissed her knuckles. She didn't say anything. She wouldn't say anything until Rose spoke; Rose knew it. Ash would give her the whole day to speak if she needed it. They lay facing each other.

"Can I tell you something?" Rose asked.

"Of course."

Rose rolled onto her back. "I haven't flown for eighteen years." She closed her eyes. "Because my parents died in a plane crash eighteen years ago."

"Rose." Ash put her arm across Rose's chest, pulling her close and kissing her forehead. "I'm so sorry."

"They loved adventure. My dad was an engineer, and my mom was a nurse. They weren't daredevils, but they'd go whitewater rafting. They took us parasailing. And my dad bought an airplane and learned to fly. He knew what he was doing. He was a good pilot. My mom was, too. They were going to some sort of rally for people who fly little planes because they have no fear of death." Rose gave a bitter laugh.

"They went over the Rockies. I was away on a year abroad. I wanted to be a music major. I was studying in Vienna. I got the call. They'd crashed. It'd taken Search and Rescue days to get to the wreck, but it didn't matter. They died on impact. People kept telling us it wasn't anyone's fault, like that was supposed to make us feel better. It didn't."

Ash tightened her arm around Rose, holding her fervently, as though someone was trying to snatch Rose away.

"I'm so sorry."

Rose loved Ash for not saying *At least they died doing what they loved.* They hadn't loved flying; they'd loved life.

"Fault makes sense," Ash said. "You can avoid fault."

"Exactly." Rose pressed her face into Ash's shoulder, breathing in the last trace of Axe cologne.

"What did you do?" Ash asked.

"I came back. I switched to a business major to be safe. Cassie moved in with her best friend's family. Ty went to live with my aunt and uncle, but she was miserable, so I let her move in with me. I…raised her. It's funny. Now she gives me advice and asks me if I know what the clitoris is. But at the time, I was her parents."

"How old were you?"

"Twenty."

"That's so young." Ash pressed her lips to Rose's forehead again. "When I was twenty, I didn't know how to open a jar without googling it."

"I got really practical really quickly. I got the job at Integral Business Solutions. They understood that I was a single mom without being a mom. They paid me more than I deserved for a college-kid receptionist."

It was strange how the tears that slid down her cheek didn't take away from the happiness of the day. It was like happiness and sadness lay on the blanket side by side holding hands. They didn't negate each other. They were both part of being alive.

"Isn't Gigi the oldest?" Ash asked after a while. "Should she have taken care of Ty?"

"Gigi is wonderful, but back then she was not the kind of person you give a sad ten-year-old to. I kept us together. We could have drifted apart, but I made us get together every week. No matter what. And we still do." Rose pictured the she-cave. Ty and Gigi bickering. Cassie in her mom jeans. The skull mugs. The love-worn easy chairs. "We came out okay. I got Ty through high school without her falling apart.

"Integral Business Solutions let me support all of us. I could help Cassie with her house. Pay for Ty's undergraduate. I once bailed Gigi out of jail because she got drunk and stripped at karaoke...at the Elks club." Rose loved them so much. "I made the right choices so there'll always be someone to take care of them."

Ash propped herself up on one elbow, looking at Rose with concern. "We can drive back if you're afraid to fly."

"We can't drive back." Rose touched Ash's lips as if to shush her. "You've got to get ready for the biggest day of your life." Rose smiled to let Ash know she was okay. "And I'm afraid of fires, earthquakes, sepsis, Ebola, identity fraud, kayaking, falling trees. It's a diverse list. If I avoided all of it, I'd never do anything."

Have I done anything?

"So if you took care of your sisters, who's taken care of you? Have you had...partners?" Ash asked tentatively.

"I did the obligatory lesbian serial monogamy thing. They were good people. I guess they tried to take care of me, but I didn't need them to." Rose held up her own leaf and looked at the lacework of veins beneath the skin. Had she ever looked at her girlfriends and lovers with the same attention she looked at this leaf or at the objects in her videos? She'd gone to all those mindfulness classes, all those Tibetan bells, but she hadn't seen them. They'd been like the Pottery Barn furniture, acceptable choices. She'd enjoyed the sex. It was nice to have someone to go to sushi with. She should apologize for being with them and not adoring them, except that'd be weird.

"They would have been lucky if you'd let them take care of you," Ash said.

"I wasn't passionate about any of them."

"Do you think you could…"

Ash didn't finish the question. There were a dozen ways she could have. *Do you think you could benefit from therapy? Hand me the wine?*

Those weren't the questions Rose answered when she said, "Yes. I'm passionate about you."

chapter 42

Leaving the garden felt like leaving paradise, but eventually there was no way to pretend they didn't have an SUV to return and a flight to catch.

"Are you going to be okay?" Ash asked as they slid into their seats and buckled their seat belts without instruction.

"I think so."

And against all reasonable predictions the plane did not crash and Rose did not die of an anxiety attack. She might even have fallen asleep for a minute, her head on Ash's shoulder.

Back in the PDX parking garage, Rose spoke her address into Ash's Tesla's navigation system. Ash took off, gracefully circling the curves of the garage with only two fingers on the wheel. Reluctantly Rose powered on her phone. Phone equaled reality. Reality equaled giving her sisters proof of life. As soon as her phone powered on, a stream of messages flooded in. She silenced the notification bell.

Cassie: *Welcome home.*
Gigi: *How was it?* 😌

Cassie: None of your bus G.

Gigi: Everything sisters is our bus

Ty: Did you? 🔍 You haven't texted all day

Cassie: Don't bother her.

Gigi: Full report!

Ty: When does Rose land?

Gigi: 10:30 p.m.

Gigi: I know you're reading this Rose

Apparently, her sisters were waiting for her to land with phones in hand.

Rose: Home safe.

Gigi replied before Rose could start another sentence.

Gigi: Well?

Ty: 🍑?

Cassie: Don't harass her.

Was she going to type it? *We had sex and it was amazing and I think I'm in love and it wasn't just the* 🍆🔍🍩🥧🥄🥥🍑 *(G I don't know what that is but now I feel dirty every time I use an emoji). And I want to make her happy. I want to spend every night with her. I want to be the best she's ever had. I think I'm really in love, and it's nothing like anything I've ever felt. I can fly.*

Rose hesitated.

Rose: Yes.

Cassie: That's wonderful.

Ty: Was it awesome?

Gigi: Did you get a Brazilian?

Ty: Was she as hot as you thought she'd be?

Cassie: She Cave tomorrow?

Rose couldn't contain her smile as she typed.

Rose: Amazing!!!

Ty: Best ever?

Rose: Top five.

What a lie. The top five were ten stories down. She might as well say it in Gigi's language.

Rose: 🧨 🧨 🧨 🔔 🔔 🔔

Cassie: Invite her over. Taco night.

Gigi: MUST MEET HER

Ty: YES!

Rose: So you can grill her about our sex life? Ha. No.

Cassie: We wouldn't.

Gigi: We will

Ty: It's a sex LIFE now. 😁

"Rose?" Ash coughed. "Rose, um..."

Rose looked over. Rose had been lost in her messages. Now she could tell Ash had been trying to get her attention for a while. Ash was also trying to suppress a grin.

"What?" Rose asked.

"I like tacos."

Ash wouldn't have taken her eyes off the road to look over at Rose's phone. There was no way. Rose looked at the screen on the dashboard. Her texts cascaded down in large, legible font.

"What the...?"

"It picked up your Bluetooth because my phone is off," Ash said, not trying to contain her grin anymore.

Rose covered the dashboard screen with her hands.

"No! How much did you read?"

"I tried not to look. Your texts are private...even if you did put them on my screen."

"I did not put them on your screen. How hard did you try?"

"I caught *taco night.* And *meet her.*"

"That's all?"

"I'd love to meet your sisters."

"I would not do that to you." Rose closed out the text

app and powered her phone off. "I would not do that to me. God, my sisters, all together? They're so excited that something interesting is happening for once in my life, they'd embarrass me."

"So I'm interesting?"

Rose snorted. "Of course."

"They'd show me baby pictures?"

"I was an adorable baby. I'll show you baby pictures."

Ash tapped her fingers to the song that was playing in the background. "It's too soon." Her smile sagged into a wistful cousin of her wide grin.

Rose wanted that grin back.

"As punishment for having a car that puts people's texts on the dashboard without asking"—Rose pronounced each word with boardroom enunciation—"I will take you to Cassie's. And they will literally kill me with embarrassment, and you, too."

"I'm hard to embarrass."

"They'll try."

Suddenly Rose loved the idea, even if her sisters would find some way to mortify her, possibly on purpose, possibly by accident. She wanted to see Ash in Cassie's kitchen, with the twins running past her and the Josten sisters all talking at once. Ash would be overwhelmed. Rose's sisters would love her.

"Gigi will tell you about waxing people. Cassie's kids will get something sticky on you. And her teenage daughter will probably ask you about cunnilingus just to embarrass Cas."

"I like them already." There was that golden smile. "I'll put it on my calendar."

When they reached Rose's townhouse, Rose wanted to invite Ash in, to throw her onto her bed and return all the glorious favors Ash had lavished on her last night. But at the same time, she needed time to take it all in, to spin around in her kitchen and marvel at what had happened. And she probably needed to do all the work she had forgotten about. Ash must have felt the same way.

"I would try to talk you into coming back to my place," Ash said when they were parking in front of Rose's house. "But I suppose I should be good. Work tomorrow. I'll try to keep my hands off you when I meet your sisters."

Rose leaned in and kissed Ash, just long enough to know Ash felt the same irresistible stirring in her core.

"Don't try too hard," she said as she drew away.

Rose got her bag out of the back seat, leaned down to blow Ash a kiss through the open window, then headed toward her door, trying not to skip.

Ash called out from behind her, and she turned.

"Only top five, eh? You'll have to teach me how to get to number one."

chapter 43

A young teenage girl with blue-green hair opened the door as though opening the door was life's great burden. But when she saw Ash, a spark of interest flashed behind the teenage boredom.

"You're the director," she said. "You're pretty. Not K-pop pretty, obviously. But pretty. Are you Aunt Rose's girlfriend?"

"I...we're..."

Ash's thoughts couldn't keep up with her racing heart. She was meeting Rose's sisters. She hadn't seen Rose since she dropped her off at her front door. She'd counted every minute. Had Rose? Now Ash was here with a bottle of wine and flowers in hand. She'd met Victoria's brother at a party where people were doing cocaine, and someone was eating shrimp off a stripper. She'd met Victoria's mother at a red-carpet event and her father in the sumptuous offices of his law firm. Victoria had met her family once and said they weren't as boring as she'd expected.

"My aunts say you're a good lover," the girl said.

"Delilah Anne!" A woman in a floral dress careened around the corner, sputtering. "If you said anything to Ms. Stewart

that I wouldn't ask her in front of your brothers, you will not
live to see sixteen."

The girl looked at her mother with big eyes. "I asked if she
was Aunt Rose's girlfriend," Delilah said innocently. "Then I
said you and Aunt G and Aunt Ty were talking about them
sleeping together."

"Delilah Anne!" the woman hissed at her daughter, but Ash
could tell she was trying not to laugh. "You go in the kitchen
and stem cilantro. Every last leaf off every last stem."

"You can eat the stems," the girl said.

"Mammals eat their children, too. Go."

The girl clomped away in heavy black boots. The woman
rolled her eyes skyward.

"I am so sorry. It's the age. She's trying to kill me with
embarrassment. You know how teenagers are supposed to be
embarrassed by their parents?" She waved Ash into the house.
"Not Delilah. She's trying to kill me. I'm Cassie. Come in."

"She's adorable." Ash handed Cassie the wine and the flowers.

"Are you sure you don't mean wicked?"

Inside the house was a cacophony of children squealing and
pots bubbling. Classic rock played on a speaker on the counter.
Rose waved from behind the island in the kitchen, and Ash
forgot how to say hello. Rose's hair was pulled up revealing her
graceful neck, and she wore a loose, spring-green dress that
showed off her curves while pretending to be modest. Delicate
emerald earrings graced her ears. Her lips were painted a soft
pink. Ash didn't think it was possible for Rose to look more
beautiful than she had in LA, but she did.

Rose's eyes met hers, and Ash was certain Rose was searching her face for the same answers Ash was looking for. *That
meant something, right?*

"Ash is speechless because my devil-spawn daughter just

told her she'd heard Ash was a good lover," Cassie called to Rose.

"Del, I will help your mother bury the body." Rose pointed two fingers at her eyes and then at the girl.

"I will ground her for life." Cassie swatted her towel at Delilah who stood in front of a massive pile of herbs. Her love for her daughter was clear in every word. "Ash brought these for you." Cassie handed Rose the flowers and the wine.

"Thanks." Rose came around the island to take the gifts. She was blushing. "I told you my family was too much."

Ash placed a chaste kiss on Rose's cheek. "I'm ready."

A woman in head-to-toe designer leaned against the counter drinking wine with clearly no intention of helping with dinner.

"Gigi." She held out a manicured hand.

Ty bounded in from the living room and gave Ash a hug as though they were already friends. Beyond the kitchen, Ash could see Cassie's husband lifting one of his children up in the air, then pretending to drop them on the sofa.

"Stop roughhousing," Cassie called without even looking.

Cassie's husband called a greeting from the living room.

Ash kept looking back at Rose.

"She dressed up for you," Gigi said.

Rose lowered her voice. "I did."

As it turned out, except for Delilah, Rose's family wasn't set on embarrassing her. The conversation started politely, everyone standing around in the kitchen. Ty asked about the challenges of being a woman director. Gigi asked about their trip to LA. Ash offered to help in the kitchen.

At dinner, conversations continued. The kids' school. Cassie's husband's co-worker who insisted on eating smoked oysters at work. Ty extolled Cassie's cooking.

"Because all you eat is sunflower sprouts," Cassie complained.

By the end of the dinner, everyone was laughing and talking as though Ash had been at their table forever. It was like eating with the crew but without the professional distance she kept between her and them. And after dinner, Cassie's husband and the kids cleaned up the kitchen, and Rose led Ash upstairs. Her sisters followed.

"Kenneth and the kids clean," Cassie explained. "And the sisters go upstairs and plan the conspiracy."

The upstairs was a finished attic, with comfortable well-worn furniture and colorful rugs. The last of the daylight shone in through skylights. Cassie went around turning on lamps, then opened a micro fridge in the corner.

"This is my spot." Rose led Ash to the love seat and they settled in. The chair brought them together. She loved the feel of Rose's body against hers. She tried not to lose herself in memories of LA lest Rose's sisters read everything on her face. Of course, if Delilah was right, they knew everything already. Rose snuggled closer; Ash wanted the moment to last forever.

"So tell us more about your work." Gigi flourished her wineglass, which looked like an artistic director had picked it to convey rustic Satanism. "What's it like? When can I be your famous makeup artist in Hollywood?"

"Mostly I film ads for the Mini Pet Mart."

"I want a mini pet," Ty said, settling herself on the opposite end of the sofa from Gigi.

"Tell us everything," Gigi said.

And Ash did, starting with the differences between producers, directors, and production designers. She described the films she'd worked on with Victoria, leaving Victoria out of the story.

"And Rose is going to help you get funding for your next project," Cassie said.

"She's stepping in for a producer," Ash said. "Handling all the details we need to have figured out before we talk to Brentworth."

"Did Rose tell you she used to film little videos? It was a kind of cooking show," Gigi said.

Beside her Rose stiffened.

Her sisters had touched a sore spot. What was it?

"My yoga studio had a class on using technology for mindfulness."

"You can call it mindfulness." Gigi laughed.

"You should show them to Ash," Cassie said.

"I did a few videos for the class. They were basically me making salads mindfully."

"I'd love to see them," Ash said.

"They were really good," Ty added.

"Ash is a professional director. I am not going to show her a video I filmed on my phone," Rose said. "And I lost those files a long time ago."

"That's too bad," Cassie said. "You really got into making them." To Ash she added, "People followed her."

"We put everyone's videos on a class YouTube channel," Rose said. "The class followed the channel."

Gigi grinned. "The mindfulness teacher turned the comments off on one of Rose's videos because people were posting dirty things."

"Will you stop!" Rose said. "Did you not get that I like Ash, and this is the dinner where you make me look good, and I show her my charming, *appropriate* family?"

Ash put her arm around her. "You don't have to show me your dirty videos."

Rose buried her face in Ash's shoulder. "They were not dirty." She sounded wan. "And I didn't make any after the class."

"Rose doesn't get excited about hobbies. It's too bad," Gigi said with a seriousness Ash guessed was rare for her. Then it was gone. "Except those little freaks of genetic engineering."

"Stop teasing." Cassie pointed a maternal finger at Gigi.

The conversation turned to other things. Eventually it was time to leave.

Ash's mind darted to her bedroom. The rest of the house was still bare, but she did have a bed. She'd made it with fresh sheets and pushed her piles of clothing into the closet. The room smelled of the lavender and lilac flowers she'd put in a vase on the dresser. When was the last time she'd bought flowers? And she'd removed the huge monitor she'd set up in the corner so she could play *Silent Spring II* from her bed. It wasn't the Benson-Lux Hotel, but it didn't say, *I was so messed up I couldn't buy furniture when, literally, all I had to do was hit BUY NOW on Amazon.* Hopefully she could bring Rose to such heights of pleasure Rose wouldn't notice if Ash shied away from her touch. Hopefully Rose wanted to go home with her.

"I like your sisters," Ash said as they lingered on the street beside their parked cars.

Above them an old oak shadowed the streetlight. Rose touched her car door handle, but she didn't open it. Ash didn't give the command for the Batmobile to open its wings.

"They're something, aren't they?" Rose looked back at the house, love and the warm kitchen lights shining in her eyes. "They're the best. They like you, too."

"How do you know?"

Rose let go of the door handle and came over to Ash. "Because I'm happy."

Ash reached for Rose's hand and pulled her closer.

"And they're watching us," Rose said.

"I don't see anyone in the house."

"Exactly. If they weren't watching, you'd see everyone in the kitchen. Nerf balls flying. The usual."

"Does that mean I shouldn't kiss you good night?" Ash asked.

"That means you should."

But it was Rose who kissed Ash, pulling her close without hesitation and threading her hands through Ash's hair. The kiss took Ash's breath away. And she felt like the hometown girl seduced for the first time. And she felt like rooftops and infinity pools. Her body and soul swooning in Rose's hands.

They finally parted. Rose asked Ash before Ash could ask her.

"Do you want to go back to my house?"

chapter 44

Rose sped across the Broadway Bridge. Ash was already parked on the street outside her town house. From inside Rose's door, the dogs let out a cacophony of howls. Rose unlocked the door and the pugs exploded out, snorting and sneezing to express that they were dying of hunger and loneliness. There was no way to make a sexy entrée.

"I have no game with these two," Rose said.

Ash knelt down and kissed Muffin on the nose. "Do you bite? Are you a watchdog?"

Cupcake thrust himself between them and licked her eye.

Ash stood up. She looked so fucking cool with her tattoo sleeve, her tailored vest, her ripped jeans. The sway of her hips, the hint of cleavage revealed by her vest. *And* she kissed Muffin on the nose. And she joked with Cassie and Gigi. And she talked to Ty like they were old friends.

"I have to walk them," Rose said apologetically.

"I'd love to walk these little mutants with you," Ash said.

Rose wished the pugs would take themselves around the block. Still once they were on the cool, dark street, she didn't mind. It felt like the world had gotten bigger, the sky higher.

Maybe her life wasn't set on a fixed course that she could never escape. Maybe she and Ash could be for real…forever. Yes, Rose would still be a business consultant telling people how to run their cauliflower empires, but she'd live in the orbit of Ash's passion and her creativity.

Muffin and Cupcake found a french fry squished on the sidewalk and began snuffling at it, their flat faces perfectly designed for scraping stuff off pavement. It was imperative that they scrape every molecule of fry off the concrete. For once Rose didn't pull them away.

"Who am I to stand in the way of joy?" Rose said and kissed Ash, the leashes dangling from her hands, her heart lifting into the sky.

Once inside again, Rose took Ash's hand and led her up the stairs to the bedroom.

"I'm trying very hard to act like a lady." Rose closed the door behind them, even though it meant in the morning she'd find two pug skeletons, their entire essence having wasted away at the devastation of being forced to sleep on the beige Chesterfield sofa instead of her bed. "But it's hard after what you did to me in LA."

Sex was fun, but she'd never thought much about sex after she'd had it. Sex was like black coffee. Some was better than others, but you didn't sit around reliving every sip. Except she'd been reliving every moment with Ash, and her body cried out for that pleasure and release.

Ash leaned over and gently bit the junction of Rose's neck and shoulder. The prick of pain undid her.

"I want you," Rose whispered.

She took Ash's hand and pressed Ash's fingers into the fabric of her dress. Ash obliged by kneading her gently. Rose's legs almost gave out. She wrapped her arms around Ash's neck and bent her knees trying to get more of the delicious pressure Ash was applying.

Then they were in bed. Rose was naked and Ash was naked except for silky boy shorts. Ash held Rose down with a palm on Rose's chest.

"Let me."

Once again, Ash kissed down Rose's body, lingering on her belly. She massaged the flesh beneath Rose's pubic hair, each swirl of her fingers tugging on Rose's labia so they brushed against her clit. Sweet, excruciating waves of pleasure every time Ash moved her hand.

"How do you do that?" Rose sighed.

She wouldn't be quite so loud this time. She'd never been a lie-still-and-think-of-the-queen lover. But in LA something inside her had opened up. She'd sung an opera of *oh gods* and *right theres*. It'd been a little extra, as Ty would say.

Then Ash pressed the heel of her hand against Rose's clit, moving in a slow, deep circle. Heat mounted in Rose's body until she was clutching the sheets. Ash placed a pillow under Rose's hips. She didn't kiss down Rose's body this time, just buried her face between Rose's thighs, pulling all of Rose into her mouth.

"Oh God!" Rose gasped. "Yes...Ash...that's so good. I want you. I couldn't wait until...this...yes."

Ash kissed her until Rose's whole body was trembling. It was so good. Rose's body arched. Her eyes squeezed shut.

"Fuck. Yes! I'm coming."

The pugs probably thought she was dying.

After Rose stopped seeing stars, she rolled Ash onto her back, pressing against her and kissing her, one hand trailing down Ash's flat belly.

"Is it because you're a director?" Rose asked.

"What?"

"That you are such a good lover. You know how to get people where you want them."

Ash chuckled. "Do you want me to call cut and get you a sandwich?"

Rose stroked the silk between Ash's legs. Ash tensed. Rose stilled her fingers.

"I want to show you how good that felt," Rose murmured, kissing Ash's nipple in between words. "If you'd like that."

"Okay," Ash said quietly.

Rose drew Ash's nipple into her mouth and pinched it with her lips. Ash lifted her chest toward Rose. The tension in Ash's body felt like desire, but it felt like Ash was bracing herself, too. Rose slowed down.

"Tell me if I get it wrong."

Rose slid her hand beneath Ash's shorts and traced the outside of Ash's labia, then parted the delicate folds, savoring the newness of Ash's body. Delicate. Beautiful. Mysterious. The feel of Ash beneath her fingers filled her with a tenderness that ached even more deeply than the pulse between her legs. Ash closed her eyes. Rose watched her face. Ash moaned in pleading gasps. Rose circled her clit without touching it.

"That feels good," Ash whispered.

Rose pressed closer to Ash's clit.

"Oh," Ash gasped as if she were surprised. "That's...that's..." Her voice trembled.

Rose dipped a finger inside her. Ash's hips bucked. Then suddenly she caught Rose's wrist.

"Don't!"

She pulled Rose's hand away. Ash sat up. She looked around like she wanted to escape.

"What is it?" Rose sat up next to her, hovering a hand over

Ash's thigh without touching her. "Are you all right? Did I hurt you?"

Ash seemed to come back to herself and pressed a hand to her face. "Fuck. I'm sorry. Can we pretend that didn't happen?"

Rose's heart swelled with concern. "We don't have to pretend because you don't have anything to be sorry about."

"It's nothing," Ash said forcefully. "Next time. I promise."

Rose wouldn't feel this aching need to hold Ash if it were nothing.

"Should I leave?" Ash said quickly.

"Sweetheart, no! Don't even *think* that you should leave." Someone would have to tear Ash away before Rose would send her back into the night. Rose beckoned for Ash to curl up in her arms. "Can I spoon you?"

Ash rolled on her side. Tentatively, Rose put her arm around Ash, waiting to feel her relax. Then she pulled her closer, pressing her chest to Ash's back.

Ash gave a little laugh. "Victoria would have kicked me out of bed if I asked her to spoon me. She hated that word."

"Too culinary?"

"Too sweet."

"Well"—Rose squeezed Ash a little tighter—"I'm not Victoria, and I feel sweet about you."

Rose's daylight alarm woke her at six a.m. with fake sunshine and the sound of birds chirping. It was not the meditative easing into the day that the SunGlo company promised. It was a hateful light and hateful fake birds because it meant morning and work. It meant tearing herself away from Ash. She turned off the alarm, moving as little as possible so as not to disturb Ash who was still asleep, the blankets covering her up to her waist, her chest bare. Her dark hair fanned out on the pillow, tangled like she'd been dancing through a magic forest and fairies had tied it up in bunches. Rose studied her.

What is it?

There were a lot of reasons why a person didn't want to be touched. None of them were Ash's fault. Not one of them would make Rose turn away. Ash opened her eyes slowly.

"I wish I could call in sick," Rose said.

And never leave this bed.

"Is that my cue to go?"

"You can stay all day long. Cupcake and Muffin would love it." Rose leaned over and kissed Ash. "I wouldn't mind, either."

Ash stretched. "I suppose I have a massive amount of work to do, too. Mini Pet Mart isn't going to advertise itself."

"I'll make us coffee."

Rose got up reluctantly. Ash fished around in the pocket of the jeans she'd left on Rose's floor.

"My phone's dead," she said. "Do you mind if I use your laptop and shoot Emma a quick email?"

Rose tried not to stare at Ash as she made coffee and Ash sat on the sofa topless, Rose's laptop on her lap, Muffin and Cupcake wedged on either side of her. The morning light brightened. Rose didn't bother pulling the living room curtains although her across-the-street neighbors could probably see Ash's silhouette. Rose didn't want to change anything. This moment was perfect. She tried to sear it into her memory because maybe she'd only enjoy this sight once or twice before Ash lost interest or moved to LA and drifted away. Or maybe this sight would become so familiar, she'd forget what it was like to see Ash in her space for the first time.

chapter 45

Ash spread a set of hastily hand-drawn storyboards in front of her customer, a solo practice lawyer specializing in small business development. Ash had almost forgotten about the appointment.

"Here are some possibilities for your ad," Ash said.

"Tell me about this part." The lawyer indicated a frame.

Ash tapped her pen beside the frame. Her body was there, holding the pen, wearing the same clothes she'd worn the night before. Her mind was on the sidewalk outside Rose's house kissing her. *Have a nice day at work. Don't work too hard. Text me. Maybe do lunch?* They were like girlfriends. Such a cute word. Could Ash have a girlfriend after everything that had happened to her? Not a tortured affair. Not a volatile lover? Not years of celibacy? But a girlfriend to walk dogs with, to send memes to, to fall asleep on the couch with? And to make love with.

"It's..." Ash studied the frame.

It looked like a robot vacuuming.

"This is you shaking hands with a satisfied client." Ash was guessing. Some of the drawings looked vaguely sexual. "If you went with this version, we'd start with a shot of you touring one of your client's shops."

Had she blown the making love part? Rose hadn't hurt her. Ash had felt an orgasm mounting for the first time in years. It had been wonderful. Then it overwhelmed her. Victoria's taunts and complaints had crawled back into her mind, which should have made her keep going. *Fuck you, Victoria!* But she'd panicked. Rose didn't seem to mind, at least not to judge. But how long would Rose be patient? A month? A year? Could Ash relax if she was worried about not relaxing fast enough?

"It looks more like..." The lawyer turned the paper around.

Yeah, it did. Ash amended the drawing. There. Now it no longer looked like the lawyer was groping her client. She described the filming process, cost, and guarantees. The lawyer signed and left. Maybe she would be Ash's last advertising customer. Maybe Ash would farm the work off on a subcontractor while she started work on her film.

Her mind spun. Her heart raced. She'd have to be in California. Could they do long distance? She couldn't ask Rose to fly. But at least they wouldn't be working together. The mistakes she made on set wouldn't be mistakes in her relationship. Her failures wouldn't hurt Rose's career. And Rose wouldn't need Ash's triumphs to succeed. The filming schedule was six days on, one day off. Ash could catch a flight out after they finished shooting, maybe at ten or twelve at night. She'd have hours with Rose before she flew back the next night. Could Rose take the time off if she came on a weekday?

Ash sat down at one of the computers and called up flight schedules. Expedia loaded slowly. What were the commuter schedules like? Nothing flew from LA to Portland after ten.

No, United did. But through Seattle. The layover was only twenty minutes. Could she make it? What were the gates?

She stopped. *Breathe.* Brentworth hadn't said yes. The pitch deck had to be perfect. Anxiety over the pitch should cancel out anxiety over the yet-to-exist long-distance relationship with Rose. Like chemistry class. Acid and alkaline. You couldn't have both in the same bowl. She couldn't panic over two mutually exclusive events. But yes she could. She forced herself to close the travel sites.

She googled *cherry covered apron*. She never watched at work—it was too private—but she had to calm down. She had to work on the lawyer's ad and edit the proof of concept. She opened Cherry Covered Apron's latest video. It was more sexual than the rest. Cherry Covered Apron ran her fingers up and down a stalk of chard. It wasn't phallic. It was more like running her fingers up and down a woman's slit. Ash turned up the audio. Cherry Covered Apron whispered, *This is the only moment that matters.* Her microphone caught every susurration of breath. Every syllable sent a shiver down Ash's back. She closed her eyes.

"You're safe with me," Cherry Covered Apron whispered.

Ash's breath slowed. She relaxed. Whatever magic spell Cherry Covered Apron cast on her vagus nerve worked.

She didn't hear Emma come in until Emma clapped her on the shoulder. Ash jumped.

"I know you watch this stuff. Let me see. Maybe I'll finally get it." Emma leaned over.

Ash tried to close the browser.

Emma swatted her hand away. "This one's dirtier than the rest."

"It's not dirty."

Cherry Covered Apron's fingers glided up the chard stalk.

"How is that not dirty?" Emma laughed. "Oh, wow, look, it's got pre-cum."

A drop of water slid down the chard.

"It's a woman," Ash protested.

There was nothing wrong with the penis—a beautiful thing for people who liked it—but Cherry Covered Apron was a lesbian. She had to be. Ash could almost feel Cherry Covered Apron's touch on her, loving and reverent.

"The chard is a girl?"

What had Ash just said? The chard was a woman? She was ridiculous. And maybe she wasn't thinking about chard. She was remembering Rose's touch.

From behind her, she heard the studio doors open. She turned. Rose stood in the doorway, two coffees in hand. Ash reached for the mouse to close out the browser, then stopped. Watching ASMR wasn't shameful. If Rose liked her, she wouldn't have a problem with this harmless self-soothing.

"Chard is like the least sexy vegetable in the world," Emma added.

"It's sexier than kale," Ash said, her attention focused on Rose.

Rose strode toward them. Her business suit seemed to swish more freely than it had the other times she'd come from work. Her smile was warm.

Emma waved at Rose. To Ash she said, "Rose is going to find out." Emma shoved Ash's shoulder.

Cherry Covered Apron was still playing. Ash swallowed back a flash of anxiety. Sharing your weird interests was part of being in a relationship, and Cherry Covered Apron had seen her through dark days. Rose would like that. She'd be glad there'd been something to comfort Ash when she could barely walk and couldn't sleep because every time she closed her eyes she was crashing into the guardrail again. Ash pushed her chair aside, not to *show* Rose the screen but clearing the way so she wasn't hiding it.

Rose looked. She took a step closer. Her eyes widened. She looked like she was going to drop the coffees.

"What, Ash? How...?"

chapter 46

Rose couldn't breathe. Ash was looking at her videos, laughing at them with Emma. After last night. After they'd fallen asleep in each other's arms. After they'd kissed goodbye on their way to work like a happily married couple. After Rose had told Ash about her parents, and Ash had told her about her accident, trust growing between them. Hanging out with Ash and her sisters, there'd even been a moment when Rose thought maybe one day she could tell Ash about Cherry Covered Apron. She could say, *When I film these videos, I glimpse another life where I did something I loved. Like you. Like my sisters. I can't tell my sisters I want to leave my job and follow a wild passion. I can't tell them I've stayed at Integral Business Solutions so I had enough money to protect them. If I do, I taint things I've done out of love. I say, I sacrificed my life for yours. I say, Feel guilty. I say, You should have said no. But sometimes at night I lie awake and calculate the cost of everything I've done and not done. The budget breaks even, but there's a line in the spreadsheet that should be filled with my dreams, and it's blank.*

Except she wouldn't say those things.

Rose's mind reeled. She saw her own hands stroking the crisp, red stalk. She stepped closer just to be sure. It was her video. How could Ash think it was okay to invade Rose's privacy? To take something like this and show it to her friend?

"Ash wants to show you this weird-ass stuff she found," Emma said, like Rose should be in on the joke. Like the worst high school bully. *I will humiliate you, and you have to laugh and take it.*

Rose's face burned with embarrassment and her eyes burned with hurt. Ash had been on her computer. She'd gone through Rose's folders, seen the video files, opened one. Maybe all of them. Then snagged them from Rose's computer—she probably had a million gigabits of memory on the fob on her keychain—and she'd shown them to Emma. They were laughing at her. Ash wasn't even worried. She looked cheerful. If she'd shown them to Emma with concern—*I think she might be into something weird*—that would at least mean Ash cared. But she was laughing the way Gigi laughed about the man who brought an econo-size lube to their first date.

Rose stared at Ash. Gigi would throw the coffees. Ty would cry. Cassie would say, *I'm going to talk to our family lawyer.* Rose did what she did best: put on her professional face and told it like it was.

"I don't think this is going to work."

Rose had to leave before she cried.

"What?" Ash looked confused.

"Is that who you are?" Rose stared at the computer screen.

Ash closed the browser. "How long were you watching?"

Now Ash had the audacity to look upset.

"Long enough."

Rose set the coffees down, then picked them back up again. What would she do with her hands?

Walk out.

"What are you doing with this stuff?" Rose demanded.

"It's nothing…" Ash said.

"Nothing?"

"Don't give her shit about it," Emma said. "It's her kink."

Ash looked at Emma. "Give us a minute."

Emma planted her feet like she might throw a punch.

"Please," Ash said.

Emma stomped past Rose, holding her gaze the whole time.

Rose's heart was plummeting down and down. Every sweet moment with Ash rewriting itself in light of this screen and Ash and Emma's laughter.

"Do you get off on this?"

Ash looked utterly convincing as the wounded lover. She twisted her hands. She stood up and took a step toward Rose and then stopped.

"I'm sorry." Ash hung her head. "I know I have issues, but it's not that bad."

Ash had been through so much. This was like compulsive shoplifting. It was a mental health issue. But that didn't make it okay to hurt the person you were with. How many times had Rose told Ty not to rescue broken women if it broke her, too? How many times had she told Gigi that if they did it once, they'd do it again?

"This isn't okay whether you have issues or not," Rose said, holding back tears. "I can't be with someone—" Rose felt like she'd been punched in the chest. All she wanted was Ash. And she was the one who was going to end it. "I can't be with someone who's going to be like you were last night and then watch these."

Ash's chin quivered. Then anger and a fragile determination came over her. She straightened. "If you actually liked me, you could have given me time."

"No." Rose should leave. There was nothing more to say. She stayed frozen in place.

"You have a right not to want all my baggage." Ash's voice cracked but her gaze was steady and there was fire in her blue eyes. "I wish I was whole for you. I wish you could fuck me with a five-pound dildo if that's what you wanted." Ash wrapped her arms around herself. "And I'm sorry I'm not ready to have sex the way you want. And I'm sorry you think watching these videos makes it worse, that it's disgusting or whatever you think." Her voice dropped to a whisper. "But are they that bad? Have you even watched ASMR? This morning when you kissed me, were you just thinking of a way to get out of this because you could have a woman who wasn't afraid to be touched? Victoria hated me when I couldn't be that person." Ash gasped back a sob. "I thought you were different."

Rose forgot that she had ever filmed Cherry Covered Apron.

"You think this is because of last night?"

Rose set the coffees down. One missed the table and exploded on the floor. She didn't even look.

"Of course." Silent tears slid down Ash's cheeks.

"Why would I be mad about last night?"

"I should have let you touch me."

"Not if you didn't want it."

Rose crossed the distance between them in two steps and wrapped her arms around Ash, holding her so close she had to remind herself that Ash still needed to breathe.

"Ash, I would never want you to do anything you didn't want to do. I was worried that I hurt you, but I would never be mad about that."

Ash pressed her face to Rose's neck.

"And I don't have the ab strength to fuck with a five-pound dildo." That coaxed a watery laugh from Ash. Rose cherished the sound. "Sweetheart, what's going on?" The endearment rolled easily off Rose's lips. "Last night was wonderful. You undid me, and then you slept in my arms and walked my pugs in the morning."

"I have…sexual dysfunction. I hate the word. Emma's always saying, *It's just like any other disorder. No one's going to hate you because you have high blood pressure.* But that's different. I let you down."

Rose wanted to hold Ash forever so nothing could ever hurt her because she loved her. It was so big and so simple. *I love you.*

"What makes you think that could ever change how I feel about you?"

Ash sniffed, her cheek pressed to Rose's shoulder.

"It's part of why Victoria left." Ash didn't lift her head from Rose's chest. "We had two things: film and sex. And since the accident, sex hurts. My body tightens up. It feels like the bruises from the accident again. At first, they thought there was soft tissue damage, but it wasn't. You don't want to hear all this."

Rose stroked Ash's still-tangled-from-sex hair.

"I want to hear anything you want to tell me."

"I saw pelvic floor specialists. It wasn't physical. It was from trauma, depression. I don't know. It hurt to have sex." The words spilled out, as though Ash had been holding everything in, and now, finally she'd found all her words. "Victoria said fucking me was like fucking a china teacup."

"I will find her and kill her." Rose didn't mean it, but if the laws around manslaughter weren't so strict…

"I want to be better."

"Did I hurt you?" Rose tipped Ash's chin up so she could search her eyes for the truth.

"It felt good, but I got...scared."

Rose stroked Ash's back.

"I'll disappoint you," Ash whispered.

"You will not disappoint me."

They were quiet for a moment, Ash still resting in Rose's arms but not clinging to her.

"You'll give me another chance?" Ash asked.

Rose stepped back. The fire had gone out of Ash's eyes, and she just looked vulnerable. All Rose wanted was to make Ash feel safe, to take her to bed and do absolutely nothing if that was what Ash wanted. But she'd given Ty too much good advice. *If someone betrays you once, they're going to do it again.*

"The videos."

"It's ASMR. I know it's weird, but it's not wrong," Ash said. "There's science behind it. Auto sensory meridian response. It's something about senses blending. Synesthesia. Something about the vagus nerve. People hear sounds and they feel tingly. It's not sexual. I mean, it can be, but..."

Ash was giving her a lecture on the vagus nerve?

"When I was recovering this was the only thing that made me feel at peace. It was the only time I could connect with my body. But it's not...I wouldn't make you watch it."

Rose stepped back. "It's the *videos*." *Focus*. "You took videos off my computer. Videos that were obviously private. And then you showed them to your friend. That's wrong, Ash."

"I would never look at your private stuff." Ash looked at her like she was waiting for Rose to acknowledge the obvious truth of the statement.

"I can see your screen."

"I checked my email. I didn't touch your stuff. Why would I?"

"Then how did you get them?"

"They're online. Rose, I would never, ever take something of yours or show Emma something you didn't want to share." Ash took Rose's hand.

Rose should have shaken her off. She didn't.

Ash pulled her to the computer. "It's a website. There's this woman. Cherry Covered Apron. No one knows her real name or anything about her. No one's contacted her and heard back. I wrote to her to say thanks but obviously she didn't write to me, either. She's a cult figure in the ASMR community." She stopped. "Do you watch them, too?"

Rose barely got the word *no* out.

"Look." Ash gestured to the computer.

Rose hadn't looked at her actual website since she set it up. There were thumbnails of all her videos. There was the URL.

"I never look at it," she whispered.

Ash had watched Cherry Covered Apron? No one watched it. No one even knew it existed. No one found websites that weren't ruthlessly marketed on social media. She posted the videos because sending them out into the massive black hole of the internet satisfied some exhibitionist impulse that she really should go to therapy and work out.

Ash's brow furrowed. "It's harmless. Why are you so mad?"

Some little part of Rose had been with Ash after the accident on Highway 101. Her voice had reached Ash through Cherry Covered Apron. In some miraculous, time-traveling way, she'd comforted Ash in her worst hours.

"Rose?" Ash asked.

"These aren't from my computer?"

"Of course not."

Rose put her arms around Ash's neck, laughing in her relief.

"You've been watching these for years?" Rose felt giddy.

"Don't judge," Ash said, not teary this time, but adorably miffed. "Everybody's got their thing."

"Yes, they do." Rose squeezed her. "They really helped you?"

"Yeah."

"Wow." Rose stepped back, looked at the ceiling, looked around the room. No one had ever seen these videos except the one person who needed them. The woman she loved. "I'm so happy."

"I don't understand."

Rose held out her hands. The same hands in the videos. Ash took them.

"For a director," Rose said, "and my lover, you're not very observant."

"What do you mean?"

Rose kissed her, then murmured in her ear, her lips brushing Ash's skin, "This is Cherry Covered Apron."

chapter 47

Rose felt a weight lift off her shoulders. She'd told someone about Cherry Covered Apron, and not just someone. Ash. Who watched and loved her videos. Ash hadn't taken them off her computer. (How could Rose have thought that? But then how could Rose have explained the mind-blowing coincidence?) The crushing sadness Rose had felt a moment before when she spoke the words that she thought would end it with Ash was gone.

Ash stared at Rose, her mouth agape.

"Rose, do you know how many people watch these?"

"You and no one else." Rose laughed.

Ash shook her head. "You have stans. You have Instagram pages that repost stills and they have hundreds of thousands of followers. I've screen-captured every video in case your site went down. You're a legend."

Ash picked Rose up an inch off the ground. Rose squealed.

"I've been in love with you since I first heard your voice." Ash set Rose down.

In love.

"You're Cherry Covered Apron." Ash held Rose at arm's length, then drew her back into a hug, then pushed her back out. "This is like meeting Dua Lipa and Kamala Harris and Hitchcock all in one day."

"There is no way those names can appear on the same list."

"And Greta Gerwig. You're the Kathryn Bigelow of ASMR. You're like the secret Céline Sciamma."

"I don't know who those people are, but I'm guessing that's not true," Rose said, but in her heart she was still spinning an inch off the ground.

"We have to skip work," Ash said. "I have to spend the rest of the day telling you what an amazing artist you are."

Rose was an amazing consultant. She rolled the word *artist* around her mind, trying it on for size. She wasn't an artist. Except the word fit even better than a tailored Marianna Villard dress. Her heart swelled like it had when Ash kissed her onstage. Anything was possible.

"I have double-booked meetings all day." She already knew she was canceling them all.

"Perfect. You tell one you had to cancel for the other and the other one you had to cancel for the first one."

"We"—Rose corrected herself—"you have a proof of concept to finish." She had to at least pretend to be responsible.

"I cannot find out that my lover is Cherry Covered Apron"— Ash's whole body was an exclamation mark—"and just go back to work! Can I tell Emma? No. I won't." Her face went serious for a moment. "This is your private life. I would never. But why haven't you told anyone? Call in sick. We'll get breakfast." She took out her phone. "I'm texting Emma that everything's fine and we're taking off."

Rose pulled out her phone. "Chloe, can you cancel my meetings this afternoon."

"Should I call someone?" The concern in Chloe's voice went beyond do-you-have-a-migraine. "What's happening?"

That's how often Rose had bailed on work. Chloe thought *cancel my meetings* meant *I am literally dying right now.*

"I'm fine." *Better than fine.* "I decided to take the day off."

Ash's idea of breakfast was a Thai street food restaurant and drinks. Ash folded her hands on the table and leaned forward.

"Your videos are amazing. I hope you know that."

"You were still laughing." And it still stung now that Rose thought about it.

"Not in a bad way," Ash said earnestly. "Emma's been teasing me about my ASMR fetish for years, but she approves. She knows what a lifesaver it was. And watching a video of a woman fondling chard *is* funny. Getting turned on by a woman fondling chard *is* weird. But that's not a bad weird. Weird is different. Weird is cool. Are those the dirty cooking videos your sisters were talking about?"

"Those were the start."

The waiter placed their drinks on the table. Ash took an enthusiastic gulp.

"The first one was a banana. I didn't mean for it to come out—"

"Sexy as hell?"

Ash pulled a piece of pineapple out of her glass and sucked on it seductively.

"You're terrible," Rose protested, although Ash sucking on a piece of fruit was kind of like the culmination of all Rose's secret dreams.

"I should have realized it looked phallic. But I was focused on the mindfulness part. I liked focusing on what I was doing. To really appreciate food and water and air and my own hands. The class talked about how technology can pull us away from each other, but if you think about it as a metaphor, it unites us, too. All those satellites and signals carrying little bits of us everywhere, making us all part of everything. Around that time, I was testing out a website editor for one of my clients. I created an account for Cherry Covered Apron because I have an apron with cherries on it. Then I recorded my first Cherry Covered Apron video." Rose felt herself blushing.

"The one where you're peeling carrots."

"God, is it still up?"

"You didn't take it down."

"I should. I didn't even have a USB mic. That was just my phone. It's probably terrible."

"People love it." Ash reached out and put her hand on Rose's. "Your sisters didn't tell me. They just said a few cooking videos. Were they trying to be discreet? You're not embarrassed of your work, are you?"

Rose's thoughts swirled. Ash liked her videos. People watched her videos. Her sisters, who shared everything with her, didn't know.

"I haven't told them."

Ash cocked her head. "But you've posted two hundred and twelve videos. It's your thing."

"I haven't kept track of how many I made."

"Two hundred and twelve. I know because I look forward to every one. But why haven't you told them?"

"You know how I said I was jealous of them?"

Ash nodded.

It felt good that have this…history with Ash. Rose had confided in Ash. Ash remembered. Rose could draw on that if she started a sentence she didn't feel like she could finish. Ash accepted her already.

"I would have told them if I didn't love doing it so much. But when I film those videos, I feel like..." That was the sentence that was hard to finish. "I feel like I want more in my life. I want to do things that I love doing, not just occasionally in the privacy of my own home, but for work. And I know that's silly because plenty of people have jobs they don't love."

"That doesn't mean you can't go after something you want." Ash squeezed her hand.

"I need to keep my job so that if anything ever happens to my sisters or Cassie's kids, and they need money, I can help. And if my sisters knew that I was working a job I didn't love, living a life that wasn't everything I want, for *them*—it would put a strain on everything. If they needed help, they'd feel guilty. And maybe I would start to resent them. If I knew they knew I wasn't happy, and they still counted on me..."

The waiter brought salad rolls and curry. Rose put a roll on her plate and rolled it back and forth, listening for the soothing sound of the wrapper sticking to the plate. She stopped when she realized what she was doing and put her hands in her lap.

"That's hard," Ash said.

"I tried doing the mindfulness exercise without the videos but there was something about being on film and pretending that people were watching that just made it...different. Better. Charged."

"*Charged* is a great word for it. Filming the fern scene... there's something about the camera...even though it's all starts and stops and breaks for lighting changes. Creating something for people to see is a thrill. And your work is elegant. That's why you had the Schoeps microphone, isn't it?"

Rose nodded.

"Nice equipment." Ash imbued the words with a hint of teasing, as though testing the water to see if Rose was ready to joke or not.

The emotions that had knotted her stomach relaxed. Suddenly she was hungry.

"Are you trying to talk dirty to me?" She touched the tip of her tongue to her lips and held Ash's gaze.

"Do you like it?"

"Yes."

"Good."

They both chuckled.

"Do you find them arousing?" Ash was obviously trying to ask in the most neutral way possible.

You spent half an hour rubbing pomegranate seeds online. No judgment.

"Not exactly."

Ash took a big bite of salad roll, chewing through her words. "I do. Some more than others. The ones with mangoes...whew." She fanned herself.

Rose blushed, but it was mostly with pleasure.

"And you're helping people," Ash added. "People like me." She grew serious. "There are people who aren't ready to see sexual content with people or who want content that's completely gender-neutral. Often I watch them or fall asleep to them because they calm me down, but when I saw the first one, it turned me on, and that was the first time I'd been turned on in a long time. Your video made that feeling safe."

The sun shone down into the valley between buildings, lighting their table. The salad rolls glowed. The yellow curry was the color of dandelions.

"What do I do now?" Rose asked.

"Whatever you want. I'm sure you could monetize this. Do a paywall. Get a distributor."

"How did you find the site?" Rose asked.

She had actually thought Ash would steal her files. Was that what love did? Make you so desperate for things to be right that you saw wrong where there wasn't any? Skip work? Tell the whole story? Apparently. Rose was in.

"I think I googled *something to bring me back into my body* or *can ASMR help sexual dysfunction*. You came right up. How many hits do you get?"

"I never look at the stats."

Ash pursed her lips, considering. "Do you have your web design program on your laptop?"

"It's web-based."

"Can you log in?"

"Now?"

From a restaurant in downtown Portland in bright daylight? She felt naked. A moment ago, she didn't want anyone to know about Cherry Covered Apron. Now...maybe she did. Her heart beat with the sudden fear of disappointment. What if Ash was wrong and no one looked at the site. What if all the comments were from trolls and bots?

"You don't have to, but if you have your computer in your bag, I could look and tell you how many people are looking at your site."

Rose logged in and passed the tablet to Ash. She followed Ash's fingers as they moved over the screen. She could feel those fingers sliding over her body.

"Here it is," Ash said, nodding with a satisfied look. "One point two million unique hits. And about twelve thousand comments, but you haven't approved them, so they don't show."

One point two million?

She'd written marketing strategies to help businesses get half that many.

"I don't want to know."

"They're good."

"Can you delete them?"

Ash looked up. "They're yours to delete." She scrolled for a while, then typed something into the search bar. "Save this one." Ash bit her lip. Her eyes got misty. She read, *"I know you don't post comments, but maybe you read them. I was in a car accident six months ago. It was bad, and then things got worse. But I wanted you to know that your site is one of the good things in my life right now. I check every day to see if you've posted a new video, and I watch my favorites over and over. I have them on a playlist and I fall asleep to your voice. It's the only way I can sleep. I'll never know who you are. We'll never meet. But I want you to know you helped me, and I'll always be grateful. Thank you, Ashlyn Stewart, Portland, Oregon."*

When Rose looked into Ash's eyes, she saw her own nakedness reflected there.

"Thank you," Rose whispered.

Ash moved to her side of the table, sat down, and placed a kiss on her cheek. "I can't believe I found you."

chapter 48

Ash had cleaned the studio. Okay, she'd cleaned up all the coffee cups, all the Red Bull cans. She'd pulled the sofa off the wall so it faced the largest computer monitor. The finished proof of concept was ready to play. She pushed the sofa a few inches to the left, then adjusted the TV screen to avoid glare, then pushed the sofa back where it had been. Adrenaline skittered through her veins. She felt like she'd drunk too much coffee. What if the proof wasn't as good as she thought? What if no one saw what she was trying to do? But the proof was good, and behind her fears, in a place anxiety couldn't touch because she was certain of her vision, Ash knew it. She'd always been like this before a first viewing: a tornado of nerves and as calm as the ocean. Maybe she was like the ocean with a tornado roiling across its surface while the depths remained still. Did tornadoes go over the ocean?

She placed her hands on the back of the sofa and took a deep breath the way Emma's pink bunny had instructed, but she didn't mind the feeling that she might fly off the screen of her life because she was so wound up. This was *her*. She was a director, like she'd always been, and she was going to keep having moments like this because she was going to keep making movies.

Rose sang out a greeting from the open studio door. She held a cake along with several bouquets of flowers, all of it looking a little precarious in her arms. Ash rushed over to take the cake. Ash set it on the worktable and opened the cake box. The cake was a creamy white. A lacework of green frosting stems, touched with red, danced around the side of the cake.

"Ferns?" Ash asked.

"No, chard." Rose gave Ash a saucy wink.

Ash gave Rose a quick kiss that would have been a long kiss except Raven, Jessica, Emma, Pilot, and Jason had arrived. Pilot air-kissed Ash and then Rose.

"You're lovely for her," he said to Rose.

There were only three more guests to come. They arrived together a minute later: Gigi, Ty, and Cassie.

"Delilah was dying to come." Cassie lowered her voice. "I told her the price of asking you about your private life was not getting to watch your preview. Life has consequences."

Ash laughed. The crew ceded the couch to Rose and her sisters. Emma hopped up on the window ledge. Pilot settled onto an office chair as gracefully as an operagoer. Ash stood in front of the large monitor.

"I am so glad you're here. I could never have done this without you."

How had she ever thought she could do it all alone? How had she forgotten: Film was the ultimate collaboration, hundreds of people (or in this case almost a dozen) each bringing their talent to the production.

Ash moved away from the screen and half sat, half leaned on the arm of the sofa next to where Rose sat. Ash rested her hand on Rose's shoulder. Rose leaned her cheek against Ash's thigh. Everything felt easy between them.

The music soared. The proof of concept was perfect.

"Play it again," Emma called out as soon as it finished.

"Wait," Ty said. "The voice-over at the beginning, that's Rose."

Rose blushed. "I have a good radio voice."

"That's more than a radio voice," Gigi said. "I want you to talk to my customers." She dropped her voice to a sultry alto. *"Waxing your jewel box will change your life."*

"Vulva!" Ty protested.

"I don't sound like that," Rose said.

"You sound better," Gigi said. "Where did you pull that voice out from?"

Ash gave Rose's shoulder a little squeeze, not urging Rose to tell her sisters, just letting Rose know she was there.

"I have hidden depths," Rose said.

The party watched the proof three more times, then toasted.

"So what's the plan?" Emma asked although everyone already knew.

"Today and tomorrow, I practice the pitch a thousand times. Then we fly to LA. My friend Mia is throwing us a pre-party to create some buzz. Then Thursday, Brentworth comes to the theater. We show the proof of concept. I talk about the film. Rose talks about the budget and the logistics." Ash stood up. "A round of applause for Rose Josten." She gestured to Rose. "I couldn't have pulled this together without her, and if I had to explain the budget and all those technical details to Brentworth on Thursday, I'd pass out."

The group gave an appreciative chuckle.

Emma said, "Do I get credit because I found her?"

"I found her at the Pug Crawl." Ash held her hand and drew

Rose to her feet. They hadn't done the pitch yet, but Ash felt like they were already stepping into a winner's circle, ready to lift their clasped hands in victory. "I couldn't do it on my own." There'd been a time when she thought those words meant she was a failure, but she wasn't, and they didn't. "Thank you for being there for me." She leaned over and kissed Rose, blessed by the cheers and whoops of her crew and Rose's sisters.

chapter 49

Tuesday morning Rose arrived early to work. She *would* finish the Baron's consultation portfolio. It was almost there. As soon as they got back from LA, she'd present it to him. Chloe would fly to Iowa to meet him, and Rose would do the official portfolio presentation over Zoom.

"How are you feeling about Beltliner?" It was Howard, leaning against her doorframe.

It was the biggest presentation of her life. She should be thinking about it every second of the day. But most of her seconds were taken up with stats for Ash's proposal and Ash's budget.

"Oh, Beltliner's fine," Rose said, drawing her attention back to Howard's jovial smile.

"That's Rose Josten. Cool as a cucumber. Do you have a minute?" Howard asked. "Closed door?"

"Sure."

Rose didn't feel even a flutter of anxiety. She might have half-forgotten Beltliner, but even distracted she was still the best consultant in the firm.

Howard closed the door behind himself and sat down. "I've got good news and I've got bad news."

Rose crossed her legs and mirrored his body language. "Yes?"

"I saw you're taking more vacation." Howard looked worried. "Everything okay?"

"I'm that person, aren't I? I told Chloe to reschedule a meeting, and she thought I was sick. Everything is fine."

"Good. Good. That's the most important thing. The bad part is this time you *have* to cancel."

"I can't."

"The Baron is coming here. He wants to meet you. He says if you're not up for flying, he'll fly, he'll *hitchhike* he said, to meet the woman who's helping him turn his company around. And he's bringing a reporter from *Forbes*. They want to do a cover story on Integral Business Solutions."

Rose grabbed the squeeze ball off her desk and compressed it beyond the laws of physics. *No. No. No.*

"They want to do the interview Thursday. It's the only day the reporter is free."

It was just like the Cauliflower Baron to plan an inescapable meeting without even asking Chloe to check Rose's calendar. He'd probably planned it in third person. *The Cauliflower Baron magnanimously decided to visit his consultant in Portland.*

"I have to be at…" *A wedding. Surgery. I'm meeting the queen of England.* The lies burned in her throat. Howard had supported her since she was twenty. He'd never talked about what Rose was going through, but he'd always made things work out in her favor. Days off when she needed to take care of Ty. An unexpected bonus when her car broke down.

"If you've got an appointment or something, we can change the time," Howard said, "just not the day."

A *Forbes* interview would be amazing for Integral. It would be amazing for Howard. It would be the crowning jewel of her promotion, the promotion that would give her the kind of job security career coaches told people was a thing of the past.

"Is there any way we can reschedule?" Rose asked.

Rose sat in the love seat in the she-cave. It felt empty without Ash pressed against her. Gigi and Ty weren't bickering. Cassie filled a death goblet and passed it to Rose. It felt heavy.

"I'm fucked," Rose said miserably. "I can't bail on Howard. This is the biggest thing that's ever happened to the company, which is going to be part *my* company. And the partnership still goes up for a vote." All the partners had given her the wink and nod that said they were voting yes, but they hadn't actually voted. "If I don't show up for this..." Rose gulped two huge sips of wine. She was never a two-gulp-in-a-row drinker. "But Ash."

Right now Ash was rehearsing her part of the pitch, waiting for Rose to come over after visiting her sisters, waiting for Rose to weave in her part. Ash had outlined a script where they went back and forth as though they were just chatting, but they were covering all the right details in exactly the right order, Ash's creative fire illuminating Rose's spreadsheets, Rose's spreadsheets grounding Ash's vision.

"Have you told her?" Ty asked.

"No."

Everyone said Brentworth was decisive. Ash would know if she'd won the pitch before she left the theater. She'd share that moment of triumph with Emma, Pilot, and Jason or she'd share her disappointment with Emma over drinks in the hotel. And Rose wouldn't be there.

"Could you just tell Howard you have a meeting in LA? You won't be in town," Cassie asked.

"I don't fly," Rose said miserably.

"But you do!" Ty hopped onto the top of the sofa, crossing her legs underneath her like a little genie.

"That's right," Cassie added. "We're so proud of you."

Gigi rolled her eyes. "Rose means she's spent years telling her boss she can't visit clients because she's afraid to fly, and he's put up with that because he loves her like a father...in a corporate-casual kind of way that doesn't involve talking about feelings...and now she wants to bail on the biggest client of her career to *fly* to LA to...what are the options? Pretend to be visiting a specialty clinic for a disease no one knew you had? Or that you're doing work for free for a secret client? Or you're going to see your lover? I know. We'll kidnap the Baron. I know people."

"Gigi, don't joke!" Cassie's face went tight with real ire.

Rose gave Cassie a wan smile.

Gigi put her wine down, looking more serious than Rose had seen her in years. "Oh, God, Rose, I'm so sorry. I didn't mean to make fun of this. I mean, this sucks. You fix all our problems and I want to fix yours but I don't know how."

"Gigi is right. There's no excuse I can give Howard that isn't a lie," Rose said, "and if I go with Ash, the truth is I'm saying *fuck you* to a company full of people who've supported me right before they decide whether or not to make me partner."

"So you're staying?" Ty's eyes said, *How could you not sacrifice everything on the altar of true love?*

"Can she do the pitch without you?" Cassie asked.

Rose wanted to say yes. Ash was a brilliant director with years of Hollywood experience. Of course she could do the pitch without her business consultant. She wouldn't crack under pressure. But Brentworth would bring a lawyer and an accountant to ask questions. Integral Business Solutions didn't make money because this stuff was simple. People hired consultants and worked with them for months, even years, because you couldn't just hand someone a PowerPoint and say, *Here's how we'll spend your twenty million dollars.*

Rose bit her lip. "Yeah?"

Ty heard the no Rose was actually saying. Ty's eyes narrowed with the disappointment as though her Disney-princess movie had ended with everyone moving to different parts of the country and taking jobs they hated in medical coding...or whatever the equivalent was for mermaids.

"Will Ash understand?" Cassie asked.

"She'd better," Gigi said.

"It'll be fine. These things happen." Rose put on a good face as she left Cassie's house.

Of course, Ash would understand. She would understand because she was not an asshole. She was not the kind of person who would say, *I'm sorry you've worked your whole life for this promotion which will finally give you the security you've longed for ever since your parents were killed when you were twenty, but you need to give up everything to help me get a job that will probably take me out of state and you might never see me again.*

Ash was so not that person. She was kind. She was embarrassed about asking for help. Rose drove the long way to Ash's house, all the way to the St. John's Bridge and back through the Northwest Industrial District, her heart growing heavier with each unnecessary turn.

Ash would understand, but this would be the end. Not that Ash would slam the door in her face. They'd go over the pitch all night, Rose coaching Ash like a tutor helping a student the night before a test they'd be lucky to pass. But Ash had lost her career and been abandoned before. Short of another car crash, Rose couldn't think of a trigger that would hit closer to home for Ash.

Rose parked in front of Ash's house and walked slowly to the door. For a moment she'd thought she could be who she was—the staid, responsible businesswoman—and still have Ash. Why did she never get what she wanted? Why couldn't the fucking Cauliflower Baron use a Doodle poll like everyone else? Why did this all seem so inevitable when just a day before she'd felt like the whole world was opening up?

"Oh my God, what's wrong?" Ash said as soon as she opened the door.

She looked lovely in sweatpants and a loose T-shirt. Braless. Her hair down.

Rose walked in and looked for a place to sit, but of course there wasn't any place except the gaming couch. It felt weird to walk past Ash, through the kitchen, across the enormous living room, and plop down in front of the Xbox to tell her the news, so Rose just stood in the doorway.

"I'm so sorry." A muddled mess of words poured out of her. She was sorry and she didn't want this…but Howard… *Forbes*…normal people didn't just show up without checking calendars. But they hadn't and she couldn't and, and, and… and the effort it took not to blurt out *I think I'm falling in love with you and I'm wrecking everything* made her light-headed.

"Stop." Ash took Rose's hands in hers, then dropped them and placed her hands on either side of Rose's face. "I wouldn't let you come with me."

Rose tried to catch her breath.

"What?"

Ash pressed her lips to Rose's in a firm, quick kiss. "You've worked your whole life for this. This is the job you want to make you feel safe, to protect your sisters."

Ash remembered.

"If you said you were missing the Cauliflower Baron for me, I wouldn't *let* you come. You're going to be on the cover of *Forbes*. And I was in Hollywood. I know about rich, powerful men messing up all your plans because they're rich and powerful and men and they can. Sometimes you get to say *fight the power* but sometimes you just have to show up because you're going to be on the cover of *Forbes* fucking magazine!" Ash clasped Rose's shoulders.

"But the pitch."

"You have twenty-four hours to teach me everything I need to know." Ash beckoned her in and gestured grandly to the sofa. "The best seat in the house. I'll get my laptop."

Ash disappeared upstairs and returned with a high-end gamer's laptop. They worked until three, Rose running numbers with Ash and quizzing her on details of the marketing plan, insurance, and schedule. It didn't feel like they were fixing the problem Rose had made. It felt like they were in it together, not just in their work tonight but in...life. Ash's pitch. Rose's promotion. Howard. Brentworth. The Cauliflower Baron. They were all part of a life Ash and Rose shared, and they were making the most of it together.

Still, disappointment made Rose's heart ache. She wanted to be at the pitch, and not just because she wanted to help Ash. She wanted to be there when Brentworth heard her voice in the voice-over. She wanted to see the part of the proof she'd edited on a screen in a vintage theater. She wanted that life.

Finally, Rose's eyes grew blurry. She pointed to a slide on the laptop but lost her train of thought.

"That...is a slide."

Ash laughed. She had the perpetual shadows under her eyes, but lack of sleep didn't seem to make her more tired.

Somewhat-tired was her permanent state, unaffected by sleep or sleeplessness.

"You're fading out." Ash closed the laptop, took it off Rose's lap, and set it aside. "I think I've got it." She hesitated. "We should probably sleep but...if you wanted to...you could...we should..."

"Yes." Yes to anything. Rose kissed Ash tenderly. "The word you're looking for is spoon."

chapter 50

Ash shielded her eyes to look at Emma as Emma plopped her suitcase down in front of her motel door. The sun hit the front of the Executive Comfort Suites with blinding ferocity.

"Why are we here?" Emma asked.

"Because this is the biggest moment of our lives."

A few doors down Pilot and Jason were letting themselves into their rooms.

"Dude, they've got a TV with rabbit ears," Jason said. "Vintage!"

Pilot stood at his open door, key in hand, looking like a man about to walk off a plank.

"Why the Executive Comfort Suites?" Emma asked.

"We can't afford the Benson-Lux."

"There are about twenty levels of quality between the Benson-Lux and here."

"Because Rose and I stayed here."

Emma put her suitcase into her room, closed the door, and walked over to where Ash was standing in front of the neighboring door.

"We have to stay here because you and Rose had sex here?" Emma took Ash's key out of her hand and let them both into Ash's room.

The air smelled like Freon and the ghost of cigarette smoke.

"We didn't have sex here."

"Are you sure I shouldn't kill Rose for not being here? You've made us stay in a hotel that probably has blood in the carpet because you're nostalgic about not having sex with Rose here."

Ash flopped on the bed.

"Why is there not a mini bar here?" Emma looked around.

"There's a landline, and I am fine."

When Rose told her, Ash had felt a moment of panic. Forget memorizing budget lines; this was the most important moment of her life, and she wanted Rose there. But Rose had her own life, and she was a rock star even if she didn't love what she did. It felt safe. If the pitch failed, Rose would still be a success. If Ash dropped the ball at work, Rose would comfort her, not fight with her because Ash had messed with her dreams. Rose wanted Ash for Ash, not Ash for what they could do together.

"I think I'm in love with her." Ash gazed at the ceiling, which was probably asbestos but seemed to sparkle as though someone had tossed a cup of glitter in the air.

"So here's the plan." Mia stood in the center of the stage.

The theater was even more beautiful than Ash remembered.

"I've set it up just like you and Rose brainstormed," Mia said. "We'll have you and Brentworth sit there." She pointed to a cluster of seats near the front-center of the audience. "We'll show the clip. Then you'll take Brentworth up to the stage." Mia whirled around in her emerald-green dress. "We'll bring the houselights up. And we've got the full boardroom ready for you." Mia pointed to the curtained wings. "The stagehands will pull it out. There's a conference table, chairs, Bluetooth screen. And of course, we'll have food and drinks and caterers to bring you anything you want. This isn't just a pitch, it's the start of a journey."

"It's amazing." Ash turned slowly. "Thank you."

Mia hugged Ash. Ash squeezed her back.

"I want this for you. Are you sure you don't want peacocks?"

"Next time."

"I'm holding you to that. You have to promise you won't disappear again."

"I promise."

"Good. Now let's talk about the pre-party tonight. We'll have the clip playing on repeat in the theater. Open bar of course. I've got an amazing DJ. He's the only one in LA who can hit that sweet spot between Daft Punk and Mozart. And I've invited all the people who believe in you, so it'll be a packed house."

Ash had remembered a good outfit this time, although the party that filled the Elsinore Theater lobby was more casual than the burlesque show. It was still a party to rival *The Great Gatsby*. People lingered around bistro tables and sat on the gilded stairs. Emma, Pilot, and Jason mingled. Ash recognized at least half the people. Actors she'd worked with. Indie directors she'd commiserated with at film festivals.

A man asked her what she thought about the new trend to return to analog film. A classmate from film school hugged Ash.

"I always thought you'd kick ass when you graduated." The woman seemed to have missed the part where Ash left the industry in shame.

The evening rolled on, relaxed and glamorous. Ash texted Rose a picture.

Ash: *It'd be better if you were here.*

Did that sound like she was guilt-tripping Rose?

Ash: *I'm so excited for your big day tomorrow*

Rose: *Don't stay up too late.*

Ash typed *I* and by some trick of algorithms and Big Brother surveillance, her phone suggested the following text could be *love you.* Ash texted *miss you already.*

Around midnight, Ash said goodbye to Mia and told Jason, Emma, and Pilot not to do anything she wouldn't do. She stepped outside to enjoy the warm night. Some of the cafés on the boulevard were closing up, and the lines outside the clubs had grown longer. She watched as a limo double-parked across the street and the driver got out to open the door for his passenger. It was strange to think that that life was still going on: chauffeurs, staff, and Jewelers Mutual Insurance. She pulled out her phone to call a Lyft, but a voice stopped her.

"Ash."

chapter 51

Of course, Victoria had heard about the party. Victoria's chauffeur stepped out into traffic and stared down another limo so that Victoria could cross. Ash's stomach tightened.

"Hey," Victoria said breathlessly, as though she were greeting a crush she hoped she might see again.

"What do you want?" Ash sounded shaky.

"I heard about your pitch," Victoria said. "They're playing your proof of concept inside. Can I see it?"

A perfectly self-actualized person would say yes. No problem. But Ash didn't have to be perfectly self-actualized. Being herself was just fine.

"No."

"Ash, I'm sorry."

Victoria hadn't changed much. Her blond hair was loose and too long, too straight, too blond. It was a trophy. Someone should invest in it like Bitcoin. *I own a one-sixteenth share of Victoria Crue's hair.*

"I heard about this, and I *had* to be here," Victoria said.

"No, you didn't. There are literally a billion other places you could be right now."

"You're still funny."

"I'm not trying to be funny." All Ash wanted to do was go back to her hotel and text with Rose until they scolded each other for staying up late and then texted some more. She looked at her phone.

Rose: *I adore you whatever happens tomorrow* 🐼🐼🐼 🖤🖤🖤

"We're still friends, right?" Victoria crooned.

The knots in Ash's stomach loosened. Victoria wasn't the bogeyman. Ash didn't have to shrink in front of her. Ash hadn't done anything wrong. And *friends?* Victoria might as well have texted, *I heard you might be getting famous again. I'd like in on that.*

"There was a time for you to show up, and you didn't." Ash's voice didn't tremble. "Why should I pretend that we're friends? So you can tell everyone you forgive me for quitting *The Secret Song* for no reason?"

"I didn't start that. It was just a good story, so people kept telling it. People like to gossip."

"Did you tell them the truth?"

"I tried." Victoria stepped forward. She wore a yellow gunnysack dress with gaping pockets as though she were going to fill them with *Little House on the Prairie* apples. Except it had probably cost eighteen hundred dollars. It swished around her, exuding fakeness.

"But their story made you the victim." Ash crossed her arms. "I bet everyone gave you a break because your ex-wife had done you wrong."

"It wasn't like that. I didn't know what people were saying about you until it was too late."

Ash's heart beat at a surprisingly regular pace. Her leg didn't hurt. Her body didn't clench up at the sight of Victoria.

Memories of their last weeks together floated through her mind like documents on paper, not like a reel she lived over and over again.

"Fine. That was a long time ago. I forgive you."

Victoria stepped closer. Her perfume was the cloying and unidentifiable scent of rich women trying too hard. "I want to explain why I left."

"You pushed me when I was hurt, mentally and physically. You told me to bear up when I was in pain. And when I couldn't, you left. It's not a complicated script."

She loved Rose's anger when she'd told Rose about Victoria. But to her surprise she didn't feel any of her own anger now, only the happy urgency of wanting to text Rose back.

"I tried to help you, Ash. Film is what you are. It's everything to you. When I met you, you were the most intense person I knew. And I fell in love with you, so I went to that space with you." Victoria reached for her.

Ash held her palm up in a stop gesture. "We're not playing that game."

Victoria wrung her hands. "I bought my way into your heart by backing your work. Would you have had time for me if I wasn't your producer? Would it have been worth tearing yourself away from the set to be with me?" Victoria opened her eyes in caricature innocence, then snapped, "That's not a rhetorical question."

Ash sifted through the memories. The nights they had fallen into bed exhausted. The few stolen moments when they got dinner at Jose and Lucy's Diner. The time they got lost in Venice and laughed with relief when they finally turned a corner to find their house. The relief she'd felt when she woke from the accident and saw Victoria there.

"Yes," Ash said. "I would have loved you off set."

"But film is who you are."

"It's part of who I am."

"I didn't force you to come back to the set for me. I forced you to come back because you needed to be that person. You were drunk on depression and self-pity. I thought leaving you would be the wake-up call you needed. Every time my phone rang, every time I got a text, I thought it would be you saying I meant enough to you that you'd become your true self again."

If Victoria actually believed that, she had the emotional intelligence of the piece of metal Ash had run over south of Centralia.

"If that's what you really thought, V, you were wrong."

chapter 52

At one o'clock, they were ready to go. Jason had checked the sound with one of the theater techs. Pilot had dusted Ash's cheekbones with blush. Ash had traded her skinny jeans and tank top for a navy sheath dress, with a matching jacket. One might almost call it a blazer. Mia was also dressed in business attire.

They stood in the lobby. A moment later, one of Mia's assistants opened the door and Brentworth strode in. Three men in suits flanked Brentworth, looking like a cross between lawyers and bodyguards. Brentworth was tiny by comparison. She looked fierce, as though the fierceness of a normal-size person had been condensed into this tiny woman.

Ash's heart raced. This was it. Everything was in Rose's immaculately designed slides. She could do this. Ash took a deep breath and put on her Hollywood smile.

"Good afternoon, Ms. Brentworth." Ash held out her hand.

Brentworth's wrists dripped bracelets.

"This is an unusual way to pitch a film." Her tone said, *Don't be wasting my time.*

I'm not.

"I can't show you *Inevitable Comfort* with a PowerPoint and an MP4. If I could sum it all up like that, I wouldn't be a contender."

Brentworth nodded, a hint of approval in her eyes.

Ash made introductions, then Mia and Ash led Brentworth and her entourage to the seats at the front of the theater. The houselights dimmed. A theater tech started the proof of concept. Rose's voice filled the theater. At the end, Raven knelt down and touched the earth, looking up at Jessica.

"Is any of this perfect?" Raven asked, perfectly transformed into her character. *"Is one leaf in this forest perfect?"*

She uncurled a fern frond and blew on the underside, releasing the spores into the air. (Although, in reality the "spores" were a hypoallergenic, cornstarch-based glitter.) Emma had filmed them beautifully, each mote caught in the sunlight like diamond dust.

"They'll land where they need to be," Raven said.

Brentworth asked to see the clip again. Then Ash invited her up to the stage where the promised boardroom had appeared like a stage play set.

"That was quite a performance," Brentworth said as they took their seats. "One of the best pieces of filmmaking I've seen. Now let's talk about money."

No warming up Brentworth with the stuff Ash did understand. Straight to business. Ash set her tablet on the table, took a deep breath—where was Emma's floating bunny now?—and called up Rose's first slide. It was a blur of numbers.

She could do this.

She heard the tap of heels echo through the theater. Brentworth frowned. Was this one of her entourage arriving late? Ash looked up. For a second the figure was lost in the shadows at the back of the theater. A step later Ash recognized

Rose's silhouette, full-figured and authoritative. Brentworth distilled confidence. Rose exuded it. She strode down the aisle and mounted the stairs. A stagehand had already rushed out a chair for her.

"I'm sorry I'm late," she said as though no one should be surprised by her presence. "My flight was delayed. Repairs. I suppose you do want them to repair the plane, even if it's a hassle."

Rose must have been terrified. Ash wanted to grab her hand. *You're here!* But what had happened with the Baron and *Forbes*? Ash tried to read Rose's eyes, but all she could see was a calm command. *Let's do this.*

"I'm the business consultant on this project."

"Ms. Brentworth is enthusiastic about the film." Ash fumbled for words. "She'd like us to get to the financials."

Rose gave Brentworth a warm, calm smile. "I think you'll like what I have to present."

Rose's recitation of information was perfect. She answered all Brentworth's questions as though they were just having a casual conversation.

When Rose was done, Brentworth held out her hand and in an amazing show of professional intuition, a caterer set a cup of coffee in it.

"That's all very interesting," Brentworth said. "Actually, it's stunning."

Was it a yes? Ash wanted to be outside with Rose, racing around the corner and hiding in a doorway so Brentworth wouldn't drive by and see them squealing and jumping up and down, hands clasped, like best friends on a playground.

"However"—Brentworth took a sip of her coffee—"you're asking for a lot of money for a niche market project." Brentworth studied Rose, then looked to Ash. "Ms. Stewart, what do you think about Ms. Josten's twenty million? Do you think that's excessive?"

They'd asked for too much. Ash glanced at Rose. "We could do it for half."

"And that is the problem," Brentworth said. "You can't. For ten million you can lose money and win at Sundance. You need twenty to make this a commercial success. But that's a big investment for something that's basically fringe."

Fringe? Ash's expression must have revealed her thoughts.

"Oh, you and I know that normal people finding love isn't fringe," Brentworth said, "but a disabled lesbian? A queer ranger-survivalist? The Midwest is still trying to get their minds around espresso. You need high production value. You need known actors. And I'm not making films for Sundance; how are you going to get a return on my investment?"

"I would love to show you our marketing plan," Rose said.

In their practice sessions, they'd presented it together, but Rose took the lead, leaving Ash looking back and forth between Rose and Brentworth. Finally, Rose opened the portfolio of curated stills, advertising mocks, and media outlets. Ash's drawings and Rose's marketing materials looked amazing together.

Brentworth flipped the first two pages. "I want to help you. Maybe in a couple of years."

Like the car crash, it took Ash a second to register the pain. That was no. She'd thought she wanted this with all her heart; she'd wanted it more. She'd wanted it in her DNA, in her bones. Every cell that made her body work wanted this chance. It was over. She thought she might pass out. The organs in her body would shut down, like lights going out in an office building. *Go home. There's nothing here for you now.*

"I could sell my house, invest in more advertising."

Out of the corner of her eye, she saw Rose give a tiny shake of her head. Ash was begging. Investors didn't like desperation.

"What do you need to say yes?" Ash had to try.

"I need to know there's an audience for this, not that you can drum up followers because they're curious what happened to half of Hollywood's *sexiest dysfunctional couple*. It's not a great line on your résumé."

Even now the mistake of building her career with Victoria haunted her.

"By the way, you leveled up." Brentworth raised an eyebrow at Rose, then dismissed the comment with a wave of her bejeweled hand. "This city breeds gossip. Everyone knows everything. What I want to know is if there's an existing market. Are there people who are waiting for this movie? Are there people who will watch it the second they know it's available?"

"We have time to find them," Ash said.

"I don't wait." With that, Brentworth pushed back her chair. "You're very talented, Ms. Stewart."

Goodbye and no thank you.

"Wait." Rose's voice held a touch of the desperation Ash felt. "Ms. Brentworth, we do have fans waiting, about 1.2 million. If you'll give me a moment."

Brentworth didn't pull her chair back in, but she didn't stand up. "I'm listening."

Rose opened a browser on her laptop and typed something. "Are you familiar with ASMR?"

"Vaguely."

There was the landing page for Cherry Covered Apron.

Rose turned her laptop toward Brentworth. "It's about the pleasure some people get from certain sounds. It's a new thing.

It's *the* new thing. What else is new in film? Special effects? Interactive menus?"

Rose smoothed the perfectly smooth cuff of her blazer. When Ash glanced at Rose, Rose's eyes were full of excitement, fear, and the question, *Am I actually doing this?*

"This is a physical reaction to audio in film," Rose said. "People experience ASMR in their bodies. I make ASMR videos, so, obviously, I understand the appeal."

Ash saw the moment Brentworth's eyes landed on the subscribed viewers number.

"I've offered to oversee sound for this production," Rose went on. "My followers will follow me wherever I go. ASMR is new, and fans of new things are loyal. They're hungry. And they've never had something like this before: a full-length film with sound by an ASMR artist."

"I thought you were the business consultant." Brentworth held up her coffee cup, and a caterer appeared out of thin air and refilled it.

The caterer offered Rose and Ash coffee. Ash shook her head. Her heart was beating so fast coffee would kill her.

"I also do sound," Rose said.

"May I watch one?" Brentworth asked.

Rose navigated to a mango video. Rose hadn't shown any-one her videos...except her 1.2 million followers, but that was different. What if Brentworth hated it? What if Brentworth walked away in disgust? Longtime artists could take rejection, but Rose was so new in sharing her art. Artists like that were snails out of their shells, tender and vulnerable. Rose was putting the most private part of her life on the table, the thing she couldn't even tell her sisters. If Brentworth crushed her, it would be Ash's fault. Ash's fault for not being good enough. Ash's fault for not thinking about followers and building a fan base. She'd pulled Rose into something Rose wasn't ready for, and she hadn't protected her. How could Rose forgive her for that? How could she forgive herself?

"Rose, you don't have to," Ash whispered.

Brentworth inched up the volume. *How beautiful. Feel the silky texture. It's luscious like you are.* Emma was right; the videos were sexy but if you weren't into ASMR they were weird AF.

Brentworth watched to the end, her face immobile. Ash held her breath.

Finally, Brentworth said, "Do sound and give my company rights to your work here, it's a yes. Next time, lead with your best assets. This can be monetized, and that will make up for any shortfalls we may experience initially."

Rose's face lit with pride. Ash felt the oxygen had been sucked out of the theater. Brentworth wasn't going to criticize Rose's work; she wanted to own it. Rose couldn't throw her grand oeuvre in to sweeten a deal with Brentworth. If she did... when she realized what she'd done... that Ash let her do it... And what if the movie was a flop and Rose realized she'd leveraged everything for a failure? If Rose kept her life separate, she'd comfort Ash through whatever fails lay ahead. She'd say, *Next time it'll be better.* But if Rose tangled her work with Ash's, eventually Ash would let her down, eventually Rose would realize she could have been more without Ash, eventually Rose would hate her and the beautiful star-speckled magic that was blossoming between them would end, perhaps before it had even really begun.

Ash could have Rose or she could have the film. The choice broke her heart, but she didn't need time to deliberate. Ash reached across the table and closed Rose's laptop. "Cherry Covered Apron isn't on the table."

chapter 53

When Rose looked at Ash, Ash's face was so full of pain and tenderness, it took Rose a second to realize what Ash had said.

Brentworth rose. "Too bad." She turned and strode away, off the stage, and out of the theater without looking back.

"I'm sorry." Ash had gone pale. Makeup blush stood out on her cheeks like a slap. "You can't give her Cherry Covered Apron."

"It's mine to give. What have I done with it all these years? Nothing."

"It's valuable."

"I don't need money. The partnership buy-in is fifty thousand dollars. I'm going to take it out of my *checking account.*"

Okay, actually if she paid the buy-in, she'd have to move it out of her high-yield investment portfolio, but technically it would spend a day in her checking account. Except she hadn't contacted the bank. The partnership was a marriage, and she wasn't in love. She was in love with Ash, with this, with the excitement of the pitch, with the texts they should be sending everyone they knew, with the drinks they should be ordering and the toasts they should be making, with the chance to make art.

"I can make more videos." Rose stood up.

"I know." Ash swiped at her hair but it was pulled up in a French twist. She looked lost in her business dress suit. Where was the ripped Bikini Kill T-shirt?

"We had the deal." Rose stared down at Ash, whose hand still rested on Rose's laptop. "*You* said no. We were all waiting for Brentworth. Would she say yes, would she say no? But you're the one. Ash, we had everything."

All those sacrifices: giving up her music degree, the long hours at Integral, the money she saved in case her sisters needed it. She'd seen a different life hanging above her head like a golden apple. And as she reached for it, Ash had slapped her hand away.

"I can't work with you," Ash blurted out.

No preamble. No *I know you thought we had something. I'm sorry you misunderstood...*

Rose's throat constricted. "I have to go."

Rose hurried off the stage and down the aisle. Ash hadn't promised her anything. Ash had barely blinked when Rose told her she couldn't go to LA. Ash might have been relieved while Rose sat in the airplane, clutching the armrests and refusing to take Gigi's Ativan because she wanted to be clearheaded for the pitch. How could she have been so stupid? She had imagined a glittering new life with Ash. Ash didn't want that life if it meant sharing it with Rose.

Ash followed her.

"What if *Inevitable Comfort* fails?" Ash gasped. "You'd have wasted your work on nothing."

"It's your choice." Rose laid each word out carefully. No

meditation exercise had ever taken the concentration it took not to cry. "It's your movie."

Out of the corner of her eye, she saw Mia and the crew peeking into the theater, then pulling back when she caught sight of them. What did they think? Ash and Rose standing paces apart. Rose with her hands balled into fists.

"I can explain...I saw Victoria."

If Ash ended that sentence with *and we got back together* Rose would give Victoria's picture to Gigi and ask, *Do you really know people who solve "problems"?*

"I loved her."

How could Ash throw that in her face?

"I don't want to hear about how much you love Victoria," Rose spat.

"I don't. That's what I'm trying to say." Ash took a few steps forward, seeming to gain courage. "I did. Once." Ash held her hand out imploringly. "But when we got into business it wrecked everything. We weren't a couple; we were a company. We were together all day every day, but we never *saw* each other. When I got hurt, she left because I was a director who couldn't fulfill the contract. And when I got better...I mean now, with you, I can see it so clearly. Victoria and I might have been happy, but that chance died the day we signed on to our first movie." Ash crossed the space between them. "I don't want to work together if it means losing you."

Now that Ash had stepped closer, Rose could see tears smearing her foundation. And Rose loved Ash for the streak of peach on her cheek. She almost broke at the sight.

"I thought we were going to grow old and buy eight pugs." Why had Rose said it out loud? Thinking about forever with a woman she'd just met was ridiculous. She clutched her arms around herself. No tailored blazer could make her feel strong now. "Was Emma right? You have to do everything on your own? You'd rather lose everything than let me help you."

"You *are* everything." Ash cupped her hands in front of her as though holding something small and precious. "I want to be a director. But I want you more."

Rose heard the crew whisper in the back of the theater. She heard the HVAC system cut in and a car honk outside.

I want you more.

"We're so new, and I don't know if you feel the same way I do. But if you gave Brentworth Cherry Covered Apron, if you had to tell your sisters about it before you were ready, if we worked together, and I disappointed you...I don't want to lose you before we've even begun. I love you."

Rose's heart did not have enough chambers for all her feelings. Had Ash thrown away her dream because she wanted Rose or because she didn't? Had Ash said *love*?

"Your videos are so beautiful," Ash implored. "They're yours. I don't want people to miss how talented you are because they're looking at some film."

"It's not some film. It's your dream."

Rose couldn't catch her thoughts any more than she could catch her breath.

"And I want you to have *your* dream. I want you to choose exactly when and what to do with Cherry Covered Apron, not tag it onto a contract to help me get what I want. I don't want to fuck it up." Ash's outstretched hands trembled.

"You just lost a multimillion-dollar deal because you don't want to hurt your chances with a woman you've known for a month?" Did Ash actually think Rose could believe that? That Rose was that precious? Worth that kind of sacrifice? "A *month*?"

Time stopped for a full second. They stared at each other.

"Yes," Ash said.

"Yes?"

And Rose Josten burst into tears.

Ash pulled her close as Rose cried the kind of tears she hadn't let herself cry since the day the Cessna went down, the kind of tears she couldn't cry because she had to be the strong one. Everything she'd wanted to do and didn't. Music. The film. And then this bigger, inconceivable dream that she was living with Ash. Ash loved her. Maybe she was crying because she was happy. She sobbed against Ash's neck.

"And what if I made the movie, and I had to live in LA and I could only see you once a week," Ash murmured into Rose's hair. "The only flight I could take after shooting goes through Seattle. One little delay in LAX. It's A11 to D7 at Sea-Tac. I mean, of course I could fly through O'Hare or somewhere farther away." Ash went on, her voice full of desperate love, the content of her sentences full of... flight schedules?

Rose swallowed a sob. "What are you talking about?"

"The flights I could take to see you if I was shooting in LA and you were in Portland. If I landed late, I wouldn't have time to get to my next gate. I'd keep missing you."

"You looked up gates for me?"

"I wasn't going to ask you to fly down to LA all the time." Ash coaxed Rose's chin up and placed a gentle kiss on the tears that had collected on Rose's lips. "I love you. Do you... you don't have to say it. You can pretend that I didn't. I just... I need you to know. The deal... Brentworth... if I only *liked* you, I'd have said yes."

Rose felt Ash stiffen. Ash was waiting. She was steeling herself for rejection. Rose had clung to her so tightly, she'd forgotten that wasn't the same thing as saying it out loud.

"I love you. Oh my God, I love you."

*   *   *

When Rose finally calmed down, she heard Mia and the crew edge down the aisle, probably waiting for Ash to give them the it's-okay sign. Reluctantly Rose left the comfort of Ash's embrace, wiping her eyes. Ash kept an arm around her.

"You didn't get it," Mia said with a sigh. "I'm sorry."

No one looked at Rose like she was ridiculous to cry over Ash's movie when Ash seemed wistful but totally at peace.

"We didn't," Ash said.

"Something will work out," Mia said.

There were hugs all around and many comments about how Brentworth didn't know a good thing when she saw it. When Emma asked why Brentworth had said no, Ash just said, "We didn't have a preexisting fan base."

Mia offered to buy drinks, but Ash, Rose, and the crew agreed they were ready to go back to the Executive Comfort Suites.

"You know Ash has terrible taste in hotels," Emma said to Rose as they piled into an Uber van. "You're going to have to break her of that. I'm just asking for a Red Lion. Something where the pool isn't a fifty-fifty chlorine-water blend."

At the hotel, Rose and Ash climbed the stairs to Ash's room, grinning at each other. The windows looked out over the problematically chlorinated kidney-bean-shaped pool. Ash lay down on the bed. Rose lay beside her. The feel of Ash's body as they cradled each other was like air and water, a necessity her body couldn't live without.

"If my colleagues knew I let a client turn down a deal with Brentworth for *love*, they'd never promote me." Rose still felt teary, but at the same time everything seemed funny and light. Ash loved her. What else mattered?

"Oh my God, your thing with *Forbes*." Ash sat up. "I forgot. I'm an asshole. You're here. You're supposed to be there. The partnership. You didn't...you didn't lose it because of me. Oh, fuck. Rose." Ash covered her face with her hand.

Rose drew Ash's hand away and pulled her back to the bed.

"I am the best consultant west of the Rockies." Rose pressed her lips to Ash's, savoring their softness, waiting for Ash's lips to part.

Ash stopped their kiss. "I didn't fuck that up, did I? You didn't...lose anything because you're here?"

Rose laughed. "In the world of lithium insurance and cauliflower, I don't lose." Soon she wouldn't have a job where she felt that confidence. Soon she'd be new and nervous. "I'm not going to be on the cover of *Forbes*, but that's okay because I'm not going to accept the partnership." The thought made Rose feel like a cloud floating higher on a light breeze.

Ash looked like Rose had just gotten a bad diagnosis.

"You're not going to be a partner?"

"What? Do you only love me in a blazer?" Rose nipped Ash's lip.

"Did you know you wanted to do sound for the movie when you came down here? And I killed the deal. I ruined it"— Ash's eyes went wide—"all." She looked like she was waiting for Rose to throw her out.

"I came down here because I wanted to help you, and I thought it would be fun, and I don't let people down just because some businessman decides his calendar is the only calendar. But it's true, when I said I'd do sound for the film, I did want that." She didn't want to say the last part. She could already see the remorse that would fill Ash's eyes, but they loved each other and that meant not hiding her passions. "I was willing to give Brentworth Cherry Covered

Apron because I'd love to do sound on *Inevitable Comfort*. I am
disappointed, but it's not your job to get me my dream job. I
have enough money for a start-up. I loved consulting for you,
and no client is ever going to be as exciting." Rose squeezed
Ash's ass. "But I'd love to help cool, woke filmmakers. And
now I can do whatever I want with Cherry Covered Apron."
She swallowed. "I'm hurt that you think I might be like
Victoria, though."

"You're nothing like her!"

"You think working with me would end our relationship."

"I'm scared it would."

Rose saw the naked, vulnerable truth in Ash's eyes.

"I want you to understand something." Rose stroked a
length of hair that had fallen out of Ash's French twist. "I
don't want to take over your life. Even if we'd gotten the deal
with Brentworth. I have a lot of things I want to do on my
own. I'm not even sure what they all are, but I'm going for all
of them. It'd just have been fun to do one project with you."
She touched her lips to Ash's to let her know she wasn't angry,
just a little sad for what could have been. "And I would never
have wanted to be your sound designer full-time. I watched
Jason work. He spends half his time begging everyone *for the
love of God be quiet!* and getting ignored."

"I shouldn't let what happened with Victoria still have
control over me. It's been too long to still have issues."

"Because I don't have any issues myself."

"Yeah." Ash looked dead serious.

"Ash." Rose put her hand on Ash's hip bone and gave her
a gentle shake. "I didn't fly for eighteen years because my
parents died in a plane crash, and my sisters think I'm going
to die alone and be eaten by my pugs."

Ash smiled. Rose's heart swelled with tenderness.

"All eight of them," Ash said, like she wasn't sure she was allowed to make a joke but desperately wanted to make Rose laugh.

"But if you and I are together, I will die with someone I love and be eaten by our pugs together. That's four pugs to eat each of us."

"I love you." Ash clasped Rose's hands to her chest. "I love you."

"You should." Rose brushed her lips across Ash's. "I'm fabulous."

Ash laughed. "You absolutely are."

"And I love you, Ashlyn Stewart. So much."

"We would have had fun working on that film," Ash said. "The way you edited the proof of concept. God. It was amazing." Ash let out a long sigh. "What would it have been like if I'd said yes?"

"The crew would be drunk by now."

"If I wasn't hung up on everything that happened... If I'd had time to think..." Ash rolled onto her back staring at the ceiling.

Excitement sparked in Rose's heart. Should she ask? "If you'd had time to think, what would you have thought?"

"If you didn't have to give up Cherry Covered Apron and if we talked about how we were going to make sure work didn't interfere with *us*... yeah." Ash closed her eyes as though searching for the answer behind her eyelids. "I would've said yes. But never if you had to give Brentworth all your stuff."

Don't rush her. It was hard. Rose's heart was rushing. "You would have wanted to work together on *Inevitable Comfort*?"

"I would have been scared." Ash didn't open her eyes. "But yeah. God, that film would be beautiful with you doing sound."

Rose rolled onto her back, too. She took Ash's hand and waited several beats. "I don't want you to say yes if your heart says no, but if you wanted to we could still do it."

"Without the funding?"

"We call Brentworth back and ask for more money."

Ash turned, looking adorably confused, and Rose was happier to explain business than she'd ever been before.

"We're bargaining." Rose rolled onto her side, propping herself up on one elbow. "She should have gone for the twenty million. Now we know she wants the film, and we want fifty, and she gets a ten percent share of Cherry Covered Apron when I monetize."

"Would she go for it?"

"She would." Rose tapped her own chest. "Best consultant west of the Rockies. I know. I could call Brentworth's office, and make the offer, and you still have time to think about it. We haven't signed anything. And if she comes back with forty, maybe we can talk to some other producers and see if we can get a better deal. We're not taking any paltry twenty million."

"That's what we asked for."

"Details." Rose kissed Ash. "I love that you accidentally played boss-ass hardball with a billionaire investor. If I read Brentworth right, she'll like it, too. She's not just investing in the film. She's investing in your passion."

The sun moved just enough to escape from behind the buildings across the street and shone into the room, turning sad-sixties-orange into sumptuous burnt umber. Ash turned to her.

"Our passion. If she invests it's in *our* passion."

chapter 54

⇶

The beds at the Executive Comfort Suites were not the kind that had springs all the way across, or at least not springs with any spring in them. Ash didn't mind. The sag in the bed rolled her against Rose, their bodies melting together as much as they could with Rose in a suit and Ash in a sheath dress. Ash wanted their clothing off. She wanted Rose's breasts pressed against hers. She wanted to taste Rose. She wanted to make Rose bless this room with her cries of pleasure. She wanted to feel Rose's hands on her back, Rose's kiss on her neck. She throbbed but it wasn't pain. It was the sweet, hungry feeling of being turned on and needy, wanting to linger and wanting to feel Rose's tongue caressing the delicate folds of her sex immediately. She wanted to have sex, and if she got scared halfway through, Rose would love her just as much as ever.

Reluctantly, Rose said, "Should you text Emma and tell the crew not to start feeling bad yet?"

"I suppose I should." Ash retrieved her phone with a sigh.

Ash: Rose thinks we may still get it. We'll talk later.

A second later, someone pounded on the door.

"I need to know now!" It was Emma.

Ash heard Jason's hushed, "Dude," and Pilot's, "Could you two be somewhat discreet? They might be enjoying sapphic love."

"I know she's having sex with Rose," Emma said to Jason and Pilot but loud enough for Ash to hear. Emma knocked again, projecting her voice. "I will get a key and let myself in if you don't answer the door. This is the kind of hotel that will give just anyone a key, and you know it."

Rose laughed an infectious laugh that Ash couldn't help but join.

"We're still negotiating," Rose called out.

"Negotiating in *bed*," Emma called.

"But we'll get it." To Ash, Rose added, "Do we have to go out there?"

Ash's body cried out, *We need to be naked on these ten-count sheets.*

Ash groaned.

"You go get a drink with them," Rose said, "and I'll call Brentworth's office and my sisters. Text me where you're all going and I'll meet you. Promise me we'll be back here tonight?"

"If I didn't think Emma was right about the key, we wouldn't leave."

But Ash didn't move. "What would you like me to tell them about me and you and Cherry Covered Apron?"

Rose pursed her lips thoughtfully. "Anything you like. Everything. I'm going to tell my sisters about Cherry Covered Apron. If you don't want to tell Jason and Pilot and Emma you turned Brentworth down, you don't have to."

"You mean tell them I was ready to sacrifice it all for love?"

"They'd probably kill you."

"I cheated death once already." It was strange how easy it was to joke about the accident. "Of course I'll tell them."

A burger, two beers, and three hours later, Ash and Rose were back in the room. The crew hadn't killed her. Their hearts were probably softened by the fact that before Rose even got to the little dive bar down the street, she'd gotten a message from Brentworth's office saying Brentworth was interested. But Jason, Pilot, and Emma were artists, too, and they got it. You didn't give away all your work. They'd toasted Rose for her self-sacrifice and Ash for playing hardball. When Ash and Emma had gone to the bar for the second round of beers, Emma had said, *Even if we don't get it, I'm glad you got Rose.*

They walked back to the hotel in the twilight. Emma, Pilot, and Jason stayed behind. Rose looked beautiful set against the purple smog and the flickering streetlights, her hair messy and her blouse unbuttoned to show a hint of cleavage, the silky collar fluttering in the breeze of a passing truck. Executive Comfort Suites only got two stars on Tripadvisor and the street was a hodgepodge of businesses that could only survive because no brand-name franchises wanted to move in. And everything was perfect.

Ash took Rose's hand. "Did you call your sisters?" Ash was glad the glow in Rose's face didn't fade with the question.

"Yeah." Rose looked a little confused but mostly happy. "They weren't mad."

"You thought they'd be mad at you for making ASMR?"

"No, for not telling them. But Cassie said it was nice that I had a hobby, and she could sew me another apron if I needed one. Then she said something about how she didn't tell us everything, either, and I think she was talking about kinky sex with Kenneth. Gigi looked the site up right away and

said the videos were freakishly sexy, but that's a compliment
from G. Ty quoted something about gender from Leslie
Feinberg. Now I feel bad for thinking telling them would be
a big deal." Rose didn't look sad. "They said I'd helped them
achieve their dreams. They said...they didn't need me to
take care of them anymore."

"Was that hard to hear?"

"No," Rose said pensively. "They didn't mean they didn't
need me like a sister. They need me the way we all need each
other. But Cassie said the one thing in her life that didn't feel
right was this sense she had that I wasn't happy. And Gigi
said she'd once counted up all the money I'd given her to keep
the salon going when she first opened and the money I used
to bail her out of jail when she had the whole Elks-club thing
and how much it would have cost if she'd gotten malaria if I
hadn't made her get all the right vaccines when she traveled.
She said I pretty much could sponge off her for life, and
she'd still owe me." Rose laughed. "And Ty just wants me to
be in love."

Back at the hotel, it was comfortable, laughing and taking
off their shoes, but Ash still felt shy as the talk quieted into
kissing. Shy and excited. Rose traced the zipper on the back of
Ash's dress.

"May I undo you?"

"You do."

"That's a yes?"

Ash nodded. Rose slowly unzipped the sheath dress, holding
Ash's hand as she stepped out of it. Ash felt Rose's eyes travel
up and down her body. She paused when she looked at Ash's
scars, but her gaze felt like a caress.

Ash put her hands on Rose's soft hips, loving the feel of
Rose's curves.

"God, you're beautiful," Ash whispered as she kissed Rose's neck.

"Why thank you."

Ash slid Rose's blazer off and placed it on a chair.

"I like your blazers," Ash said.

"I'll have to tell Gigi."

Rose caressed the back of Ash's head where her hair was shaved. Ash's skin tingled. She leaned into Rose's touch.

Rose led Ash to the rumpled sheets, but Rose went to her briefcase and dug around and produced a small box. "I got you a present. You don't have to use it." She held it out.

It was a flat, roundish vibrator that fit perfectly in Ash's palm.

"I went to Satisfaction Guaranteed and asked them if they had something for someone who... wanted something gentle."

The vibrators Ash had had with Victoria were bigger affairs, dildo-shaped with rabbit ears, some with suction, one that thrust. She'd enjoyed them once. She took the vibrator out and turned it on. It hummed in her hand, gentle and innocuous.

"Thank you." When they lay down, Ash tucked it into the underwear she was still wearing. "Hmm." She held her hand over the vibrator, pressing it against herself. "I like it."

She kept it there as Rose lay down and they kissed for a long time. When it was clear Rose wouldn't make another first move, Ash reached around and unclasped Rose's bra with one hand. Rose looked at Ash for confirmation then fumbled with Ash's bra. Ash helped her. Rose caressed Ash's breast, rubbing a hypnotizing circle against Ash's tightening nipple. Then she drew Ash's nipple into her mouth.

"I want you." Ash squirmed and sighed.

"I want you, too." Rose kissed Ash's belly.

Ash felt the kiss reverberate through her. "Please."

Rose kissed down Ash's stomach, around her hip, across the surgical scars on her thigh.

"You're so beautiful," Rose whispered. She spent a long time stroking Ash's thigh until Rose's hands gliding over her legs became sweet teasing. Ash was wet. The vibrator was a sweet frustration, buzzing against her clit but not satisfying anything.

"Stop me if it's not right," Rose said seriously.

Then she took the vibrator away. Ash gasped a protest at the sudden absence even though she wanted what came next. Then Rose kissed the delicate skin beside Ash's vulva, caressing her outer labia, running them through her fingers like she was touching the petals of a flower...or chard. Everything felt lovely. Rose ran her tongue in slow circles around and around Ash's opening. It felt amazing. Ash moaned.

"That feels good." Ash's breath sped up, her body soaring with pleasure. *Harder. Faster.* Every fiber of muscle in her body seized. Her back arched. She needed to come, and she hadn't for so long. Was she taking too long? She was thinking too much, a jumble of images tumbled through her mind, senselessly landing on Emma's pink bunny. *Breathe in.*

"I...please...now...I can't..." She couldn't get there. She wanted it too much. She felt brittle. She was shattering into pieces.

"I got you," Rose whispered.

From somewhere in the sheets, Rose found the vibrator again, placed it between Ash's thighs, and moved her own leg over Ash's. "Yes?"

"Yes." Ash pulled Rose on top of her, pleasure rising as Rose settled her thigh between Ash's legs, the vibrator pressing against Ash, Rose's full body pressing her down. She couldn't shatter with Rose's glorious, soft weight holding her safe and still. Rose thrust against her. Ash ran her hands through Rose's hair, tightening her grip as Rose moved faster.

"Yes! There! Please!" She clutched Rose's back. "I need it so bad." She ground against Rose's leg. The world expanded, then distilled down to a single point of pleasure. "I need you." Then her body broke into blossom and she was floating off the screen. And when she finally sank back down, melting under Rose's body, Ash was laughing.

"That was so good." Tears welled in Ash's eyes but they were tears of happiness. "I thought I'd never feel that again. And I did. I do. With you." Ash was beaming and wiping at her eyes. "It was so fucking good. It was. So. Fucking. Good."

Rose rolled off her, still holding all of Ash in her arms, kissing Ash's forehead and her temple and her cheek. Ash could feel Rose's grin.

"Don't be smug," Ash protested, although she loved the idea of Rose being smug because Rose had brought her to a screaming orgasm.

Rose kept kissing Ash's face. Ash felt bathed in Rose's love.

"I'm not smug," Rose chuckled, sounding a tiny bit smug. "It's just... I don't think I've ever been this happy before."

epilogue

Rose couldn't stop looking at Ash. She glowed in her iridescent, ripped jeans and silver-pink leather jacket and worn-so-thin-you-could-see-her-bra Human League T-shirt, every color picking up the shades of Rose's Marianna Villard dress. Which, unlike Cinderella, she got to wear twice. They had looked magnificent striding up the Oscars red carpet, pausing for the occasional photographs. They weren't making the cover of any tabloids, but enough people had wanted their attention that only now, at the Elsinore afterparty, were they able to say ten consecutive words to each other.

Ash sipped a peach Bellini.

"You don't even like this stuff." Rose kissed the hint of peach on Ash's lips.

"But it goes so well with our outfits." Ash put an arm around her. "You go so well with my outfit. You go so well with everything in my life."

Rose breathed in Ash's perfume. If someone could have bottled the essence of this night—the lights, the fame, the feeling that it was theirs for the taking and yet it had no hold on them—that's what it would have smelled like. Rose almost asked Ash what it was. Funny that she didn't know. She'd seen the bottle on Ash's real-furniture dresser. There was still so much she wanted to learn about Ash and there was so much about their lives together that felt blissfully familiar. She kissed Ash.

"Come on, you two," Mia said affectionately. "It's time for a toast."

The party guests quieted.

"I am so honored to host the *Inevitable Comfort* afterparty," Mia said. "One of the best films I've ever seen."

The party cheered.

They hadn't been nominated for an Oscar but no one cared.

Brentworth lifted her champagne flute, her gold bracelets sliding down her birdlike wrist. "To *Inevitable Comfort*, a very good return on my investment."

Even if they'd won every Oscar on the roster, it wouldn't have made Rose as happy as she was to see Ash smile, at home and relaxed in her world, surrounded by people who recognized her gifts and loved her for her kindness and her humor.

"To our producer," Ash returned. "And the 1.2 million people who came just to hear Rose's voice-over."

Rose gave a little bow. There were more toasts, hugs, handshakes, and praise. Rose's sisters gathered around Rose and Ash.

"I can't believe we're here," Cassie said, still goggling at the theater.

"Believe," Gigi said.

"So I won't die alone and get eaten by my pugs?" Rose shot Gigi a look.

"Did I say that?" Gigi sipped her drink innocently.

"Yes," Rose and Cassie said in unison.

Ty would have joined in, but she'd met Emma at Ash's

studio when they'd watched the proof of concept and was now hopelessly in love with Emma which meant she couldn't talk to her or look in her direction.

"So what's next?" one of Ash's old friends asked.

Ash gestured to Rose to go first. There was so much. Every ASMR conference, podcast, and production company wanted her. She was coaching a new ASMR artist and consulting for a queer history museum. Plus furnishing the apartment they'd rented in LA. And of course, basking in Ash's success, one of Rose's favorite new hobbies. Five producers fighting Brentworth for Ash's next production. Ash's latest script dancing off her fingertips as she typed late into the night. And of course, flying back and forth between LA and Portland. Assuring Muffin and Cupcake that she still loved them even though Ty had joint custody. But for now...

"We won a trip to the New Destination Resort," Rose said. "We're going to listen to the waves and drink tropical drinks on the beach."

"But not with LED lights in them," Ash said. "No one knows what those things are made of."

Someone said, "Lots of people know."

Ash said, "But do they *really*?"

Ash turned to Mia. "Thank you. I presume you rigged the game for us?"

"I might have pulled some strings behind the scenes." Mia winked. "But I couldn't help you with the answers."

Ash beamed at Rose. "We are obviously perfect for each other."

The DJ struck up his signature blend of Daft Punk and Mozart.

Ash put her arm around Rose. Rose savored the touch, her body alight with anticipation of Ash on top of her, her lips on

Ash's body, their moans of pleasure, and the way they melted in each other's arms. Then there'd be the sweet pleasure of falling asleep together and the pleasure of kissing goodbye in the morning as they both set out for their respective days filled with dreams, projects, challenges, and laughter. And the pleasure of coming home to each other and lounging on the gloriously comfortable, hideously gaudy couch that Ash had found at a vintage resale boutique called Nineties Landline. And talking about the past and the future, about work and family and pugs and measuring spoons. The pleasure of being two separate people who were always on the same team, loving and helping and supporting each other through everything.